Henry C. Van Schaack

Memoirs of the Life of Henry Van Schaack

embracing selections from his correspondence during the American revolution

Henry C. Van Schaack

Memoirs of the Life of Henry Van Schaack
embracing selections from his correspondence during the American revolution

ISBN/EAN: 9783337230562

Printed in Europe, USA, Canada, Australia, Japan

Cover: Foto ©Andreas Hilbeck / pixelio.de

More available books at **www.hansebooks.com**

MEMOIRS

OF THE LIFE OF

HENRY VAN SCHAACK

EMBRACING

SELECTIONS FROM HIS CORRESPONDENCE

DURING THE

AMERICAN REVOLUTION

BY HIS NEPHEW

HENRY CRUGER VAN SCHAACK

Author of the LIFE OF PETER VAN SCHAACK, LL.D.; HENRY CRUGER—the colleague of
Edmund Burke; CAPTAIN MORRIS, OF THE ILLINOIS COUNTRY, etc., etc.

Superanda fortuna ferendo

CHICAGO
A. C. McCLURG & COMPANY
1892

PREFACE.

History is indebted to biography for a large share of its choicest beauties, and of its enlivening, if not its most valuable, materials. Where the memoirs of an individual exhibit the type of a class, they become history itself, and are such in all but the name. Well-meant contributions of this description, to our biographical literature—at least to the extent of their interest and value—cannot fail, therefore, to be appreciated by those who take pleasure in historical researches.

Under no circumstances can the details of personal biography become more useful and important to the historian than in the elucidation of the motives, principles and conduct of the unsuccessful party in civil war. Fairly to judge of their characters and principles of action we should be made acquainted with the precise positions in which they stood; we should aim to occupy the points from which they viewed passing events; we should know their history; we should become familiar with all the details of their origin, their education, their associates, their habits and pursuits, and with the early as well as later influences to which they were subjected; and we should inquire particularly into the persecutions (or what they deemed such) experienced by them in their own persons, or in those of their connections and friends, at an early stage of the contest, as well as with the other excesses of those who, claiming to be the only true supporters of the cause of liberty, unfortunately often acted in direct contravention to its principles.

The author of this work is believed to have been the first individual in the United States who so far ventured to encounter hereditary prejudices as to publish the life of one who had been on the unsuccessful side in the American revolt. Without any pretensions to authorship, he felt himself constrained, on that occasion, by his situation (having come into possession of materials deemed interesting and valuable for historical purposes), and particularly by a sense of filial duty, to assume a responsibility not likely to be discharged by another. A sense of obligations similar in their character, though not so imperative, pointed to the preservation of the manuscripts incorporated into this work.

Although it is not claimed for the subject of this sketch that he was a very great man, it is asserted that he was a remarkable man, and an admirable specimen of that venerated class of noble-minded men known to us as "GENTLEMEN OF THE OLD SCHOOL." Although not highly educated, nor ever called into any very elevated public station, Henry Van Schaack was, for twenty-five years immediately antecedent to the revolution, in various official stations of respectability and usefulness, under the Crown or the Province. His associates, also, show him to have been a man of mark in his day; and although his life would not have been written for the mere purpose of elucidating character, and irrespective of its position as a revolutionary biography, it is submitted that our ante-revolutionary history cannot well be written without greater aids, than the historian now possesses, from biographies of the character presented in this work. As a revolutionary biography, it is doubted whether there are many instances in which, at this period, as full material for biographical sketches of American loyalists exists, as are to be found in this volume.

Mr. Van Schaack lived in eventful times, and passed through

popular convulsions and revolutions of the gravest character, with which he was more or less identified.

An actor in three different capacities—lieutenant, paymaster, and commissary—in the war by which the Canadas were subjected to the British crown; an Indian trader for ten years before and immediately after that event, extending his operations, at that early period, to Detroit and Michilimacknac ; the unjust object of popular violence at the period of the Stamp Act; a loyalist in the Revolution and subjected to proscription, imprisonment, and exile, by reason of his political sentiments; a citizen of Massachusetts during Shay's rebellion, and active in quelling that alarming revolt, of which his immediate neighborhood was a prominent theatre; his career was not destitute of variety or incident. It was prolonged to a period of upwards of ninety years—1733 to 1823. What a world of history, written and unwritten, has been enacted during this period! Unless the author has greatly misjudged, the papers of Henry Van Schaack will form an interesting contribution to the memorials of that history.

H. C. Van Schaack.*

Manlius, N. Y.

* Appendix A, page 221.

CONTENTS.

MEMOIRS

OF

THE LIFE

OF

HENRY VAN SCHAACK.

CHAPTER I.

Henry Van Schaack was born at Kinderhook, in the then county of Albany (now Columbia), and province of New York, in February, 1733. He was the oldest son of Cornelius Van Schaack, who was a merchant and reputable citizen of that place for a long time, an elder in the Dutch Reformed Church, and for many years a magistrate and colonel in the provincial militia. The late Peter Van Schaack, LL. D., whose name occupies no obscure place among the eminent men of his day, was his youngest brother, and the youngest of a family of seven children.

The Van Schaack family, whose ancestors were early settlers on the banks of the Hudson, are of Holland, and not of German, descent, as the pronunciation of their name by many as if spelled Shaak, on the supposition that it was a German name, has led some persons to infer. It is known that the family in Holland were respectable. One of their ancestors was burgomaster (an officer like our mayor), and member of the city council of Enkhuysen, an ancient city of Holland, and another was minister of the gospel at Lutjebrook, a village in the north part of Holland, in the quarter of Hoorn, and they spelled their name Schaeck.*

But little is known of the juvenile history of the subject of this sketch.   It was principally by the force of his own native strength of mind and quickness of parts, improved by attention, perseverance, judicious reading and close personal observation, that he became a man of extensive general information, and attained a high degree of respectability and usefulness in society.   The facilities for improving the mind, in the interior of the province of New York, were exceedingly limited when Henry Van Schaack was a young man.   He attained his majority previous to the establishment of any college in the province.   King's college did not go into operation until about the period of the commencement of the "seven years'war," which necessarily checked for sometime the progress of educational improvement.   It was chiefly from their native powers of mind and active energy of character, and not from facilities for mental cultivation, or any finished course of study, that the leading characters of Mr. Van Schaack's day became distinguished.   The knowledge they possessed was derived from the diligent reading of a few choice books, and a careful study of the characters they portrayed, in connection with close observation in their intercourse with the world. They were men of thought and reflection, and hence probably arose that manly self-dependence and vigor of mind, as well as that originality and simplicity of character, for which the prominent men of that day became distinguished, and for which, as well as for their cardinal virtues, they are now venerated by posterity.

Mr. Van Schaack was emphatically one of this class, being a self-taught man, and having no other education than that afforded by a common school in the country at that early day. At the age of fourteen he was placed as an under-clerk in a merchant's counting house in the city of New York.   It was by self-discipline in this situation that he laid the foundation

* The master founder at Woolwich in 1779, who communicated these facts to Peter Van Schaack, was a Dutchman by the name of Verbergen, and had married a lady of this name. There was an officer in the 55th regiment by the name of John Schaack.

of that admirable address for which he afterwards became distinguished. Having at mature life, by his various good qualities, secured in an eminent degree the respect and confidence of the great and good men of the land, comprehending in the number the leading statesmen and the public men of his day, with whom he was fully able to cope in argument, and who took marked delight in his society. Mr. Van Schaack was asked by a friend to explain how he had overcome his early disadvantages; he replied: "I have informed you that in early life I studied the lives of living characters, and learned to copy from the virtuous and most respectable their manners and examples. Subsequently I read the best authors on history, geography, religion, morality, and general science, preferring the style of Johnson, Addison, and the best English writers of that age. If I did not comprehend the subject by reading once, I would review and examine until I did understand it, confining myself to a few choice books. I found great advantage in taking notes, and expressing the principles and sentiments of the author in my own language. This not only enabled me to form my own judgment, but it was a great aid to me in composition, by thus learning to arrange my ideas on paper. My custom on this subject, if I did not satisfy myself on the first attempt, was to burn the paper and try until I did succeed. I improved much in this art by early epistolary correspondences with respectable gentlemen—ah! and ladies also—in various parts of the country." Here Mr. Van Schaack closed his remarks by saying, "Sir, you see here on my table a dictionary" (putting his hand on the book). "From my boyhood, whenever I found a new word, or any doubt respecting the orthography or definition of a word, I always refer to that standard."

In 1755, at the age of twenty-two, we find him a lieutenant in a company of provincial troops, of which Philip Schuyler (afterwards the renowned General) was captain, in the expedition commanded by Major General (afterwards Sir) William Johnson against Crown Point. The severe and sanguinary conflict between a body of provincial troops under Colonel Ephraim Williams and an ambush party of French and Indians, by whom they were surprised near French mountain, on the eight of September, 1755, and the subsequent defeat of the latter and capture of their commander on the same day, in an attempt to storm General Johnson's lines, are interesting and well-known events in our colonial history. Mr. Van Schaack was one of a detachment of two hundred and fifty men, commanded by Captain Maginnis, which went up the same day from Fort Edward to the relief of the provincial troops. In their march to the English camp, near the southern extremity of Lake George, they encountered the retreating French army while the latter were engaged in pillaging the dead (about three hundred in number) of Colonel Williams' party, whom they had surprised and slaughtered in the early part of the day. The detachment, after a severe engagement, which lasted nearly two hours, defeated the enemy in this third conflict or the same day, and secured a safe junction with the main army. Lieutenant Van Schaack is particularly mentioned in the published accounts of the day as having "distinguished himself in that action." On his arrival at the English camp at Fort George in the evening, bringing the welcome intelligence of the second defeat and ultimate rout of the French army, Mr. Van Schaack was conducted to General Johnson's quarters. Here an interesting scene was presented. The commanding officers of the two opposing armies had both been wounded in the conflicts of the day, and were now occupying the same tent; the Baron Dieskau reposing upon General Johnson's bed—a scene not unworthy the pencil.*

At this period scalping parties of French and Indians, from Canada, made frequent incursions as far down the east banks of the Hudson as Kinderhook and Claverack. There were repeated cases of individuals being scalped and killed, or carried into captivity by these marauding parties.

---

* The author is indebted for the principal part of these facts to a minute made by the Honorable James Kent, 14th July, 1816, of a conversation had by him on that day with Mr. V —— S——, and deemed by him worthy to be placed as a note in Smollett's History of England. To this note Chancellor Kent afterwards made the following addition. "I dined with H. Van Schaack at Mr. Vanderpoels, (at Kinderhook) July 4th, 1821, and he said he was eighty-eight years old the preceding February, and he repeated the same here and was lively, hearty, well, smoked and drank well, and was as intelligent as ever."

Instances of marked bravery and heroism worthy of record were also exhibited by individuals in the defense of their persons and their homes. Three members of the family of Joachim VanValkenburgh were captured by the French Indians and two of them murdered. His wife also fell into their hands, and while they were conducting her away, Van Valkenburgh shot the Indian in the back who was leading her and recovered his wife.*

The English as well as the French, at this period, gave rewards for the scalps of both sexes, the former being driven into this cruel measure by the practices of the latter, and the influence it gave them with the savages.

There was a small stockade, dignified with the name of "Fort," at Kinderhook, to which the neighboring inhabitants were accustomed to resort for refuge in case of approaching danger. On one occasion of an alarm given in consequence of the approach of a party of Indians, mothers with their children and all the females in the neighborhood, repaired to the Fort for safety. It so happened that all the men in the vicinity were absent at the time. To disguise their weakness, under the lead of a Mrs. Hoes, a brave Dutch vrouw who volunteered to command on the occasion, the women, occupying a position where only the covering of their heads could be seen by their invaders, put on men's hats and made great noises. The Indians, deceived by these indications of strength, did not venture to attack the feminine garrison.

In 1756, and for several years afterwards, Mr. Van Schaack was paymaster to the New York regiment. For a portion of the time he also held a special commission from the governor of the province to act as "paymaster and commissary of the musters," and was obliged, in the performance of the duties of his office, to visit the military posts on the frontiers where the troops were stationed. Oliver Delancy, Beverly Robinson and John Cruger, who resided at New York, were paymasters and commissaries to the force of the colony, and had the principal disbursement of the one hundred thousand pounds voted by the Assembly for the campaign of 1758. Mr. Van Schaack

Vide Appendix.

was then their agent at Albany, at which point a large portion of the expenditures and business was made and conducted.

From 1756 to 1769 Mr. Van Schaack resided in Albany and was engaged in merchandizing at that place during nearly all that period. In 1761 he imported goods on his own account from London. A great portion of the articles thus ordered were designed for the Indian trade, in which he was engaged for about ten years. He had a trading establishment at Oswego (then known as Fort Ontario) and set up another at Niagara, upon the capture of that post by Sir William Johnson in 1759.

Upon the termination of the seven years' war, and the transfer to Britain of the French possessions on our northern borders, a more enlarged field for enterprise was opened to the colonies, in the less dangerous spread of their settlements, and in an unrivalled intercourse and trade with the aborigines, and Mr. Van Schaack's activity and enterprise led him to extend his operations in the Indian and fur trade. He opened trading houses at Detroit and Michilimackinack, whither he made repeated journeys, and he spent several winters in those remote regions, then regarded as the *ultima thule* of British America.*

At this period he was connected in business with Edward Cole, an intelligent and enterprising gentleman, of an ancient and reputable family residing at New Port, Rhode Island. Colonel Cole, who subsequently was employed in Indian matters by Sir William Johnson, commanded a regiment under General Wolfe at the siege of Quebec, and also at the capture of Havanna, under the Earl of Albemarle.

The furs and peltry were brought down in the bateaux from Detroit to Fort Shosher and conveyed by land carriage around Niagara Falls to Niagara, there re-shipped and borne from thence down Lake Ontario to Oswego, up that river and through the Oneida lake and Wood creek to the Mohawk, and

---

* Mr. V. S., when at Detroit, redeemed a white boy from captivity by giving the Indians a silver tankard for him The lad grew to manhood, was established in business by Mr. . S. and was known by the name of "Tankard."

down that river to Schenectada, which was the starting point
for the ascending bateaux and where there was a block house.
There were four portages or carrying places in the route, and
the same vessels continued through. The bateaux usually
carried from two to five tons, and the freight was first transported over the carrying places, and the bateaux were then
relaunched and reladen.

In some instances, after the conquest of Canada, Mr. Van
Schaack shipped furs from Quebec, but generally from New
York, and insurances were invariably ordered, in advance, in
London. Many of these consignments were large and amounted
to several thousand pounds.

It is melancholy to notice the immense quantity of ardent
spirits which were forwarded at this period to the vicinity of
the military posts to be sold to the soldiers and Indians. British spirits, Jamaica and St. Croix rum, as well as Maderia
wine "for the officers," almost invariably formed part of the
loading of the ascending bateaux. Large quantities of shrub
were also ordered from Philadelphia for the use of the army,
being deemed a very necessary beverage when the troops
should take the field.

In May, 1762, General Amherst prohibited spirituous
liquors from being sent up among the Indians, not long after
which time quantities of those articles were returned from
Albany to New York as unsalable, in consequence of this
order.

On looking over the names of the leading men of business
in the colony, at this period, it cannot escape observation that
of those who were men in years and of experience, a large
portion afterwards espoused the royal cause in the contest with
the mother country. It is natural to suppose that strong attachments were formed among men who had lived and labored in
intimate intercourse with each other in the comparative infancy
of a people, and that after having been harrassed by wars with
the French and savages, against whom they had fought side
by side for so many years, they should have desired peace and
tranquility, and particularly that they should have had a
strong aversion to engaging in a war with a government for

which they had so often contended, with whose prosperity they considered that of the colonies to be identified, whose institutions they had been accustomed to venerate and to whom they still looked up as to a mother.

In 1760 Mr. Van Schaack was married, at Albany, to Jane Holland, a lady possessing many rare and estimable qualities. Her father, Hitchen Holland, was captain of one of His Majesty's independent companies of foot, and was stationed at Fort Ontario (now Oswego) in 1753, and for several years afterwards. He resided at this time on his farm on Cherry Hill, near Albany.*

Mr. Van Schaack's connections with the army as a lieutenant, paymaster and commissary, and his, frequent visits to the frontier posts, in the discharge of his official duties and in the prosecution of his business, brought him into intimacy with many of the officers of the English army, with whom were many worthy and high-minded men, with whom a lasting friendship was formed. Being intelligent, lively, open-hearted and full of anecdote, and having a lady to preside at his table who possessed the same good qualities, his company was much sought for, and his house on Cherry Hill overflowed with visitors, called there by his great hospitality.

Among the officers referred to, with whom interesting friendships were thus formed, were Richard Montgomery, then a captain, and Lieutenant Launcelot Hill, who was for a time stationed at Oswego. Both of these gentlemen, at the close of the French war, returned to their native Ireland. The former had caught the enterprise of the new world, and returned shortly after to America, and forming a matrimonial connection, fixed his residence on the banks of the Hudson, until the disastrous expedition against Canada, which will ever possess a melancholy interest from the circumstances of his untimely death. On his way to Canada in the summer of 1775, General

---

* The paternal grand-father of Mrs. V. S. came from Ireland, and was a captain of one of the Independent Companies in New York. He had three sons; Edward, Henry and H.... en. Edward was, in 1731, and for many years afterwards, mayor of Albany, and subsequently may r of New York, and one of His Majesty's council. He died in 1756, and was succeeded in the mayoralty by John Cruger. Henry was, for many years, high sheriff of Albany county and a master in chancery. He died in or about 1776.

Montgomery called to see his early friends, the Van Schaacks, at Kinderhook. On this occasion, as if anticipating his melancholy end, he gave Mr. Van Schaack several tokens of remembrance which are still preserved in different branches of the family.

The strength and sincerity of the friendships which were formed at this interesting period are illustrated by the following letter, written from Ireland and received nearly thirty years after the period referred to. It was superscribed "Peter Van Schaack, Esq., or any of that family in New York, or elsewhere." The entire letter is here given:

"LIMERICK, 17 April, 1791.

Launcelot Hill, formerly an officer in the 55th Regiment, now settled in Limerick, Ireland, has very great pleasure in hearing of the present prosperity of the province of New York, where he spent some happy years before the unhappy troubles commenced, and where he received such civility and acts of friendship as will never be forgotten by him while he remembers anything. He is at a loss to know to whom to address this but if any of his worthy friends the Van Schaacks are still in being, he begs a line from them to let him have the pleasing account of the welfare of his friends in New York, on the river and at Albany."

Such friendships could only have their base upon solid merits in the parties to them, and in a sincerity and simplicity of intercourse to which the calculating spirit of the present day, and our riper age as a people are comparative strangers. The intercourse thus renewed was kept up for many years.

Mr. Van Schaack, as was his father before him, was a man of close investigation and a shrewd observer of men and things. He had a very retentive memory and related many interesting occurrences in our colonial history during the life and times of that extraordinary man, Sir William Johnson, with whom he was on the most friendly terms, and corresponded about colonial affairs. He was a frequent guest at Johnson Hall, which was, during the life-time of its original proprietor, the seat of the most extended hospitality.*

---

* It has been intimated that there was some mystery connected with the death of Sir William Johnson. The following authentic account of that event is taken from a manuscript left by a Judge of the Supreme Court, who was holding a circuit at Johnstown at the

Major Van Schaack was attached to the expedition, fitted out by General Bradstreet, at Albany, in the state of New York, in the spring of 1764, against the Indians of the North West. His two particular friends, Captain Richard Montgomery and Captain Thomas Morris, both officers in the Seventeenth English Regiment of foot, were also in that expedition. From Niagara, Major Van Schaack wrote a letter to his brother Peter, his junior by fourteen years, and then pursuing his studies in King's College, New York, in which letter he gave a long extract from the writings of an author, whom he described as "Mr. Shakespeare," the extract being the admirable advice of Polonius to Laertes, his son, as found in the play of Hamlet. On the arrival of the military expedition at the mouth of the Miami river, about fifty miles from Detroit, General Bradstreet despatched Captain Morris, with an escort of friendly Indians, into the wilderness (now Indiana), to negotiate with the hostile savages there, and reconcile them to the recent change of jurisdiction from France to England, consequent upon the treaty of 1763. Here a very singular incident occurred. One of the visited Indians, known as Little Chief, of his own motion, presented to Captain Morris a volume of Shakespeare's plays!

On his return to England, in 1768, Morris took back with him that precious volume of Shakespeare and evidently cherished it through life. Being a literary character of considerable note, he published in 1791 a volume of his compositions, and among them was one which bore the title of "A letter to a Friend on the poetical elocution of the Theatre and the manner of acting the Tragedy." In this letter, published twenty-six years after he received the Indian gift, Morris thus feelingly alludes to it by expressing a doubt as to whether the world

---

time, and who was at the funeral, which was attended by upwards of two thousand people: "Being Superintendent of Indian Affairs, and some jealousies being infused into the heads of the Indians by designing people, Sir William directed a meeting at the Hall, consisting of the Sachems of the six nations. They all attended. It was in July, 1774. The author was present. Sir William opened the treaty about ten in the morning. He made a long speech, pronounced with all the spirit, activity and energy of the Indians. He was heard with great attention. When he had ended he retired to his chamber; drank some wine and water, sat himself down in an elbow chair; he leaned his head against the back of it and expired without a groan."

ever afforded him a "pleasure equal to that of reading Shakespeare at the foot of a waterfall in an American desert."*

Popular violences, growing out of the passage of the Stamp Act, broke out in the city of Albany, as in other parts of the continent. Mr. Van Schaack was at this time postmaster and an alderman of the city, and a leading man of business. The jealousy of the populace was highly excited in regard to every prominent individual to whom the office of stamp distributor was likely to be tendered. The bare suspicion that Mr. Van Schaack had applied for the office, or would accept it if tendered to him, was the sole justification for a wanton destruction of his property, by those who called themselves "The Sons of Liberty.†"

The following communication, which appeared in a ‡ newspaper of that day, carries with it an air of candor, and probably contains a pretty correct version of the affair. As an illustration of the temper of the times, as well as a specimen of "genteel" treatment, after the requisitions of the mob had become satisfied, this paper possesses historical interest:

"MR. PRINTER:

Amidst the general disquiet that now fills the minds of the Americans, occasioned by the Stamp Act, and the several justly concerted measures that have in different parts been put into execution in consequence of this uneasiness, in order to repel from the land of liberty the dangerous invaders thereof; we desire that the following transactions by the Sons of Liberty, in the city of Albany, against some persons who have laid under the suspicion of having made application for the too well-known detestable office, may by your paper be made public.

ALBANY, January 8th, 1766."

"On Saturday, the 4th instant, a number of the Sons of Liberty, at Mr. Williams', tavern keeper, in this city, taking into consideration the repeated informations they lately received

---

* That volume was probably an Indian trophy of Braddock's defeat at Fort Du Quene, now Pittsburgh.

† Benjamin Franklin nominated persons for stamp officers (5 Bancroft, p. 250). Richard Henry Lee (afterwards a signer of the Declaration of Independence) solicited the office of stamp distributor.

‡ The New York Gazette, or the Weekly Post-Boy, of 22d day of January, 1766. The motto at the head of ths journal was, "The united voice of all His Majesty's FREE AND LOYAL subjects in America. Liberty and property and no stamps "

from every quarter, of too considerable a number of their fellow
citizens having applied for deputations in the stamp office, and
resolving not to be behind hand with their brethren in opposition to the chains of slavery, sent billets to the several gentlemen there accused, to speak with them at Williams'.   All
attended but Mr. Hanson, who, being waited on at his own
house, gave under oath immediate and ample satisfaction that
he neither had applied nor never would accept.   Messrs.
Macomb, Gamble and Stephenson confessed applying, and gave
assurances under hand that they never would act, also promised
to swear at any time when required.   Mr. Van Schaack denied
application, and declared upon honor that he never had, but
upon being requested to declare that he never would, he refused,
urging that the gentlemen might look upon him on equal footing with themselves, and that it would be unjust to oblige him
to put it out of his power to take a post of profit which the rest
of his fellow citizens were at liberty to accept.   The Sons of Liberty answered that they could not look on Mr. Van Schaack as
on an equal footing with themselves, as the very reserve argued
some degree of inclination, the minutest portion of which was
utterly inconsistent with their sense of liberty, and utter abhorrence of any post, how profitable soever, so subversive of the
very foundations of human happiness.

On Monday evening, the Sons of Liberty, in a considerable
number, again met and were considering on measures, when
Mr. Silvester, brother-in-law to Mr. Van Schaack, waited on the
company and expressed his concern that so near a friend of his
should by any means have drawn on himself the resentment
of the Sons of Liberty, and asked whether he might not be
useful in the mediation and accommodation of the matter.

The company gave Mr. Silvester for answer that they had no
further demands to make of Mr. Van Schaack than were generally required of all suspected persons on the continent, to
wit, that he not only never had, but also that he never would
apply or act.   Mr. Silvester had half an hour to bring Mr.
Van Schaack's answer; but returned reporting he was gone
home, a mile out of town, which the company taking as an
implied declaration that Mr. Van Schaack undervalued their
notices, determined to visit him in a body, and the number of about four hundred marched in very regular order to his
house which the servants opened and informed them he was
not at home but had gone to Mr. Schuyler's. The boys searched
the house in every room, and not finding him, no entreaties
could prevent their committing some outrages on the furniture,
windows and balcony; which latter, though a very elegant

piece of work, was entirely demolished. The more moderate were obliged to draw off, to induce the company to follow them.

They then visited Mr. Schuyler's and inquired for Mr. V. S. there. Col. Bradstreet (out of a window) assured the company that he valued liberty as much as any of them; said Mr. Van Schaack had been there, but was gone to town to the Mayor and authority; which declaring on his honor, the company left the house and marched to town, the boys drawing Mr. Van Schaack's sleigh along with them, demolishing it piece-meal, till they came to Capt. Bradt's, where they got hay and wood, and setting fire to it went blazing with it to town.

Coming to the Mayor's they knocked and inquired for Mr. Van Schaack. The Mayor declared on honor he was not there, on which they returned to the tavern, where some mentioned Mr. Jacob Vanderhuyden as a person suspected of applying. The company sent for him and required the same satisfaction as of the others. Mr. Vanderhuyden offered to swear, but refused to sign any paper, which caused much heat; but his oath was at length accepted, as he ever declared he never had applied.

Tuesday morning notes were found on many public places desiring the Sons of Liberty, and all that had any business with them, that had ever appeared, to meet at Williams' at five in the afternoon, to consult measures to treat the cause of liberty. At five Mr. Silvester again attended and signified Mr. Van Schaack's entire compliance; begged the honor of the gentlemen in protecting Mr. Van Schaack from any insult, which was to a punctilio performed, and Mr. Van Schaack gave the following affidavit:

'Albany ss: Henry Van Schaack being duly sworn deposeth and saith, that he has never made application to Mr. McEvers or any other person or persons whatsoever, for any post in the stamp office, either in this colony of New York or any other place on the American continent, and that he never will make application or accept the same.

HENRY VAN SCHAACK.'

'Sworn this 7th day of ⎫
January, 1766, before ⎬

    JOHANNES VAN ZANTE, ⎫ Justices.'
    PETER LANSINGH, ⎭

Mr. Van Schaack was hereupon saluted with three cheers, and genteely conducted to his lodgings.''

Mr. Van Schaack's losses in the Indian and fur trade led to pecuniary embarrassments, and he was eventually driven to the necessity of giving up his effects to his creditors. On this trying occasion, the brothers unanimously agreed that everything they could do to make the dividend respectable should be done, that the creditors might be convinced of the honor of the family."*

In addition to the stations held by him, as before mentioned, Mr. Van Schaack was postmaster at Albany from 1757 to 1771, a period of fourteen years. The salary was eighty pounds per annum. His successor, John Monier (who had before been his deputy), received a commission, and complains in a letter to him, that "the thirty pounds a year you allowed me would be better than the allowance I am to receive; at least I fear so, for I am to have twenty per cent. on the net proceeds of my office; no office rent, firing, candles, papers, wax or twine to be allowed. It's true the officers must pay for their letters, which will make some odds."

Previous to July, 1770, the accounts of the Albany postoffice used to be "settled with His Excellency, the General of the King's troops;" after that period, with the postmaster-general at Philadelphia.

Mr. Van Schaack was deprived of the office of postmaster in consequence of his removal to Kinderhook, which took place in 1769. In the spring of the next year he was appointed a justice of the peace and one of the quorum, upon the recommendation of his friend Sir William Johnson. A contemporary, in a letter dated a few years afterwards, speaks of his "judicious conduct since he had been in the administration of justice in these parts and as having gained the universal good-will and applause of all the neighboring towns."

At the first district meeting after his removal to Kinderhook,

---

* His business correspondent in London, under date of 1st April, 1766, says "The sale of beavers has been greatly affected by the results of the late cursed Stamp Act." The same gentleman wrote to him the 7th of February, 1768, at Detroit: "Many plans have been laid before this Government in order to form Detroit into a separate government, but the sentiments of our Ministry seem to tend to modes of economy, and are adverse to any increase of expense. In short, the late behavior of the colonists is such as has incensed our great folks, and made them shy to adopt any measures, however calculated for the good and interest of the provinces."

he was also chosen supervisor of his native town; in which office he was continued for six years by annual re-election (and he also held the office of magistrate), until the administration of the laws was interrupted by the revolution.

It was characteristic of the subject of this sketch to enter with marked diligence and zeal upon the performance of every duty which devolved upon him, and to exert the whole force of his character to the attainment of any given end of public or private good. There was no half way about any of his movements, and no dodging of responsibilities or of danger. Shortly after receiving his appointment of magistrate he issued a notice that a law passed on the 22nd day of October, 1695, against the profanation of the Lord's Day, would be strictly enforced by him, and calling upon all public officers and all well-disposed citizens to the exercise of vigilance in bringing offenders to punishment.

As preliminary to the introduction of the following letters, which become interesting and valuable from their undoubted accuracy and candor, it should be mentioned that the writer, Peter Van Schaack—who was younger by fourteen years than the subject of this sketch—was at this time twenty-two years old, and had just finished a course of legal studies in the office of William Smith, then one of the most distinguished lawyers in the city of New York. That gentleman, in a conversation with Colonel Schuyler, described his late student as "the first genius of all the young fellows at New York."

The better to understand the graphic description of an interesting scene in the Provincial House of Assembly contained in the first of these letters, it will also be proper to mention that Philip Livingston (afterwards known as one of the signers of the Declaration of Independence) resided in the city of New York, and had been an unsuccessful candidate in that city for a seat in the legislature at a recent exciting election. He was then chosen a representative for the manor of Livingston, which, at that time, was entitled to a member. When Mr. Livingston attempted to take his seat in the House, he was excluded on the ground of non-residence. A letter dated a day previous to that which follows, says, "he was met in the hall below the Assembly by about twenty of his friends, who huzzahed him thrice, and then conducted him to his house. People are divided in sentiment, but the major part approve of the conduct of the House."

[FROM PETER VAN SCHAACK.]

NEW YORK, 14th May, 1769.

DEAR BROTHER: I had yesterday the pleasure of reading your very agreeable letter of the 8th instant. The contents are truly interesting.

I wrote you that Mr. Livingston was dismissed from the House. I heard a small altercation between Col. Schuyler and Mr. DeNoyelles on that occasion. The Col. told the House that as they had admitted non-resident freeholders to vote, they ought to preserve a consistency and admit them to sit as representatives, if they were returned as such, since the same act excludes both (this is the common observation). He then said, in an oratorical way: "I beg it as a favor that the House will show the distinction. I want information—I pray for information. I will vote against Mr. Livingston, if the house can convince me that there is a just distinction between non-resident ELECTORS and ELECTED. People out of doors will complain; they will censure this house when it is NO MORE. Gentlemen, people will scrutinize your conduct, and if they find you act without reasons, they will stigmatize you, when they are not afraid of your resentment."

Mr. DeNoyelles rose up and said: "Col. Schuyler, you mean by these threats to INTIMIDATE this House, and your speech is more calculated for the by-standers than for any INFORMATION to this House. Can you suppose any member ignorant that his conduct is known out of doors? No member here but CHOOSES the public should be acquainted with it. For what other purpose have we unanimously resolved to have the doors open? But your observations are nothing to the point in question. Why don't you answer my arguments?"

I should have told you that this gentleman had, before Col. Schuyler spoke the last time, and upon his once before PRAY-ING FOR A DISTINCTION, given some reasons to show why a representative should be a resident, and why a freehold ought to give a right to vote even to non-residents; during which he observed: "The House is the ABSOLUTE judge of its own members, and the act which is made to regulate the election of members in one part, falling short of, in another, suiting with the reason upon which the House judges, may in part be received and partly rejected. A freehold should give a right of representation. Every man who has such an interest in the community as the law prescribes, should be entitled to vote whether resident or not. From this no evil can result. But to admit non-resident representatives is pregnant with many evils. The landed interest in time will be disregarded, and our boroughs, manors, etc., will be bought. This is the case in England. The city of London furnishes representatives for two-thirds of the kingdom. These people being in the interest of the minister, he can carry any point, as we know by sad experience."

Excuse incorrectness. I cannot do justice to Mr. De Noyelles speech. Whether you will altogether approve of it, I don't know. I should not mention it in my present hurry, but that it is in pursuance of my scheme of communicating everything that passes in the House. I shall carry up all the acts of the Assembly, votes, etc.

Yours in a great hurry,   P. V. S.

[FROM THE SAME.]

NEW YORK, Dec. 20th, 1769.

DEAR HARRY: I was much surprised at not receiving a line from you by the post; the more so, as I expected the petitions down. However, this should not have prevented my writing had I had materials and time for a letter.

On Sunday, a good deal of noise was made on account of some anonymous papers, filled with the most violent and indecent expressions, charging a combination between the Governor, Council, and the ascendent party in the House of Assembly, the DeLanceys, to trample upon the liberties of the people, in order, as they said, on the part of the Lieutenant Governor, to keep his peace at home, and on the part of the DeLanceys, to prevent a dissolution. The mighty occasion of this was that a vote had passed the House (*nemine con.*) to grant to the troops two thousand pounds; one thousand thereof to be taken out of the treasury, the other one thousand to be drawn out of the money expected to be emitted in a short time by law. One of those papers contained an invitation to the TRUE SONS OF FREEDOM to meet at the Liberty pole on Monday morning, and from thence to repair to the House of Assembly, to oblige the the House to retract their vote. A number, to the amount of about three or four hundred men, met and appointed a committee to draw up instructions to their members to the above effect. The people who met were not of the more respectable part of town. Of the committee John Lamb is one (strange!). They have this morning delivered their instructions. It is not expected the members will regard those instructions because they were not the sentiments of the major, or the more respectable part of the city.   Much is said on both sides of the question, and people's minds are heated to a great degree.

The minority allege that troops are a useless expense to the colony; that their residence here is a burden to the city; is productive of luxury, and tends to enhance the prices of provisions in an intolerable manner; that they are a tax upon us, and may perhaps be instrumental in enforcing the most unconstitutional acts of Parliament.

The other party say that these are the mere suggestions of a malevolent, disappointed faction; that in a FORMER ADMINISTRATION, when a CERTAIN PARTY prevailed, those moneys were granted without murmur; that they have been granted at a time when we were threatened, in the over-bearing terms of ministerial language, to have our House of Representatives annihilated unless we complied; that a requisition could never be complied with promising greater advantage to this colony; for that now we had the highest assurances that a compliance will procure us that so-long-wished-for object, a paper currency, for which the country cries aloud, and which has been thought so highly necessary that an address has been presented to Sir Henry Moore, most earnestly begging him to solicit his Royal Master for leave to give his assent to a bill for the purpose; and that Sir Henry has been extolled to the skies for exercising his influence to effect this; that an additional reason for a paper currency now is, that the colony is indebted, through means of the deficiencies of the late treasurer, in the sum of thirty thousand pounds, which, unless we have an emission (which being by loan will enable the colony to replace this deficiency in a manner least burdensome), must be supplied by a tax on the colony; that besides, of the two thousand pounds now granted, one half is to pay off the arrearages already incurred, and that if no money is granted to the troops, without which no emission will take place, individuals, who have trusted the troops upon the faith of the government, must suffer.   But if the granting a supply now is so disagreeable, why, when the matter has been under consideration near three weeks, were no objections before raised?   Why endeavor to fix a stigma on the House after passing a vote which they knew would take place and took no pains to prevent?   Why attempt to reduce the city members to the disagreeable dilemma of receding from this vote, or of drawing upon them the unjust censure of disregarding the sentiments of their constituents?

These considerations have operated so powerfully, that the

dream is over, and men are come to their senses, and those
who favored the scheme are now ashamed of it. The House
has voted those papers scandalous libels, and addressed his
Honor to offer a reward of two hundred pounds for any person
discovering the author, etc.

John Lamb is this day to be had before the House. The
charge preferred against him is, that he acted in consequence
of a proposal contained in one of those libels, and therefore
may be supposed to have been AIDING AND ABETTING it.
Poor Johnny has done himself more mischief than the glory he
will reap is likely to compensate.

Some people say that these libels were the LAST WORDS
AND DYING SPEECH OF AN EXPIRING FACTION, but I believe the
gentlemen in the minority will not rest the matter here. They
conceive themselves ill used, and will, I believe, cut out more
difficulties for their opponents. It is remarkable that scarce
any public business is done—motions succeeding motions—
puzzling each other; though, indeed, more of this, in my opinion, is chargeable upon the one than the other party. Guess
which I mean.

I am in a hurry.

Your aff. Bro.,   P. V. S.

[FROM THE SAME.]

NEW YORK, Dec. 25, 1769.

DEAR HARRY: I received your letter enclosing the petitions, etc., and shall take the necessary steps to answer the
ends proposed by my townsmen. As to your letter to the
Governor, I shall not deliver it, because, in the first place, I
expect to stop the bill before it goes out of the House, and, in
the next, it is improper. I have known Sir Henry Moore to
be extremely censured for not passing a bill which had gone
through both Houses, when his only reason was that he had
received a letter from Col. Beekman intimating that an opposition would take place. To ask improper favors may be a bar
to those that are proper.

There is the most perfect concord between the different
branches of the legislature, notwithstanding a number of
attempts to destroy it. I have told you that a scheme was on
foot to raise an opposition to the Assembly's conduct in voting
money to the troops.

The more respectable part of the town discountenances those
attempts, and I doubt not the bill will pass through the House,
but not without opposition. Your man of candor, Col. Schuyler,

acknowledges that he was for granting money last session (in the administration of Sir Henry Moore), but now he says he has more maturely considered the matter, and thinks it wrong. Mr. De Noyelles told him, "Yes, Col. Schuyler, you have had great reason to change your sentiments: politics are changed since the last session."

Your member has distinguished himself by his singularity. When the libels, which I have mentioned to you in a former letter, were under consideration, all the House resolved them to be scandalous libels excepting only the COLONEL.

De Noyelles is a charming fellow: he has silenced some gentlemen from ranting as they used to do. He is really sensible.

His Honor, the judge, is again returned, and OUT TURNED, also. He had his indenture several days without presenting it, with a view, as his opponents thought, to take an occasion, when the House was filled with his friends, to present it. The other party, therefore, to prevent a surprise, sent an order to the clerk of the Crown, to know if any and what return was made to the writ issued to the Manor of Livingston. His answer was that Robert R. Livingston was the member returned. It was then moved that Mr. Justice Livingston should be directed to attend the House. His Honor, who was in the House, begged leave to speak a few words, and observed that there might be more Robert R. Livingstons, and therefore why would the House force HIM to appear? (This was to stave off, as was supposed by his opponents.) Mr. De Noyelles then said, to prevent mistakes, he moved that the returning officer for the Manor might be ordered to attend and acquaint the House which Robert R. Livingston it was. THIS WAS THE THING. Mr. L. then produced the return, in order, as he said, . to save the expense of the officer's attendance. Mr. Livingston's enemies say he lessened himself much by this conduct.

Give my duty and respects, love and affection to all my friends, and wish them a happy New Year for Betsy.

Your aff. brother,   P. V. S.*

[TO GOVERNOR TRYON.]

KINDERHOOK, 12th September, 1772.

SIR: Agreeable to the promise I made Your Excellency at Canajoharie, in the beginning of August last, I now take

---

* Several other letters in the series, possessing historical interest and relating to this period, will be found in the life of Peter Van Schaack, p. 6 to 12.

the liberty of enclosing a map of that part of the county of Albany, lying between the north bounds of the Manor of Livingston, and south of the upper part of the Manor of Rensselaer.*

I must observe to Your Excellency, that it is from actual survey, but it is only intended to give a general idea of the county, and the limits of such particular patents as have occasioned much controversy for a number of years past. The lines of the Westenhook patent are not laid down upon this map, and for this obvious reason: No evidence can be procured to establish the boundaries of it, it being the most obscure and unintelligible description perhaps ever known. If this imperfect sketch gives Your Excellency any insight into this remote part of the Province I shall think myself extremely happy.

The ambition I have of sustaining such a character as to merit the continuance of the notice of government, makes me hope that the freedom of the application I am going to make to Your Excellency will be pardoned. I therefore beg leave to acquaint you, sir, that I am well informed that means have lately been taken, in a very private manner, to obtain signers to certain papers that have a tendency to affect my character in the public offices I sustain. As it is surmised that those papers are directed to Your Excellency, and conveyed by the way of Albany, I hope an application (if any such papers be delivered to Your Excellency) for a knowledge of their contents will be considered to proceed from motives extremely justifiable, when I tell Your Excellency that I have had the honor of serving the Crown and the Province, with an unsullied character, since the year 1755, in different capacities.

The occasion for Mr. Van Schaack's vindication of his character, contained in his letter to Governor Tryon, had well-nigh led to a duel, at that time, between the lieutenant of 1755, now known as MAJOR Van Schaack, and his former captain, who, as we have seen, had become conspicuous as Colonel Schuyler. The two gentlemen were much alike in disposition, being both men of high spirit and marked courage and energy, entertaining nice perceptions of honor, as well as jealous of their reputations; the former impetuous, and the latter described as "hot,

* This territory included the district of Kinderhook and several other towns. In a letter from Mr. Van Schaack to Sir J. William Johnson, dated 24 Nov., 1760, he says. "the inhabitants between the south boundaries of Rensselaerwick and the lower bounds of Kinderhook, east into the woods to the west line of Massachusetts Bay, can make out at least one thousand men able to bear arms."

violent, and indiscreet." They were also about of an age, having both been born in the same year.

Col. Schuyler had reported to Col. Guy Johnson (upon information on which he no doubt relied, but which proved to be erroneous,) that Mr. Van Schaack had attempted to influence the action of Clisors, who had been appointed to summon a jury in an important land trial before the Supreme Court, in which controversy the two gentlemen were probably interested. The charge was met on the part of Mr. Van Schaack by that frank burst of indignation, which is the dictate of conscious integrity in a man of spirit, and the authority for the aspersion demanded. An explanation, dated at Saratoga, was made, and pardon asked, accompanied by the remark: "Be assured, sir, that I shall never decline a personal explanation (in whatever sense you may use the word) that you may think proper to call on me for. You know where to find me, and I shall be at Albany about the 25th of next month."

Good sense prevailed in the matter, and the early friendship, based upon highly meritorious traits of character in both, which had long subsisted between these gentlemen, although in a measure interrupted, for several years, by controversies in regard to conflicting land patents, and by the disturbing causes of the revolution, was, immediately after the latter event, revived in its pristine vigor, and continued through life.*

The controversies in regard to land titles, growing out of conflicting patents and vague descriptions in grants, particularly in the matter of their boundaries, had become a very serious evil for some years previous to the revolution. Whole

---

* Many admirable and commanding traits of character have justly been accorded to General Schuyler. But that constitutional ardor of temperament and vehemence of feeling. to which Chancellor Kent adverts, in his historical discourse, as characterizing General Schuyler in early life, no doubt often led him into extremes. Some exhibitions made by him in his early legislative career, border on knight errantry, and, at this day, excite a smile. A letter to Mr. Van Schaack from his brother, dated New York, 27th February, 1769, contains this paragraph: "The dispute between Col. Schuyler and brewer Anthony (Mr. Gouverneur's son-in-law) was briefly this: The latter had said, at the Coffee House, that the aim of the Colonel's motions in the House was popularity, and added something which I forget. The Colonel immediately armed himself with his sword, went to the Coffee House and other public places thus arrayed. I saw him come in this manner into the House of Assembly, 'tis said in quest of Anthony, not meeting with him, he called upon him at his own house, where he (the Col.) says Anthony asked his pardon.

communities became involved in them, and were arrayed in clans, under their respective patentees and grantors; and there were instances of voyages to England to procure their adjustment by the Board of Privy Council.*

The following paper (written probably in 1773) is from the pen of Peter Van Schaack, who was professionally employed in very many of these controversies, and they doubtless formed the school in which he laid the foundation for that profound learning in the law of real estate for which he afterwards became distinguished. It possesses historical interest and will not be out of place here:

"Among all the subjects which are proposed to the attention of the public, I do not know one of more serious importance to the well-wishers of this colony than the present precarious situation of our landed property; I mean with respect to the disputed titles. There has not perhaps been a greater obstruction to its growth and opulence than this circumstance, and while we lament the hardships we receive from our mother country, the evils arising from the subject of this paper are perhaps not less severe, though less general, than those which are produced by the invasions of our natural and constitutional rights by the British Parliament.

"The courts of justice have long been filled with controversies about disputed boundaries. The inaccuracy of former times prevented that precision in the descriptions which would have prevented the present disputes, and the proprietors of such patents, taking advatage of these uncertainties with which they abound, have extended their claim beyond their right, and ask for indulgence due to transactions in the infancy of the colony. In these circumstances, there are many sufferers, either such as hold their possessions within those controverted lines under a sense of the lands being vacant in law as well as in fact, or else under the sanction of the government obtained in posterior grants of the same lands.

"In this situation is much of the landed property in this colony. The consequence is an almost endless scene of lawsuits

---

* The father of Chief Justice Savage went to England in 1774 for this purpose.

between the claimants, while the lands lay, in **great measure** uncultivated, and the actual possessors are deterred from making improvements by the uncertainty whether they will be preserved in their possessions by the successful party or not.

"The case of the subsequent patentees is the harder, not only on account of the expenses and trouble attending the grant of lands, but also as the benefits arising from the indulgence of His Majesty's Council are lost. It is well known that this Board, for prevention of the mischief just now hinted at, upon every application for grants of lands, gives an opportunity to the prior claimants, if there are any, to assert their titles, and then, after solemn argument and upon mature deliberation, determines whether the land petitioned for has or has not been before granted. Is it not extremely equitable, that the man who knows of those proceedings and neglects to assert his pretensions, should be barred of his right, if he has any; and is not the supposition more natural, that in his own opinion he has no right? And, if this is so, should the discovery afterwards of a circumstance affording a color for a new and extensive claim be indulged?

"I do not, however, mean to charge the courts of law with any wrong in receiving such claims. It is out of their power to reject them. But this evil seems to merit the attention of the legislature.

"Nor is the evil confined merely to the actual possessors and the claimants under subsequent patents. Those very landholders, against whom the mischiefs before mentioned are chargeable, will experience the disadvantage, and perhaps gentleman of large estates whose equitable conduct has hitherto justly secured them, may hereafter be involved in the general ruin. The inaccuracies of their patents may expose them hereafter to the prerogative construction of vacating the Royal Grant for uncertainty. Some late instances of the conduct of the administration may convince us that the large possessions in this Province have excited their attention and jealousy. However disagreeable this doctrine may be, it certainly has not been hitherto extended too far, nor can we reasonably apprehend so many evils from it, as from the present

situation of our titles. It can injure but few landholders of enormous extent, whereas at present the evil extends to hundreds and thousands. Besides, should the Crown vacate some grants, it is most likely that in the future grants they would prefer those who by their manual labors had rendered the land more beneficial, or who have the authority of later patents fairly and openly obtained, and strengthened by the general sense of the country of the vacancy of the lands, to support their claim.

"In short, the encouragement of old dormant claims can never be advantageous to a community. The discouragement of them is, and has always been, so considered by the legislature.

"The evil above mentioned is growing, and calls out aloud for a remedy; and it is much to be wished, that the method of settling contested boundaries in other cases might be adopted in these, by commissioners to be chosen by the parties, and that the legislature would do so either upon application of all parties, or, if some perversely refuse to do it, without their consent; as their dissent must be construed to flow from a sense of their defects in title.

"Similar methods in their consequence are used to settle contests between different colonies, nor are instances wanting when different patentees have submitted to the same equitable mode of decision; a mode preferable to the verdict of twelve ignorant men, often unacquainted even with the language, and for the most part totally ignorant of legal proceedings, most of which evils may be prevented by choosing persons in the above manner."

CHAPTER II.

We have now arrived at a period when the revolutionary movement began to assume an interesting and portentous aspect. In pursuance of a circular-letter addressed to the supervisors of the different towns throughout the colony, by the committee of correspondence appointed in the city of New York, on receipt of the "alarming news from England" of the passage of the Boston Port Bill, the "freeholders and inhabitants" of the district of Kinderhook assembled on the 21st day of June, 1774, and adopted the following resolutions:

"*Resolved*—That in the present critical situation of the colonies in relation to the mother country, the appointment of committees of correspondence in the different colonies appears to us to be a measure highly expedient, as best adapted mutually to communicate to each other the earliest intelligence of such matters as may affect their common interest; to concert such a plan of conduct as—being the result of the united wisdom of all the colonies—will best promote their common benefit, most effectually secure their constitutional rights and liberties, and prevent rash, crude, and inconsiderate measures.

"*Resolved*—That as we have the fullest confidence in the wisdom, prudence, and moderation of the committee of correspondence appointed for the city of New York, it is our opinion, that the inhabitants of the whole Province may, with great safety, rely on their adopting only such measures as shall have our common welfare for their object; but, although we think, for these reasons, that the appointment of distinct committees for the different counties may at present be dispensed with, yet, if the sense of the other districts of this county should be in favor of a committee, we shall readily acquiesce in that measure.

"*Resolved*—That Henry Van Schaack and Mathew *Goes, junior, be appointed by this district to consult with the representatives of the other districts upon the expediency of

---

* This name is pronounced as if spelled Hoes.

appointing a committee for this county, and to nominate on our behalf the persons of whom such committee shall consist."

At a meeting of a county committee held at Albany, on the 13th of August, Robert Yates, Henry Van Schaack and Peter Silvester were nominated as delegates to represent the county in the Continental Congress, subject to the approval of the different districts, who subsequently signified a wish that only one delegate should be sent. Col. Philip Schuyler was thereupon appointed. At the same meeting, August 23rd, a resolution was adopted, "that the resolves of the city and county of New York should be read to the people in each district by their respective committee-men, who are ordered to take the sense of their districts on the same."

At a meeting held a few days afterwards, August 29th, in the Kinderhook district, to take action upon the New York resolves, "Mr. Goes and Mr. Van Schaack informed the meeting that Col. Schuyler had, before the committee of correspondence, on the 13th instant, declared, in express terms, his disapprobation of the above resolves, and in particular against the following words contained in them, viz: 'That it is our greatest happiness and glory to have been born British subjects.' The question was then put, whether it would be proper that those resolves should be adopted, IF COL. SCHUYLER GOES FROM THIS COUNTY AS A DELEGATE to the general Congress at Philadelphia:"

"*Resolved*—That as we acknowledge ourselves British subjects, it would be altogether improper to instruct Col. Schuyler with resolves which hold up principles that tend (as he thinks) to enslave us.

"*Resolved*—That if instructions for a delegate or delegates, or another set of resolves, are offered to the consideration of the committee of correspondents at their next meeting, such instructions or resolves ought to be laid before the several districts within this county before any delegate or delegates attend the Congress from the body of the city and county of Albany.

"*Resolved*—That Matthew Goes, junior, and Henry Van Schaack have acted right in giving their votes against paying delegates to go from the body of the county of Albany, as this district could with great safety have confided its trust in the delegates that are appointed for the city of New York."

Col. Schuyler declined the appointment of delegate to the Continental Congress, in consequence of ill health, and the county committee resolved to adopt "the delegates and resolves of the city and county of New York."

The New York loyalists were disappointed by the proceedings of the Congress of 1774. They had united in the measure of sending delegates to that body, to bring about a reconciliation with the mother country, as well as to procure redress for admitted grievances. The deliberate sanction, by that Assembly, as one of its first steps, of the "Suffolk Resolves," well-nigh destroyed all hope with moderate men of effecting any good through the medium of a Congress.*

The resolutions referred to were adopted at a meeting of delegates from every town and district in the county of Suffolk, in the colony of Massachusetts, held at Dedham, September sixth, 1774. They were adopted by the Continental Congress on the seventeenth of the same month, and entered at length in their proceedings.

The preamble to those famous resolves commences by referring to "the power but not the justice, the vengeance but not the wisdom of Great Britain, which of old persecuted, scourged, and exiled our fugitive parents from their native shores, and now pursues us, their guiltless children, with unrelenting severity;" and, pointing to the government of the mother country as the author of all their grievances, it proceeds to anticipate the honor which would attach to their efforts, "if

---

* In the draft of an unpublished letter from Peter Van Schaack to the Rev. John Vardill, then in London, dated New York, 3rd January, 1775, we find these passages: "The proceedings of the Congress must have reached you several weeks ago, and have by this time no doubt passed through the ordeal of a critical examination. How they have been received is a subject of anxious concern to us all. The spirit they breath, is, I am afraid, little calculated for the meridian of Great Britain. Their CLAIMS are clearly enough stated, but as for CONCESSIONS I am afraid you will search for them in vain.

The announcing the resolutions of the county of Suffolk to the public, under the sanction of a resolve of approbation and adoption from the Congress, astonished everybody. From your ideas of what the utility of a Continental Assembly would consist in, you must have been surprised at such a measure. Indeed the members from this city deny that it was INTENDED to adopt those resolutions.

I dare say you have been equally surprised, instead of a petition or memorial to PARLIAMENT to find a warm address to the NATION at large. There must be some fatal distemper in the body politic which can render such a remedy justifiable or necessary. An appeal to the people from the supreme power of the empire, seems to imply the actual dissolution of the government."

we arrest the hand which would ransack our pockets; if we dissarm the parricide who points the dagger to our bosom; if we nobly defeat that fatal edict which proclaims a power to frame laws for us in all cases whatsoever; if we successfully resist that unparalleled usurpation of unconstitutional power, whereby our capital is robbed of the means of life; whereby the streets of Boston are thronged with military executioners; whereby a murderous law is framed to shelter villians from the hands of justice," etc.

Among the propositions laid down in connection with this denunciatory prefix, was one declaring the allegiance of the colonies to the King, to rest solely in a covenant or compact between them and His Majesty.

By another resolution, it is declared that no obedience is due from the Province to the acts of parliament complained of. By a third, the Justices of the Superior Court of Judicature, Court of Assize, etc., and inferior Court of Common Pleas are denounced as "unconstitutional officers," and a pledge is given to "support and bear harmless all sheriffs and their deputies, constables, jurors, and other officers who shall refuse to carry into execution the orders of said courts;" and the future suitors in said courts are stigmatized as "enemies of their country." By a further resolve it is "recommended to the collectors of taxes, and all other officers who have public moneys in their hands, to retain the same, and not to make any payment thereof to the provincial county treasurer until the civil government of the Province is placed upon a constitutional foundation, or until it shall otherwise be ordered by the proposed Provincial Congress." The eighth resolution denounces the persons who had accepted seats at the Council Board, by virtue of a mandamus from the King, in conformity with a late act of the British Parliament, as "obstinate and incorrigible enemies of their country," unless they publicly resigned their seats "on or before the twentieth instant of September."

By another prominent resolution, the inhabitants of the different towns and districts who qualified, were urged to use their "utmost diligence to acquaint themselves with the art of war as soon as possible, and for that purpose to appear under arms at least once a week."

It is surprising that a body, from which emanated such dignified papers as were the addresses of the Congress of 1774, should at this delicate conjuncture have deliberately sanctioned proceedings so little calculated to ·lead to a reconciliation, accompanying an order for their publication with an "earnest recommendation to their brethren of perseverance in the same firm and temperate conduct as expressed in the resolutions."*

To a liberal and unprejudiced mind, it cannot appear strange that many individuals, who had concurred in the measure of a general Congress, should have withheld their unqualified approval of the proceedings of this body, regarding them as the "heralds of war" rather than the "harbingers of peace."

It cannot be doubted that the class of persons above referred to, perceived, as they honestly thought, at that early day, and in the proceedings of that memorable body, as well as in other public movements, a fixed design to shake off the dependence of the colonies on Great Britain. That there was warrant for the inferences thus drawn by loyalists, seems now to be conceded; and the admission gives them at least a claim on our charity, if it be not a compliment to their sagacity. A respectable authority argues that "the Suffolk county proceedings was in point of fact and almost in form, a declaration of independence."†

[FROM ELIJAH WILLIAMS.‡]

"GREAT BARRINGTON, Dec. 1st., 1774.

DEAR MAJOR: "A New England trick" has long since (in your Province) become proverbial. I used to hear the phrase made use of with some degree of emotion, thinking it not gen-

---

* Journals of Cong., p. 19.

+ New York Rev., No. 19, p. 37.

‡ This gentleman was a graduate of Harvard University, and bore the title of Colonel. He also held the office of High Sheriff of Berkshire county, under the colonial government, and, for many years after the revolution, represented the town of Stockbridge in the legislature of Massachusetts.

erous to characterize a whole country from the conduct of a few worthless emigrants, which I supposed was the case. But I must confess I begin to alter my mind, and to think my country had no injustice done it; and if we have any men of virtue and honor among us the number is so small that it will not be sufficient to support the credit of the country.

People now show themselves daily more and more, but I hope they will confine the most of their tricks to their own Province, and not increase the bad opinion that our neighbors have heretofore conceived of us. But, pray is it not something in our favor, that a sanction is put upon some of the worst of our conduct by the Continental Congress?

Pray give me your opinion of the productions of that august body.

The New England tricks prove very prejudicial to me. Out of six or eight hundred pounds, and above half of it in what are called good hands, I cannot, since law has been set aside, collect enough to support my little family with decency, but must have suffered if I had not had a good stock of provisions of my own; for you may as well find a saint in Barrington as a man who will part with anything without the cash.

I am now under the necessity of advancing a little money to carry on some of my business to advantage, and, as I can collect none here, I am necessitated to apply to you for some help. If you can send me fifteen or twenty pounds, I should be very glad. I must suffer greatly if you cannot help me. I should be glad if you would let me have one hundred weight of German steel. I shall want some more by and by, and I should be glad to know if you can supply me.*

No news in our last papers except the dissolution of parliament, which perhaps you have had before now. Mrs. Williams begs you to salute Mrs. Van Schaack, and to be yourself saluted with her compliments, and so does

Your humble serv't,

E. WILLIAMS.

---

* Mr. Van Schaack was at this time engaged in merchandizing at Kinderhook, between the inhabitants of which place and the people of Berkshire county there was an extensive business intercourse. The exports of Berkshire were usually conveyed to Kinderhook Landing, on the Hudson, and there shipped for New York, and the city supplies for that region were returned by the same route. At a period somewhat earlier than this, the Dutch settlers on the Hudson were very distrustful of their eastern neighbors; a state of feeling probably in a measure growing out of the early disputes in regard to colonial boundaries, which had been attended, on several occasions, with forcible invasion and bloodshed, on the part of some rash New Englanders. So great was this prejudice, at one period, as tradition informs us, tha the Dutch landholders about Kinderhook refused to sell a foot of land to a New England man, and they afterward confidently maintained that they never were troubled with smut in their wheat until the Yankees came among them.

In explanation of some allusions in the foregoing letter, it may here be remarked, that judicial proceedings were suspended in Berkshire county from 1774 to 1780,* and the inhabitants of this county, who were the "first to put a stop to courts" at the beginning of the revolution, were very backward afterwards in consenting to have them resume their functions.†

"At the opening of the courts in Great Barrington, in August, 1774, a body of fifteen hundred men assembled, on an apprehension that the judges were to proceed to act under the new regulations appointed by the parliament of Great Britain, and although they were informed that the act of parliament for that purpose had not arrived, and consequently the business of the court would be conducted in the usual way, still they would not allow the judges to proceed; giving them to understand it was required they quit the town immediately, which was complied with."‡

These violent measures, thus resorted to for arresting the proceedings of the courts, were afterwards relied upon as a proper and justificatory precedent for a similar course to procure redress of their grievances, by the promoters of Shay's rebellion.

* Hist. of Berk, p. 104.
† Ibid, p. 125.
‡ American Archives, 4 series, 1 vol., 724.

The following anecdote is related by John Adams, and, coming from a prominent Whig, gives to it a marked interest. The occurrence took place in the Autumn of 1775, (as would seem from his diary), when he was on a visit to Massachusetts, during an adjournment of the Continental Congress: "An event of the most trifling nature in appearance, and fit only to excite laughter in other times, struck me into a profound reverie, if not a fit of melancholy. I met a man who had sometimes been my client, and sometimes I had been against him. He, though a common horse-jockey, was sometimes in the right, and I had commonly been successful in his favor in our courts of law. He was always in the law and had been sued in many actions at almost every court. As soon as he saw me he came up to me and his first salutation was, 'Oh! Mr. Adams, what great things have you and your colleagues done for us! We can never be grateful enough to you. There are no courts of justice now in this Province, and I hope there never will be another.' Is this the object for which I have been contending? said I to myself, for I rode along without any answer to this wretch. Are these the sentiments of such people, and how many of them are there in the country? Half the nation, for what I know; for half the nation are debtors, if not more, and these have been in all countries, the sentiments of debtors. If the power of the country should go into such hands, and there is great danger that it will, to what purpose have we sacrificed our time, health and everything else? Surely we must guard against this spirit and these principles, or we shall repent of all our conduct. However, the good sense and integrity of the majority of the great body of the people came into my thoughts, for my relief, and the last resource was after all in a good Providence."—Life and works of John Adams, 2 vol., page 420.

CHAPTER III.

In the correspondence, to which the reader's attention will now be invited, we find one brother disclosing his sentiments to another without disguise, and in the confidence of fraternal intercourse. Can we doubt the truthfulness and sincerity of opinions coming to us in this artless shape, or question the purity of motive of the writer in communicating, under such circumstances, his conviction, at this early period, that "people had got to that pass that they did not consider the qualifications of a King, for that they would have no King."

[TO PETER VAN SCHAACK.]

"KINDERHOOK, 16 January, 1775.

DEAR PETER: Yours of the 6th I received last evening. I suppose by to-morrow evening you will be satisfied that I have been by no means inattentive to the several matters you have so warmly recommended to my notice. I am grieved to the heart to find that politics wear so unfavorable a complexion throughout the continent. The dispute with the mother country is carried on with too much acrimony. The proceedings of the Congress have left no back door open for a reconciliation. I am sorry to inform you, that some of the citizens of the metropolis of this county (Albany) are impatient and vehement, and there is but too much reason to apprehend that many of them wish to shake off the dependence on G. B. Notwithstanding all I could do at the meeting of our last committee, the majority insisted upon instructing our members to adopt the resolves of the Continental Congress. I urged the impropriety of it with all my might. I told them that every good man ought to do his endeavors to think of a reconciliation, instead of widening the breach; that perhaps when the House met, some conciliating plan might be suggested and approved, and that by instructing their members such a salutary measure might be thwarted. The meeting was small, but with all I could do the majority, by one, carried the point. It appeared grating to Schuyler, who sat by all the time of the debates, which lasted more than an hour. I think I can see clearly, some designing men in this country make a handle of those resolves to procure a dissolution.

Our committee of correspondence will be dissolved on the 20th instant, the members of the old committee to propose an election of a new committee, in their respective districts. I am pretty certain that our district will drop all committees and all committee-men, and confide in their legal and constitutional representatives, to remonstrate and petition for redress of grievances. King's district the same, I believe. Do not fear those people. They are peaceable, dutiful subjects. They have always been so and will, I dare say, continue in the same disposition of mind notwithstanding the Attorney-General's assertion to the contrary. I hope you and Mr. Jay may think it your duty to draw up a statement of these people's case, and let it be published under the signature of Capt. Baldwin, with all the affidavits, without respect of persons.

The Westenhook commissioners have acted so arbitrary a part that they ought to be exposed. They have been trespassers, and after that, when they were avowedly parties, acted judicially, and committed people to gaol, who attempted to keep them out of inclosed lands upwards of sixty years in possession.

Just now David Pratt informs me that there is a report that some people out of the Massachusetts province are coming over to forbid the justices of King's district from acting as magistrates. It seems these gentlemen are too alert to grant their precepts against offenders when they come over the line.*

They were greatly threatened when that nest of money-makers was destroyed. These gentlemen were then too active to bring offenders to justice, and there would actually have been rescues if it had not been for the spirit and unanimity of the people of that district in general. They voluntarily went in companies of thirty, forty and fifty men to guard the prisoners and protect the officers. Not an instance of greater regard of the laws can be shown in any one district where people have gone to support government than these people. But to return; if these people from the other side of the line come over, and it is known when they set out, it is more than probable that a

* The territory known as "King's District" was situated between Kinderhook and the Massachusetts line, and is now embraced in the towns of New Lebanon, Chatham and Canaan.

number of them will get into gaol. Mr. Pratt says their people are greatly exasperated indeed.

God knows what the event of all this will be. I suppose the Sons of Freedom in the other county are greatly displeased with the inhabitants of King's District for asserting that the King is supposed to be present in all of his courts. I believe they have got to that pass, that they do not consider the qualifications of a King, for that they will have no King.

If our country does not take great care and be resolute to repel force by force, it is most probable we shall be troubled with these people. These people mean, I believe, hostile measures against this colony, if their points cannot be carried by fair means. Their large and sudden strides will prevent them the accomplishment of their views. Other colonies will be alarmed.

I shall take this up to Albany. If anything new occurs you shall hear from me.

Yours,   H. V. S."

[TO THE SAME.]

"KINDERHOOK, 21st January, 1775.

MY DEAR BROTHER: I returned last evening from Albany, where I have finished the dispute Col. Cole and I had with Fonda.

It is but too true that our committee have instructed the members to adopt the resolves. If the proceedings of the committee were shown, it will appear that not above five, or six, or seven of the members give the instructions. The meeting was thin, and those who were there had not consulted their constituents. This was an objection I raised. One or two of them declared they would take instructions on themselves. It was at length put to vote. I was in the minority.

The people in this district had a thin meeting yesterday. The meeting was advertised by Matthew Goes and myself, to acquaint the people that the old committee was dissolved, and to know whether they would go to the choice of a new one. They were unanimous against it; committees of correspondence, proceedings of the delegates, etc., not having answered the great object of a reconciliation with the mother country, which our people have all along had in view.

In haste, adieu.   Yours aff.,   H. V. S."

Egbert Benson, well known as a prominent champion of the revolution, was upon terms of great intimacy with

Mr. Van Schaack and his brothers. A marked friendship, as pure and sincere as it was close and lasting, begun in early life and only slightly disturbed by political differences, for a short period, during the revolutionary war, subsisted between them for considerably more than half a century, and was only terminated as the parties successively descended in good old age to honorable graves.

A letter from David Van Schaack to his brother in New York, dated at Kinderhook, 15th January, 1775, contained these passages:

"Would you believe it, that Benson is so warm a Son of Liberty as to produce the following lines to me? 'In short, if we are but firm and unanimous among ourselves, we need not fear Lord North, nor Lord Mansfield, nor all the lords and devils upon earth; but the mischief is we have some among us FRIENDS TO GOVERNMENT, as they call themselves, who, with their coolness and moderation, or rather with their baseness and treachery, I am afraid will ruin our cause. Thank heaven you and I are not of that number!*

"Is it not amazing that a man of his sense and goodness should so far lose himself as to become a dupe to principles the most pernicious to everything good and valuable. I suppose the Farmer's unanswerable performance has helped these sentiments out of his profession. To see the madness, folly and extravagance into which our modern patriots and Sons of Liberty run, is enough to make a well-meaning person shudder at what may be the consequences."

[FROM PETER VAN SCHAACK.]

NEW YORK, 25th Feb., 1775.

DEAR BROTHER: Your letter by Mr. Benson arrived but last night. * * * * *

As to politics, it is impossible to conceive what will be the end of the present troubles. Should the mother country fail in asserting her supremacy, this colony will be eternally odious,

* It is not certain but that Benson, who must have known the political moderation of his correspondent, purposely wrote this letter to fix his friend on the popular side.

and yet it is impossible that we can unite in the violent measures of our neighbors on either side of us. In some of the
Southern colonies, they are raising money and levying troops,
with a design, as they say, to defend themselves. This was
just the cant of the republicans in the last century. Indeed,
all the present manœuvres have a tendency to the same unhappy catastrophe. It becomes us, however, to behave so far
cautiously as not unnecessarily to make ourselves odious.
Your resolves do not quite please me.

There are many people in town here of the moderate party
who will abide by the ASSOCIATION. Indeed, a non-importation
and non-consumption are what we expected they would agree
to. It is a peaceable mode of obtaining redress. It should
have a fair trial, especially the former. The usefulness of the
latter is not likely to be so very important, but it will prevent
smuggling more effectually than all the navy of England.

I shall leave off drinking tea, and though I advise no body
out of my own family to do so, yet I think the less publicly
they declare against this the better. Many windows will be
broken, I fancy, on this score, if not much worse consequences.
I would not go into a WRONG measure for the sake of union,
but innocent measures, I think, should be acquiesced in.

I am, with my unfeigned respects, with Betsy's, to my father
and mother, your wife, etc., etc.

Yours aff'y.   P. VAN SCHAACK.

[TO WOODBRIDGE LITTLE, AND OTHERS.]*

"KINDERHOOK, 8th March, 1775.

GENTLEMEN: I have flattered myself that the mode of
conduct pursued by me, respecting the present unhappy

---

* "Mr. Little was a lawyer by profession, I believe, of quite respectable standing, and I
think King's attorney for the county when the revolution came on. His town (Pittsfield) and
county (Berkshire) was composed mostly of very zealous Whigs, particularly the clergyman
of the parish, the Reverend Thomas Allen, as who then, as also in the federal and demo-
cratic times thereafter, pursued Mr. Little (as he and his friends at least thought) pretty
warmly and inexorably. However, there was no love lost between them. I believe that
Mr. Little had to submit to some inconvenient and annoying personal restraints during the
period of the revolution; but as his integrity of purpose was never questioned after the scares
of the revolution had passed, he resumed his former standing in society, and was much
employed in the municipal concerns of the town and as its representative in the legislature.
Being a member of the Board of Trustees of Williams' College, and having himself no child,
he left, by his will, the bulk of his very considerable property to that institution." [Letter
to the author from the Hon. Ezekiel Bacon, of Utica, who was a native of Berkshire, for
several years its representative in Congress, and in 1811, Chief Justice of the Circuit Court
of Common Pleas].

disputes between Great Britain and her colonies, would have secured me the well-wishes of the people in Pittsfield, instead of incurring their censures. But, it seems, reports are raised and spread against me with the greatest asperity imaginable, in order to draw the popular resentment of your place upon me. The agreeable connection that has long subsisted between a great number of reputable inhabitants of Berkshire county and my father and his family, makes me desirous of removing unjust and ill-grounded suspicions respecting my public conduct on the present alarming dispute the unhappy colonies are engaged in with the parent state.

The reports invented and propagated against me are, I hear, as follows:

First—That certain letters have been sent from Gen. Gage and Col. Williams, of Hatfield, to me, to be forwarded to Canada, to draw a military force from that quarter, and that I am to make a junction with that force, to imbrue my hands in the blood of my countrymen, the people of Berkshire.

Second—That I have engaged and influenced the people of King's district to enter into resolves injurious to American liberty.

Third—That I have prevailed on the inhabitants of this district to agree in measures similar to those in the above district.

Fourth—That I have abused people in Pittsfield, by advising some of them to be sued, BECAUSE they acted in opposition to those laws of parliament so universally opposed throughout the colonies, etc.

I shall reply to these several malicious charges distinctly, that you may remove any prejudices yourselves or neighbors may have conceived against me, and that you may be convinced those reports are founded in malice and falsehood.

In answer to the first article, I reply, upon the word and honor of a man who values both highly, that I have neither directly or indirectly heard either from General Gage or Colonel Williams about this matter, nor do I know of any letters having been sent by these gentlemen to Canada through any other channel.

The second charge is equally false and injurious. The whole foundation for the calumny is simply this: Some people in Kings, and a neighboring district to it, had formed a plan to put a stop to courts of justice, under the specious pretence of their laboring under oppressive hardships, by being continually harassed with law suits carried on by creditors living in your county, who avoided the payment of their own debts by the courts of justice being stopped there. But, in fact, it appeared that the real design was to screen themselves from paying their just debts to people living in both provinces. In consequence of this a district meeting was held on the 24th of December last. The result of that meeting soon after appeared in Mr. Gaines' newspaper, to which I refer.*

The foundation for the third charge is as follows: Mr. Abraham Yates, junior, chairman of a committee of correspondence, directed a letter to me in the following words:

'ALBANY, 24 January, 1775.

SIR: At a meeting of the new committee of correspondents, agreeable to the resolution of the former, this committee, after having appointed a chairman, a clerk and a sub-committee, to manage the ordinary business, ordered that letters be written to the supervisors of the districts that did not associate at this meeting, to desire them if no committee be appointed to urge the district thereto, and should a committee be already appointed, that then the supervisor will be good enough to send this letter to them, but, in either case, an answer is desired directed to your most humble servant,

AB'M YATES, Jr.

To Henry Van Schaack, Esq.,
Supervisor of the District of Kinderhook.'

To this letter I replied as follows:

'KINDERHOOK, 6th Feb., 1775.

SIR: Your letter of the 24th of January I did not receive until the first instant. The subject-matter on which you have written, is, in part, answered by mine in company with Mr. Goes, of the 23d ultimo, to the chairman of the committee of correspondence at Albany. As the new committee, by your letter, seem desirous of having the sense of the districts who have not sent committee-men, I shall request of the inhabitants of this district to meet sometime next week, in order that the sense of the people may be obtained collectively, on a matter that may be important in its consequences. I am, sir,

Your most humble servant,

HENRY VAN SCHAACK.'

In consequence of what precedes I requested the inhabitants to meet on the 16th of February last, and at that meeting

---

* See Appendix B.

the foregoing letters were fully considered, and, upon the
question being put whether the meeting would agree to the
choice of a new committee, it was unanimously voted
to have no committee, because the people could with safety
rely upon their representatives (then convened in general
Assembly) to make a statement of the grievances the colony
labors under, the more so as the journals of the House informed
the meeting that the Lieut. Governor, in his speech to the Assembly, recommended it to them to 'examine the complaints of
their constituents with calmness and deliberation, and determine on them with an honest impartiality, and that if they
found them to be well grounded, to pursue the means of redress
which the constitution has pointed out. Supplicate the throne
and our most gracious Sovereign will hear and relieve you with
paternal tenderness.'

The Assembly, in answer, say they will 'with calmness and
deliberation pursue the most probable means to obtain a redress
of our grievances.'

Again, we found by the journals of the House, that Col.
P. Livingston, on the 31st January last, moved that a day may
be appointed to take the state of this colony into consideration,
to enter such resolutions as the House may agree to on their journal, and in consequence of such resolutions, to prepare an humble, firm, dutiful and loyal petition 'to our most gracious
Sovereign.' Mr. DeLancey immediately after moved 'that a
memorial to the Lords, and representation and remonstrance to
the Commons, of Great Britain, may be prepared together with
the petition.' The House agreed to both motions *nemine con-
tradicente*.

For these reasons, the people of Kinderhook were unanimously of the opinion, that a petition to the King, and a
memorial and a remonstrance to the Lords and Commons from
the House of Assembly, would have more effect than any steps
a committee in the county could take.

The last charge is so trifling, and beneath the attention of
the town of Pittsfield, that a repetition of it seems almost unnecessary. However, lest the retailers of scandal and detraction
might impute my silence to want of means for a justification,
I shall say a few words on that subject also, altho' my letter is
grown already to an enormous length.

My brother David, it seems, has, after waiting a great
while for money due from Mr. David Noble, of Pittsfield,
thought proper to arrest him in this county. Hence a story
has been raised, that I should have advised the suit, because
Mr. Noble had been chosen a captain in Pittsfield to oppose

British acts of parliament. To this I answer, that Mr. Noble was in jail before ever I heard of the suit being commenced. Had I given the advice I would not care how public it was. There is nothing criminal or offensive to the town of Pittsfield in the advice; but the motives said to have influenced me are so trifling and absurd that I am amazed it can be believed.

I find I am blamed by some people for treating Mr. James Easton, of Pittsfield, with language injurious to this gentleman in his present elevated station.*

I will here be a little particular, in order to show from whence this report took its rise. There is an account against Mr. E. in my books since May in the year 1773; the payment of which I have had a right to expect for sometime past. At last I drew an order on him, which not being honored with acceptance and at the same time the refusal being accompanied with unpleasing† * * * *

To show with what little propriety Easton could object to being called upon to pay his debts, at this time, the following advertisement issued by him is placed before the reader:

"Whereas the subscriber has closed his book accounts, all persons therefore indebted to him, by note or otherwise, are now once more earnestly requested to discharge the same in cash or country produce. Those who are conscious to themselves that they ought to have paid one, two or three years ago, may expect trouble from the Court of Conscience, who will sit immediately upon the reading of this, and acquit or condemn on the best evidence, and finally execute judgment, unless they discharge the same forthwith. And 'tis to be hoped no one will take the advantage of this time we are fallen into, and neglect to pay, remembering the court will sit constantly, and they liable to indictment, arrestment, and what is still worse, is that they are obliged to turn evidence against themselves. Those who will escape the court, trial, judgment and execution aforesaid, will doubtless exert themselves to make payment. Their conduct will then bear reflection, while otherwise it will not, and it will give pleasure to their very good friend and

Humble servant,

JAMES EASTON.

March 1st, 1775."

---

* Easton had been chosen a militia colonel and was a tavern keeper in the town of Pittsfield. He was one of the party from Berkshire who joined the "Green Mountain Boys" in their expedition against Ticonderoga two months after the date.

† The rest of this paper is unfortunately lost.

"To the, Gentlemen who compose the Convention of Committees of the several Towns in the County of Berkshire, to be held on the third Tuesday of April, 1775, at Stockbridge:

KINDERHOOK, 14 April, 1775.

GENTLEMEN: Jahlcel Woodbridge, Esq., has transmitted to me. as supervisor of this district, certain resolves said to be entered into by 'a convention of committees from the several towns in Berkshire county, held at Stockbridge, on the 23rd day of March, A. D. 1775.' Tho' the convention have ordered them to be directed to me as supervisor, yet I do not look upon myself warranted to call a public meeting in consequence of them, well knowing that the greater and better part of the inhabitants of both districts would be displeased to be called together on such an occasion, more especially as our annual stated meeting is so near at hand as the month of May next. It is most probable, we shall then hold up to public view proceedings which (though unjustifiable upon principles of Christianity, law, humanity, or even that of Congress itself) have this advantage that they are altogether singular.   This part of their merit I shall pass over unnoticed.

As I mean, gentlemen, to treat you in your conventional capacity with all possible lenity, I shall pass over what I apprehend to be the true reasons which influenced your deliberations, and confine my observations to the ostensible one, viz., that it did 'appear to your body that the inhabitants of Kinderhook and King's districts have been drawn into act contrary to the association of the Continental Congress, which you are induced to believe was gone into by the artful insinuations of persons disaffected to the rights, liberties, and privileges of North America.'

As you mean by these your resolves to transmit the inhabitants of two districts to posterity as enemies to our most gracious Sovereign and his vast extended empire, I hope, in the plenitude of. your conventional power, you will suffer one of the proscribed individuals to offer a few remarks on your proceedings, that they may go in the 'Gazette' with the resolves, lest the British parliament should take measures to carry ministerial vengeance against 'the enemies of the rights and liberties of North America and the whole British empire.' What a terrible situation shall we be in, if all the military force at Boston is sent against these devoted districts.

If you are really in earnest in these your resolves, you would have done well to have pointed out, in the first place, in what instances the people of Kinderhook and King's districts had violated the association, and, in the second, that by such conduct they could with propriety be held up to the present and future generations 'as enemies,' etc. Mere assertions in matters of such importance will not do. Authentic proof is required of you. If you fail in this, your ostentatious resolves will operate no further, it is hoped, than among yourselves.

Should the intemperate spirit which occasioned the extraordinary production under contemplation be a little subsided by the time you meet again, as a convention, I hope to make it appear that you far exceed the limits assigned by the congress of your appointment. The eleventh article does by no means warrant your resolves. It enacts, or recommends, 'that a committee be chosen in every county, city and town, by those who are qualified to vote, for representatives in the legislature, whose business it shall be, attentively to observe the conduct of all persons touching this association, and when it shall be made appear, to the satisfaction of a majority of any such committee, that any person WITHIN THE LIMITS OF THEIR APPOINTMENT, has violated this association, that such majority do forthwith cause the truth of the case to be published in the Gazette etc.

You will observe that this article of the association prescribes no rule of punishment to those who do not appoint committees, nor even to conventions of intolerable committees who exceed all bounds of justice, discretion, and even of humanity. If you have recourse to the 14th article, that, you will see, regards whole colonies and provinces. In short, it is difficult to know upon what principles you have proscribed two whole districts, and at the time when you are so very condescending as to be induced to believe, 'that the inhabitants of these districts had gone into a violation of the association of the congress by the artful insinuations of persons disaffected to the rights, liberties and privileges of North America.' Admitting, upon your own principles, that you, as a conventional body, consider that we are within the limits of your appointment, does it not argue unchristian principles in you to treat the innocent with the guilty indiscriminately, as ENEMIES TO THE RIGHTS AND LIBERTIES OF NORTH AMERICA AND TO THE WHOLE BRITISH EMPIRE'—and that, too, without taking one step to convince us of our error.

It has been suggested that we have in two instances offended, whereby we have subjected ourselves to your displeasure. The first is that the use of tea is not discontinued. The second, tha t we have not participated in the appointment of a committee of correspondence. Why you should confine your rigid patriotism to these districts only, is a question which may hereafter be answered; especially since the committees of inspection in the city of Albany, Schenectady, Rensselaer-wick and Claverack (with everyone of these districts people of your own county hold commercial intercourse) suffer tea to be disposed of and drank as usual.

As to the second charge, true it is we have not participated in a committee of correspondence since the month of January last. The people of both districts unanimously agreed to rest a state of their grievances with the House of Representatives. This, you will remember was at a time when our Assembly 'was not dissolved contrary to the rights of the people,' and at the time when the representative of our most excellent King did not check the House for 'attempting to deliberate on grievances,' but, on the contrary, were encouraged to make 'their dutiful, humble, loyal and reasonable petitions to the Crown for redress.' This being a short but true state of facts, and for which we are like to be treated as 'enemies to the continent and the whole British Empire.'

As I have reason to hope these resolves may be rescinded or that it will be made to appear that they did not pass UNANIMOUSLY, I shall rest observations I had to make on the conduct of several people of your county touching the association; and conclude my letter with praying to Almighty God that the present unhappy differences between the parent state and her colonies may be removed; that a cordial reconcil-iation may take place, and that a permanent constitution may be offered to, and approved of, by the colonies, and that you may all be forgiven at the great day of judgment for your cruel and vindictive spirit towards us.

H. VAN SCHAACK."

[TO PETER VAN SCHAACK.]

KINDERHOOK, 28th April, 1775.

DEAR BROTHER: I have received your letter, and had previously to it received the melancholy news from Boston.*

This shocking affair draws a cloud over all our prospects in this life, as it will in all probability not only ruin America, but pull down Great Britain after it. The cruelties committed by the soldiery have annihilated the very name of Tory in New England. I plainly foresee that that province is in such

---

* The account of the battle of Lexington.

a state that next year there will be famine. No labor is done. The farms lie uncultivated, and everything is sad.

I by all means approve of your coming up here. If any where, we shall preserve peace here. We are, and have been, very circumspect for a long while.

I am, with anxiety and great concern for Great Britain and America,

Yours sincerely,

DAVID VAN SCHAACK.

[TO PETER VAN SCHAACK.]

KINDERHOOK, 29 April, 1775.

DEAR PETER: The melancholy accounts from Boston had reached us before your letter to David got here last night by the post. It fills every good human breast with sorrow to see the unhappy situation this county is in. A storm threatened us when the news first came, but I fancy everything subsides again.

I am happy to find you and your family intend us a visit, to be out of the noise of your townsmen. Beaver Hall (this is my house) I hope may be the place you intend to retreat to. You and Betsy may be assured of a hearty welcome. I trust we shall be able to preserve peace and good order in spite of every effort to the contrary. Your presence would contribute towards it. By saying that you and Betsy, etc., I mean your whole family. God bless you and yours and be assured that EVERYBODY here will be happy to see you all.

In haste,

Your aff. brother,

H. VAN SCHAACK.

The inhabitants of the district of Kinderhook had withdrawn from the committee of correspondence in January of this year, for the alleged reason that they had found by experience that those committees had not answered the salutary purposes they were intended for by the well-meaning part of the county; and "because they had not been productive of proposing one single thing that has had a tendency of promoting a reconciliation between the mother country and the colonies."

But when the "melancholy news" arrived from Boston announcing the shedding of blood at Lexington, they were again roused to action by an urgent invitation from the county committee, and they again assembled, and chose Henry Van Schaack, Matthew Goes, junior, Peter Vosburgh and Peter S. Van Alstyne, delegates to represent them in the district and county committees. Mr. Van Schaack accepted his appointment with great reluctance, in obedience to the urgent desire of his fellow citizens, whose confidence he enjoyed in an eminent degree, as is shown by his re-election at this period, for the sixth time in succession, to the office of supervisor, at a full meeting of his townsmen, "with only two dissentients."

[TO PETER VAN SCHAACK.]

KINDERHOOK LANDING, 18th May, 1775.

DEAR PETER: I have received all of your letters which you have from time to time written, but their particular dates I cannot attend to, as many of them were destroyed lest visitors should lay their hands on them.

I have been threatened from different quarters with visits, but I have hitherto escaped; owing, I hope, to the uprightness of my conduct. When threatenings were thrown out by some, others entered into an examination of my conduct, and as soon as it was properly investigated, violences abated. Upon the whole I believe I am considered a considerable of a liberty-man. I have endeavored to inculcate moderation and temper. Those in this county, as well as some in the other province, who have been violent are cooling fast. Some of the most violent Whigs in Berkshire are sueing for a reconciliation. Whatever the event may be, I hope it will appear, when the spirit of factious violence abates, that my conduct in the most convulsive moments, has been such as will meet the approbation of those who are friends to liberty and good government. A volume of this when I see you. Expect to hear of intolerable ingratitude from some of those who have been cherished in our bosoms.

You will doubtless hear before this comes to hand that our district has joined in a committee of safety, protection and correspondence, sorely against my will, for many reasons. Necessity has no laws. I made all the interest in my power not to be one of the deputies. There is no knowing what spirit the deliberations of the congress may be influenced by. I fear the worst, and at the same time I am thoroughly convinced that Great Britain will lower us in spite of all we can do. The fishing bill must make us knuckle.

What think you of the taking of Ticonderoga? The regular soldiers passed by my door last Tuesday. Strange sight to see Britons led into captivity by Americans! This step of the Connecticut people has alarmed many violent Whigs in Albany. I hope our Provincial Congress will consider it as an unjustifiable invasion and treat it accordingly.

Levelling principles are held up in Spencertown. In short, the county is convulsed everywhere. God knows what the end will be.

Pray, ask Silvester what Col. Schuyler said when the secret expedition to Ticonderoga was first discovered to the committee at Albany. I am not sure whether he will tell you, but this you may be sure of, that he lamented his being obliged to go to the congress, otherwise he would have taken the honor to himself of reducing the Fort!

Adieu. Yours in haste, but

Affectionately, H. V. S.

A letter dated at Kinderhook 16th May, 1775, contains this paragraph: "The Ticonderoga garrison just now passed through here, under a guard of men, to Hartford jail. The officers go down without a guard, and just now stopped at Goes'. I really think our Provincial Congress should resent the insult of taking a King's Fort within our province, and carrying the garrison into another province prisoners of war, in a high and public manner. Our province is a great deal too low. I hope Governer Colden will write the Governor of Connecticut on the subject. The regulars in passing through here expressed their surprise that a King's Governor should allow King's troops to be carried through here prisoners of war and not be rescued. This fatal affair will bring destruction on our frontiers."

The taking of Ticonderoga, although it immediately followed, was not exactly suggested by the affair at Lexington, as the relative dates of those occurrences might seem to indicate. The capture of that Fort had been secretly projected by the "Green Mountain Boys" several weeks previous to the occurrences at Lexington, and its execution only deferred to await the commencement of hostilities. This is shown by a letter from John Brown (known afterwards as Major and Colonel Brown), who was a member of the Massachusetts Provincial Congress, and had been dispatched by that body to Canada to promote the revolutionary movement in that province. He wrote from Montreal to the Boston committee of correspondence under date of 29th of March, 1775, as follows: "One thing I must mention, to be kept a profound secret. The fort at Ticonderoga must be seized as soon as possible should hostilities be committed by the King's troops. The people in the New Hampshire grants have arranged to do this business, and, in my opinion, they are the most proper persons for this job. This will effectually curb this province and all the troops that may be sent there.*"

In the conflicting accounts published concerning the Lexington affair, and in which each party sought to fasten upon the other the responsibility of commencing hostilities, it is not surprising that the seizure of Ticonderoga and the forcible removal of its garrison should have been condemned as unjustifiable, by those who deprecated all violent measures.†

[FROM JOHN SERGEANT.]

STOCKBRIDGE, May 23, 1775.

SIR: I send you inclosed the paper you gave me sometime since. I have neglected sending it for want of a safe opportunity. I have shown it to several gentlemen. They correct but one thing in it, which is the asserting that the King has a right to make courts. Perhaps you might satisfy them what you meant by it, etc.

In haste,

Your most obedient and humble servant,

JOHN SERGEANT.

---

* American Archives, 4 series, vol. 2, p. 243.

† Governor Turnbull disavowed it as a public measure, and treated it as a private expedition, although the "number of gentlemen from Connecticut," who formed a part of it, included several members of the legislature of that colony.

CHAPTER IV.

It was on Sunday, the twenty-fifth of June, 1775, and just ten days after he had been appointed General and Commander-in-Chief of the army of the United Colonies, "raised or to be raised for the defense of American liberty," that George Washington, accompanied by his recently appointed military associates, Major-Generals Lee and Schuyler, arrived in the city of New York from the Continental Congress, then in session at Philadelphia. Amid the rattling of drums and the display of colors, they landed from the Jersey shore, and were received upon the beach by a large assemblage of people, with all the éclat which the novel capacity in which they appeared was likely to excite in the burning breasts of the "Sons of Liberty." Under the escort of a military detachment, ordered out for the occasion, the three distinguished champions of freedom were conducted to their quarters "amid the repeated shouts and huzzahs" of the attending multitude.

On the morning of that same day it was announced in the city, that a ship had arrived at Sandy Hook, having on board Governor Tryon, just returning to resume the administration of the government after a year's absence in England. What more proper occasion than this, at least with one portion of the excited community, for the exhibition of feelings of loyalty, for which preparations were made now in anticipation of his landing?

The royal deputy reached the city in the evening of the same day, and landed at the Exchange, where he was joyfully welcomed by the provincial and city authorities, and by an "immense number of the principal men of the city," and conducted by them, preceded by a detachment of military, to his lodgings in the Broadway, amid "universal shouts of applause," including (as we are told) the loud acclaims of many of those who had before formed the escort of the three *pro*-liberate generals.

The reception which was thus given to these high dignitaries, occupying such different and conflicting positions, had been ordered, in part, by the Provincial Congress, which was in session on the day of these occurrences—for these exciting times "knew no Sundays." A public display on the occasion would almost seem to have been invited by the Commander-in-Chief himself, doubtless that so rare an occasion might not be lost for imparting dignity to the cause in which he was embarked, or for infusing new animation into the popular mind.

In justification of this latter inference, we find an entry in the journals of the Provincial Congress, on the morning of the twenty-fifth of June, acknowledging a "letter from General Schuyler, dated at New Brunswick, June 24th, 1775," informing this congress, that General Washington, with his retinue, would be at Newark this morning, and requesting this congress to send some of its members to meet him there, and advise the most proper place for him to cross Hudson's river on his way to New York.*

A committee, of whom the lamented Montgomery was one, was appointed to proceed to Newark agreeably to this invitation: "And information being received that Governor Tryon is at the Hook and will land at about one o'clock, Col. Lasher was called in, and requested to send one company of the militia to Powle's Hook to meet the generals; that he have another company at this side of the ferry for the same purpose; that he have the residue of his battalion ready to receive either the generals or Governor Tryon, whichever should first arrive, and to wait on both as well as circumstances will allow."

On the morning of the next day, the Congress appointed a committee to call on General Washington to ascertain "when he would be waited on by the Congress with their address." The hour of half past two o'clock in the afternoon having been designated, the congress waited on the Commander-in-

* Journals N. Y. Provin. Cong., 1 vol., p. 54

Chief at that time in a body and presented him their address, which had been reduced to writing and was directed "To His Excellency George Washington, Generalissimo of all the forces raised and to be raised in the federated colonies of America." To this address the Commander-in-Chief made a suitable reply, of which a copy was obtained (as appears by the record) "to prevent mistakes."

These ceremonies having been completed, Washington and Lee proceeded on their journey to the seat of war, already rendered conspicuous by the battle of Bunker's Hill; while Schuyler remained in the town to make preparations for the expedition against Canada, of which he was the chosen leader.

The instructions given to the latter, by the Commander-in-Chief, on assigning to him the Command of all the troops destined for the New York department, required him "to keep a watchful eye on Governor Tryon,"* and, but for the fact that such an interference might be deemed an infringement of the powers of the Continental Congress then in session, Washington more than intimated the propriety of seizing the person of the royal Governor, in case he should be found "attempting directly or indirectly any measures inimical to the common cause; albeit," he remarked, "the seizing of a Governor would be quite a new thing, and of exceeding great importance."†

During his stay in the city, Schuyler lodged with a friend in Broadway nearly opposite the Governor's mansion. The two gentlemen were well acquainted with each other, the former having been at the head of the government for several years, and the latter well known as a "COLONEL" in the provincial militia, and as a somewhat conspicuous member of the general Assembly. They had often been brought into official intercourse, and it was even said that the provincial Colonel was under some obligations to the royal representative for favors received. However this latter fact may be, in view of the recent return of the last named gentleman, after so long an

* Washington's letter to Schuyler, dated New York, June 25, 1755.—Amer. Arch., 4th series, vol. 2, p. 1084.

† Ibid.

absence from the country, it was natural that an interview should take place, although not a little awkward, whether we consider the new position in which the late colonial legislator was now placed by his recent military appointment, or the particular business which occasioned his detention in the city.

Accordingly (as Tory tradition informs us), the congressional General, desirous of paying his respects to the royal representative, but not at all disposed to throw aside the trappings which attached to his own elevated position as a Major-General in the American army, appeared at the door of the Governor's mansion "dressed in the regimentals of rebellion," and sent in word that "General Schuyler had called to see him." The Governor, little loath to compromit his allegiance to his royal master, or his own official dignity as Captain-General, Governor-in-chief and Vice-Admiral of His Majesty's province of New York, by recognizing a military commission emanating from such an "illegal body" as the "rebel congress," returned for answer to the message of his waiting guest, that he "knew no such man as GENERAL Schuyler."

No further attempt was made for an interview, and the two gentlemen probably never met afterwards.

Having completed, so far as practicable at New York, his arrangement for the invasion of Canada, Schuyler proceeded to Albany, where, on Sunday, the ninth day of July, a public reception was given to the "third Major-General of the American army."*

He was received here, upon his landing, with great ceremony, and the honors due to his rank and elevated station were accorded to him without stint or reserve and in the best style known to this ancient Dutch city. Under the escort of the city troop of horse, of the association company, and of the city and county committee of safety correspondence and protection, and attended by the principal inhabitants of the city, the General was conducted to the City Hall.

Here the committee presented a patriotic address, to which (as the record informs us) "a polite answer" was returned by

---

* This reception gave rise to some ludicrous scenes, illustrating the extreme jealousy of liberty, which are elsewhere recorded.—Vide life of Peter Van Schaack, p. 68.

the General. The company thereupon proceeded to the King's
Arms tavern, where, albeit it was Sunday, "a grand entertain-
ment was provided."*

* Amer. Arch., 4 series, 2 vol., p. 615.

CHAPTER V.

The removal of Mr. Van Schaack's brother Peter with his family from the city of New York to Kinderhook in May of this year suspended their correspondence, and deprives the biographer of the valuable and authentic historical materials which a continuance of their written inter-communications at this interesting period would have furnished. We are translated into the next year to find matter worthy of note.

[JOHN HARRIS CRUGER TO PETER VAN SCHAACK.]

NEW YORK, 4th March, 1776.

DEAR SIR: Last week I had the pleasure of your letter of the 8th ultimo. Your friendly invitation to the distressed of this place at this season, does the greatest honor to your hospitality. I do not know of any of our friends that have not already (like good generals) secured a retreat when they are forced to fly. If any should come within my knowledge, I will acquaint them with your humane sentiments. Many of our inhabitants, members in the lowest circumstances, have brought on themselves unnecessary expense and trouble by flying most precipitately out of town, subject in the country to the greatest impositions. I have seen no occasion, as yet, to quit the town, nor do I believe there will be any, unless troops arrive here from England, which, with me, yet remains a doubtful case; and whenever they do come they will meet with a warm reception, as we are preparing batteries in several places. One is finished in the Broadway from Weatherhead's house to the opposite side of the way; another on the wharf, at Ten Eyck and Seaman's store, Coenties dock; a third is building on the bank behind Lambert Moore's house, commanding the North river; and a fourth on poor Jacob Walton's point, at Belleview, to the entire ruin and destruction of everything, the house being common barracks for between two and three hundred men. Jacob was wholly dispossessed in three days' time. He is gone on Long Island, with all his family, to Mosquito Cove, where a house was taken for him. His case is truly hard, to say no more of it.

I have this morning bought you "Common Sense," and send it herewith. It is the first time I have seen the pamphlet, and I have not time now to read it. I am obliged to hurry, for fear of missing this opportunity.

My love to Betsey, and best wishes for your happiness, is all I have time to add at present, save the strongest assurances of esteem and regard of, dear sir,

Your very affectionate,

J. H. CRUGER.*

[TO THE NEW YORK CONVENTION.]

KINDERHOOK, ALBANY COUNTY,
22nd March, 1776.

GENTLEMEN: A difficulty has arisen in the execution of my office as Justice of the Peace, under the Five Pound Act, which induces me to apply to your Board. I have hitherto issued precepts as usual, when applied to for the recovery of debts,

---

* This gentleman was a brother of Mrs. Peter Van Schaack, and he was a son of Henry Cruger, senior, whom he succeeded as a member of His Majesty's council in the province of New York, on the resignation, by the former, of his seat at the council board, in 1773. Henry Cruger, junior, Mayor and Sheriff of Bristol (England), and who was twice elected a member of Parliament, was his brother. When the Revolution broke out. John Harris Cruger was Chamberlain of the city of New York, and he appears to have been at first a moderate loyalist. He married a daughter of Oliver DeLancey, and was appointed a lieutenant-colonel of the first battalion of DeLancey's brigade, on its organization, in 1777. His wife was at her father's house in Bloomingdale when it was plundered, set on fire and destroyed, in the dead of night, by a small party of American soldiers in the Autumn of 1777, by whom she and the other females in the house were most inhumanly treated. The Council of Safety severely condemned this act of the soldiery in wantonly destroying a private dwelling. In their letter to Governor Clinton, dated Hurley, December 16th, 1777, they say: "The information which we have received, as well in your Excellency's last letter as by other channels, of the burning of General DeLancey's house, gave this Council great uneasiness. We think this a most unequal method of waging war with the enemy, because neither we nor they can possibly destroy anything but what are properly our own houses, and we fear that so conspicuous an example as the burning of Mr DeLancey's mansion house will be industriously followed by the enemy, to the ruin of many of the good subjects of this state. For those reasons, sir, we most earnestly entreat your utmost exertions to put a stop to practices, on our part, which may be attended with the most destructive retaliations by the enemy.' —Journal N. Y. Provin. Cong., 1 vol., p. 1101.

Col. Cruger's subsequent military career was quite conspicuous. At the close of the war he went, a permanent exile, to England, while his brother Henry, who had espoused the American cause in Parliament, came over to America, and was shortly after chosen a member of the New York Senate. Such are the strange positions into which different members of the same family were cast by the Revolutionary conflict.

within my limited jurisdiction, though I have always, since the commencement of our public distresses, endeavored to dissuade parties from a prosecution, where the debtor's default arose from inability; but where I have been assured that the demand of protest process by the plaintiff has not proceeded from litigiousness, but as a means of obtaining a just debt, which was not detained from inability, but from an expectation of evading payment through the feebleness of the law, I have readily exercised the powers of my office.

Notwithstanding these, my principles, I have given offense, and on Saturday last I was visited by sundry persons, who said they were a committee from a larger number in the northeastern part of this district, who had come to a resolution, that the law for the recovery of debts before a magistrate should cease in this district; and yesterday, when I happened to be from home, about thirty or forty men came with a design to compel me to a promise, of desisting from the further exercise of my office in civil suits. The objections they made are of a general nature, and by no means confined to me, for no peculiar hardship or any oppression is complained of, nor has any resentment been shown against the plaintiffs; but they say that in the present situation of the country they ought not to be compelled by law to pay debts, and that while we are fighting against the King (I state their objections) it is absurd to use his name or authority to enforce the payment of debts.

Your Board will at once perceive the dilemma to which myself, and indeed all who are concerned in the administration of justice, are reduced by their principles, and the compulsory methods threatened of carrying them into execution. For my part I have remonstrated that no order of the Continental Congress, the Provincial Congress, or the general county committee, has passed for a cessation of law, and that when either interferes I shall doubtless be freed from such applications. They, on the contrary, argue that silence of the Congress must be taken to bein their favor, from the evident reasonableness of their objections (which I have already stated), and therefore that it is incumbent on those who are advocates of the laws going on to get an express declaration to destroy what they suppose to be the implied sense of the congresses. At present, while the one party complains of the hardship of paying debts, the other thinks it equally hard to be restrained from the only effectual means of enforcing their just demands.

Upon the whole, it would be of public benefit that your Board, which, except the grand Continental Congress, is the only competent power to decide these differences, should express its sentiments upon this important subject, for it is that by which all sides profess themselves ready to govern themselves.

I am, gentlemen,

Your most obedient servant,

PETER VAN ALSTINE.

Although we have not yet experienced the inconveniences above set forth: yet, being exposed thereto from the nature of our offices as magistrates, we beg leave therefore to join in the above representation.

PETER VOSBURGH.
H. VAN SCHAACK.
ANDRIUS WITBECK.

In the afternoon of the 17th of June, 1776, Mr. Van Schaack, while several miles from his home, was arrested, upon an order issued by the county committee of safety, placed under guard, the privilege of writing his family denied him, and he with sixteen others of his neighbors, who were supposed to have the most influence, were the next morning conducted to Albany, and there immediately committed to jail without any previous examination.

"The seventeen persons who were apprehended upon the mandate before mentioned were kept imprisoned for seventeen days (all offers of bail being rejected) and then discharged, the committee declaring that the charge against them was NOT OF SUFFICIENT WEIGHT to require defence. There was to be punishment, however, though there was no guilt; for notwithstanding their declared innocence, they were charged with the expense of a Major and a party of fifty odd men, to parade through the district, though not a man but would have attended upon the slightest notice. Nor was this yet sufficient; but the charges were to be accumulated by transmitting the bill of costs to the committee of another district, who employed an officer, who levied his mileage in addition to the original charges, and all this without any request from the committee for payment or any intimation that they were to be paid."*

* Miscellaneous papers in Sec of State's office, vol. 36., p. 514 to 518. See also Life of Peter Van Schaack, LL D., p. 477.

It is probable that these apparently arbitrary proceedings had been adopted by the committee upon misinformation, dictated by malicious motives on the part of some restless and vindictive spirits, who were aiming at notoriety. Their evident tendency was to sour the feelings of those who were the subjects of them, while they were well calculated to drive them into an obnoxious position.

The minutes of the county committee evince the existence at this period, of a great share of alarm and suspicion, and the members of their own body were not exempted from such distrust.*

The aspect of public affairs was threatening and discouraging. The expedition against Canada had signally failed, and the American army, greatly reduced by the small pox, desertion, and the expiration of their terms of enlistment, was retreating, with the army of Sir Guy Carleton in hot pursuit. An invasion of the state, also, by a powerful fleet and army, under Admiral and General Howe, was daily anticipated. The county of Albany, at this time, was a "frontier county" and on that account the more exposed. Under these circumstances, the county committee of safety, aiming no doubt to comply with the recommendations of the Continental and Provincial Congresses, proceeded to remove from their borders into the neighboring states a large number of persons, including not only those who had been guilty of overt acts in opposition to the public measures, but individuals who had done nothing criminal, their only offence resting in the apprehension of the committee, that their "influence, IF EXERTED, would be used against the American cause."

About the twentieth of July Mr. Van Schaack was again arrested by an order of the committee and taken to Albany, and after ten or twelve days imprisonment, he was sent from that place, with nineteen other persons, to Hartford, in Connecticut. Accompanying a letter from the committee to Governor Trumbull was a list of the "crimes" of which the persons

---

* "RESOLVED, upon motion, that it shall not be permitted to any member or members of this Board to become bail for any Tory or disaffected person whatsoever."—Committee Records. June, 1776.

therein named had been guilty. The one assigned against Mr.
Van Schaack was in these words: "A disaffected person, corres-
ponding with the Tories in Connecticut."*

[TO THE ALBANY COMMITTEE.]

ALBANY, TORY JAIL., 1st August, 1776.

GENTLEMEN: We have just now received your letter of
this date, by which we find that, contrary to the most reasonable expectations, we are forced to go off to-morrow morning.
The reasons for our expectations are so forcibly pointed out in
our former letters that we shall forbear to recapitulate them
now, and only observe, the same severities are still exercised
respecting the admittance of those who have business with us; so
that at this hour we are in no situation to do anything.

As this probably will be the last time you will be troubled
with letters from us, we hope you will excuse us for requesting to
know whether we are to go with or without a guard from here
to Col. Hoffman's Landing, as we purpose to go by land from
here, provided there are no objections. Should there be any,
on account of sending a guard with us, and you are disposed
to take sufficient security, we conceive (as we are to maintain
ourselves) the Board will have no objection to our transporting
ourselves in the cheapest manner, so that our persons are
delivered according to the tenor of your orders. If this be
refused, can we have a pass for a couple of men to take out
horses down to Red Hook?

As we have been confined for a long time, and for sometime past treated as malefactors, christian charity obliges us to
believe that your board have received information concerning
us of a very criminal nature indeed; and as we are entirely
to guess from whence such information proceeded, we now
request that our crimes may be stated, and the accusers names
mentioned, that we may have an opportunity, as well in Connecticut as here, to clear our characters of any aspersions that
may be before your Board. Should the crimes of which we
are supposed to be guilty, or stand accused of, justify unremit-
ting severities with which we have been treated in our confinement, we dread the reception we are to meet with in a country

---

* Several persons were returned as being "disaffected persons, who had refused to sign
the new association." Benjamin Greenman was returned simply "a disaffected person."
—Journals N. Y. Provin. Cong., 2 vol. 493.

where we are strangers and friendless. We mean, should we be transferred unheard and unquestioned.

We are, etc.,

H. VAN SCHAACK,
JOSEPH ANDERSON,
JOHN MUNRO, &c.

[TO THE NEW YORK CONVENTION.]

HARTFORD, 12th August, 1776.

GENTLEMEN: As you preside over the state of New York, at this critical and very alarming juncture, for the safety and welfare of its inhabitants, it gives me a right to inform you that I have been transported hither unheard, unquestioned, and contrary to the principles of the Bill of Rights published by the honorable the Continental Congress, in September, 1774, as well as subsequent resolves by that Board.

As the post is this moment going off, I have no time to state at large the grievances I labor under. I shall therefore be brief, and acquaint you that I am conscious to myself that I have neither said nor acted in opposition to the measures pursued by the united councils of the continent, or those recommended by the provincial councils. It therefore appears hard, that the most sacred rights I hold in society should be violated. I have been sent hither under every appearance of guilt, without being allowed an opportunity of knowing the crimes for which I have suffered transportation.

That I may not be charged with neglecting to apply for knowledge of my supposed crimes to that power which inflicted the punishment, I take the liberty of inclosing a copy of a letter wrote to the Albany committee, signed by myself and others in the same situation.

As I have suffered a long confinement, torn from my family and friends, my affairs going to ruin, and obliged to maintain myself at a very great expense in this state, and now under orders to go to New London (what punishments will follow these, God knows, but proceedings so vague and loose promise nothing but indefinite punishment), to you, gentlemen, as the guardians of these rights which are held valuable in society, I now appeal for a stop to further punishment, by suffering me to appear before you, there to be condemned or acquitted. As I am known among many of you, gentlemen, I hope this can be granted without any apprehensions of my deviating from my parole. Should there, however, be any doubts, I will readily be at the expense of a guard to conduct me to you.

I remain, with great respect, gentlemen, in haste,

Your most obedient servant,

H. VAN SCHAACK.

Upon the receipt of the two preceding letters, they were ordered by the convention to lie on the table for the perusal of the members, and the minutes of that body discloses no further action in reference to them.

The convention at this time was in a very unsettled state. General Howe, who had been lying at Staten Island for several weeks, made a descent upon Long Island with his army on the day the above letters were received, and the convention, a few days afterwards, dispersed, having first resolved itself into a committee of safety, which latter body migrated from the city of New York to Harlem; thence to King's bridge; the house of Mr. Odell, Philip's manor; and from thence to Fishkill, where the convention was reorganized.*

The favorable impressions made by Mr. Van Schaack upon the strangers with whom he was suffering exile in Connecticut are shown by the following extracts from a letter written to him fourteen years afterwards by the Reverend Elijah Parsons. It bears date 14th of June, 1790, at East Haddam; to which place Mr. Van Schaack had probably been sent by Governor Trumbull:

"Very often, sir, both while our public dissensions lasted and since the establishment of peace, I have inquired after you and was always rejoiced to hear of your safety in the time of war, and your happy settlement and prosperity at Pittsfield since quiet and independence have been given to our country. Anecdotes of you and Dr. Munro are often recurring to my mind. I never ride by the pond but I think of the many hours you passed there in fishing. I have often recollected the full satisfaction you gave Captain Percival, on the subject of your refusing to fight; and when I consider the good humor and cheerfulness you always manifested while with us. I am persuaded you

---

* The public records of the colony had been ordered by the convention to be transferred, for safety, from New York to Kingston, sometime previous to this.

enjoyed yourself with more ease and contentment than almost any other gentleman under the same predicament could have done. This was owing to a certain original cast of mind which you inherit from nature, and must always be a source of happiness to him who possesses it, in any reverse of fortune.

"In regard to myself, sir, I often look back to the time when you lived here with regret and self-condemnation for the narrow spirit which had too much influence over me; and, instead of assuming any merit for my attention to you, I am sorry that it was not doubled, and I am sure it would be, were the same scene to be acted over again."

We here find a Whig of the Revolution, many years after that event, reproaching himself for his contractedness and illiberality, during the contest, towards those of opposite political sentiments. The fact is not without interest.

In October of this year (1776) Mr. Van Schaack was permitted by the county committee to visit Kinderhook to attend the death bed of his father, in the seventy-first year of his age, after which he repaired again to Connecticut.

About this period he made his will. It contained the following singular provision:

"Item. I will and desire that I shall be buried in forty-eight hours after my decease, in the dusk of the evening; and in case the physicians or surgeons who may attend me, or be in the neighborhood where I die, should think that by opening my body any discoveries may be made that may prove useful to my fellow creatures, I hereby expressly order and direct that they shall have free leave to make use of a carcass that would otherwise prove useless."

Mr. Van Schaack probably remained in Connecticut until the ensuing winter or spring. We find him at Kinderhook in May, having probably been permitted to return to his home, by Governor Trumbull, on his parole of honor. He was then brought before the commissioners of conspiracies at Fishkill, on the supposition that he had returned to the state under a resolution of the convention allowing those who had been sent into other states to return to their homes, on condition of taking a certain prescribed oath of allegiance.

The commissioners allowed him to return to his residence to arrange certain business matters, and on his second appearance before them, on the seventh of June, he was dismissed on his parole of honor, "that he would, within twenty days from that date, remove into the states of Connecticut or Massachusetts Bay, and become a subject there, or surrender himself to this Board."

It is probable that at this time he went into Massachusetts, as the following clause in a letter written in 1783, to his friend Sedgwick, who resided in Berkshire, no doubt relates to the early successes of Burgoyne: "In times of danger, when a victorious invading enemy was approaching, I lived among you quietly, and I hope my conduct then will one day be considered in a favorable light, and impress conviction, that people in my situation and of my principles would be of no injury to be incorporated with the citizens of your county."

In the extracts given on a preceding page from Mr. Parson's letter, that gentleman refers to the satisfaction Mr. Van Schaack had given in conversation "on the subject of his refusal to fight." His great difficulty, and it was that which mainly deterred him from participating in the revolution (as declared by him to a friend in after life), was the oaths he had taken as a public officer. These oaths were of the most solemn character, and copies of several of them were found among his papers at his decease.

He had not only repeatedly taken these oaths, but he had been in the habit of administering them to others, having been united with Sir William Johnson in a commission issued by Lieutenant-Governor Colden, in 1770, empowering them to administer the oaths of allegiance, supremacy and abjuration, etc., to all officers, civil and military, in the county of Albany. A parchment roll is still in existence, commencing with his entering upon the duties of magistrate in 1770, which contains the original signatures of individuals to a general oath of allegiance and abjuration administered by him. We find on it subscriptions during each of the four subsequent years, and three as late as May, 1775.

It is not strange that a conscientious man, who, in the

fear of God, had himself taken these solemn oaths, and who, in the discharge of his duty as a magistrate, had so often administered them to others, should have felt restrained by them from taking up arms against the King to whom he had thus sworn to "bear faithful and true allegiance," and to "defend to the utmost of his power against all traitrous conspiracies and attempts whatsoever, which should be made against his person, crown or dignity."*

The sentiment of allegiance and loyalty was with many an absolute religious sentiment. To determine when a man is absolved from his oath of allegiance is generally an embarrassing and, not infrequently, a profound question.

---

* These quotations are the language of the oaths.

CHAPTER VI.

"There is no word," according to Montesquieu,* "that admits of more various significations, and has made more different impressions on the human mind than that of liberty." So grotesque is the shape which the idea of this principle has assumed, as we are informed by the same eloquent writer, that "a certain nation, for a long time, thought that liberty consisted in the privilege of wearing a long beard."†

The people of the united American colonies had been fostered in the principles of freedom; and a knowledge of their constitutional rights had been widely diffused by the discussions which preceded the revolution.

The sentiment of liberty prevailed to a great extent, but it was in many respects crude and incongruous. The jealousy, also, which entered deeply into its composition, often caused it to assume the most fantastic shapes; and the illustrations we have of it furnish many amusing and ludicrous scenes, imparting to our revolutionary story an air of romance, and in some instances, wearing the aspect of knight errantry.

Among its other phases, a leading characteristic of the spirit of liberty, as then exhibited, was its exclusiveness; denying to others a participation in that freedom which it so largely appropriated to itself. For it is not to be denied, that those who were strenuously contending for liberty of opinion and action, and were the loudest in sounding their sanctity, were often unwilling to concede the same rights to others. There was no little truth as well as severity, in the remark made by a loyalist, in reference to various acts of lawless violence of which the revolutionary party in the colony of New York were

---

* Spirit of Laws, 1 Vol., p. 218.   † Ibid.

guilty in the first two years of the war: "These are the people who are contending for liberty; they engrossed the whole of it to themselves and allowed not a tittle to their opponents."

An "excess of the spirit of liberty" was often displayed, particularly in the early stage of the conflict, in acts of open violence—in the destruction of printing offices; in burning individuals in effigy; in tarring and feathering persons, and in riding others upon a rail; in committing loyalist publications to the flames; in the breaking of windows, and destruction of furniture, and other injuries, to the private dwellings of obnoxious individuals; in midnight attacks upon printing offices, to destroy the manuscript and derange the type of intended answers to publications of the popular writers, and in various other acts of open as well as secret violence, not to say personal outrages, terminating in death.

Thus "unlimited freedom" was, on many occasions, "confounded with political liberty," and, in view of acts such as these, can it be deemed strange that moderate men should have come to the conclusion that "license" was often meant when they cried "liberty."

In view of such proceedings, there was significance in the answer of a loyalist farmer, when permission was asked, by his Whig neighbor, to cut a valuable tree standing on the land of the former: "Why do you ask?—you are for liberty—why do you not go and take it!"

Some of the popular measures of that day although "avowedly in defence of liberty, absolutely violated the freedom of society, by demanding men, under pain of being stigmatized and of sustaining detriment in property, to accede to resolutions, which, however well meant, could not, from the apparent constraint they held out, but be very grating to a free man."

It is a melancholy feature, also, in the contest which led to our independence as a nation, that the revolutionary party should have deemed it necessary to visit with punishment due only to crime, the mere expression of opinions honestly entertained by those who doubted the expediency or propriety of many of the public measures, but who, as we have reason to know, had the welfare of their country at heart as much as the violent authors of those measures.

Men were, also, not only sent from their homes and imprisoned within the state, on suspicion merely, but they were banished to other states, and there incarcerated among strangers for an indefinite time, without trial or an opportunity for self-defence.*

On the 3d of Sept., 1777, Egbert Benson, one of the commissioners of conspiracies, informed the council of safety, that many of the persons "confined on board of the fleet prison were apprehended on SUSPICION of having joined the enemy— ordered that Mr. Benson, together with Major Van Zandt and Mr. Harper do proceed to the fleet prison and examine the state prisoners lately apprehended to the northward, and that they be authorized to discharge such of them as they may think proper."†

In violation of a great principle, and yet perhaps from a political necessity (deemed by the actors equally forcible) "the fears of one class of men were made the measure for the rights of another."

Among the assigned causes for fining, imprisoning and banishing individuals, were the following: "Speaking disrespectfully of the Whigs in general, and discouraging to our present cause; uttering unbecoming talk against the American cause; testifying disapprobation of the measures they (the Whigs) were pursuing; speaking diminutively of the authority of a committee; a refusal by an individual to sign the 'association,' which contained an explicit engagement, in advance, to support future and unknown measures of the Congress; an

---

* This was a great evil, and in some instances operated, no doubt, very oppressively. The revolutionary tribunals sought to alleviate it, but their records establish the fact. The minutes of the committee of Conspiracies, under date 21st January, 1777, show, that "a petition to this committee, from divers persons prisoners in Springfield jail was read, praying that they may be sent for and tried. RESOLVED, that WHEN PROPER COURTS OF JUDICATURE SHALL BE ESTABLISHED IN THIS STATE FOR THE TRIAL OF OFFENCES AGAINST THE SAME, the above-named petitioners and all others in the like predicament with them, will receive a fair and impartial trial for the several misdemeanors with which they stand respectively charged; and that in the meantime no greater liberty be allowed them than what humanity may require."
—Com. Records Library of N. Y. Historical Society.

† Jour. N. Y. Provin. Cong., 1 Vol., p. 1004.

affirmative answer, extorted from an individual, quietly pursuing his peaceful avocations, to the question whether he considered himself bound by his oath of allegiance to the King; or a refusal to answer such question.''

Mere differences of political sentiment, particularly in an individual of influence or distinction, though wholly unaccompanied by overt acts of a dangerous character, was termed "disaffection;" and this undefined offence was often adjudged to be a sufficient ground for imprisonment and banishment to another state. In several instances of such incarceration and exile, it was assigned as one reason for the punishment, that the culprits had "celebrated the King's birthday," and in their jollity on that occasion had "drunk the King's health," and sang "God save the King."*

This was on the fourth day of June, 1776—just one month previous to the Declaration of Independence—until which event the contest was professedly carried on as a war "between subjects and their acknowledged sovereign."†

It was the Declaration of Independence by the Continental Congress, as historians concede, that severed the colonies from their allegiance to the British crown, and until that event, no such authoritative measure had been adopted by any body representing the associated colonies, as would have advised the commonalty of the criminality of the acts above numerated. For if these were criminal, at the period referred to, then the Continental Congress itself was at fault, inasmuch as at this very time THEY were hesitating in regard to the propriety of such declaration, some of its leading members solemnly contending in debate, that the people "had not yet accommodated their minds to a separation from the mother country;"‡ and, moreover, in the city in which Congress was assembled, and in the public worship which many of its members attended,

---

* "His drinking the Kings health the fourth day of June last can likewise be proved."— Jour. N. Y. Provin. Cong.

† Marshal.

‡ The delegates from New York, in the Continental Congress, expressly declined to sign the Declaration when it was adopted, for the reason that they were not empowered so to do —their INSTRUCTIONS CONTEMPLATING A "RECONCILIATION."—Life of Jefferson.

prayers "for the King and all the royal family" were put up on every Lord's day up to the fourth day of July, 1776.

Thus, while members of Congress, if not that body itself, were publicly PRAYING for the King, the committees organized by their direction were incarcerating and banishing individuals for "drinking His Majesty's health," and for exercising their vocal powers by singing the national anthem, which contemplated His Majesty's "safety!"

It will be somewhat difficult, at this day, to discover the principle upon which rested the distinction by which public prayer for the King was tolerated and practiced, when singing the national air—"God save the King"—was punished as criminal. May it not have been that the former presupposed His Majesty to be a great sinner (a fact fully believed by the "Sons of Liberty," and of which they entertained no doubt), while the spirit of song is usually employed to commemorate virtues—which, in this instance, were as firmly believed not to exist.

It may, moreover, be urged on this head, that there is a Divine command to "pray for your enemies," but we have no such injunction to sing their praises.*

The revolutionary substitution of new governments for the old dynasty, was attended with many embarrassments, and some of the irregularities referred to, must probably be regarded as among the indications that the public mind was ripening for a Declaration of Independence. The councils of the United Colonies had, indeed, from the first, exhibited an anomalous

---

* The Rev.William (afterward Bishop) White, who was then assistant minister to Dr. Duche, the chaplain of Congress, in the parishes of Christ Church and St. Peters, Philadelphia, and whose sentiments are known to have been friendly to the Revolution, continued the prayers for the King and royal family until the Sunday, inclusive, previous to the Declaration of Independence. After that time he ceased to do so, and took the oath of allegiance to the United States. The following resolution was adopted at the meeting held by the Rector and vestry of the parishes referred to on the fourth of July, 1776: "Whereas the honorable Continental Congress have resolved to declare the American Colonies to be free and independent States, in consequence of which it will be proper to omit those petitions in the liturgy wherein the King of Great Britain is prayed for as inconsistent with the said Declaration; therefore,

RESOLVED—That it appears to this vestry to be necessary, for the peace and well being of the churches, to omit the said petitions, and the rectors and assistant ministers of the united churches are requested, in the name of the vestry and their constituents, to omit such petitions as are above mentioned."

aspect. In practice they had repeatedly exercised the highest acts of independent sovereignty, while in their petitions and public addresses they professed undiminished allegiance to their sovereign. They had, in the first year of hostilities, levied a war of invasion against the Canadas, which were distinct portions of the British dominions, with which they had no political connection, while the language of their published proceedings indicated the highest attachment to the parent state, and only sought a redress of their own grievances.

Such are, perhaps, the natural incongruities growing out of a state of civil war: of a people verging from a condition of colonial subjection to an independent state of national existence. It is by the chastening and enlightening progess of time and experience alone, that wisdom, moderation and mercy become the "final and permanent fruits of liberty."

The LADIES of the revolutionary period, also, had THEIR ideas of liberty. When the wife of a soldier, absent on duty, was notified by her landlord to vacate the premises occupied by the family, she wrote to her husband to go to his commanding officer and "see whether D. has any right to turn me out of door, since you have listed to go and fight for liberty. Why" (says this heroine) "should not I have liberty whilst you strive for liberty.*"

The ladies of that day, in no insignificant manner, evinced at times their impatience of what they conceived to be arbitrary restrictions upon their rights and privileges. In defiance of the solemn regulations of congresses and committees, they claimed the privilege of drinking tea—a right as it must be conceded, "inestimable to them, as it has proved formidable to tyrants!" In the exercise of a manly (if the term may be allowed) spirit of independence on this subject, the ladies of Kingston, in county of Ulster, surrounded the building in which the revolutionary committee of safety was in session, and there proclaimed that "if they could not have tea, their husbands and sons should fight no more."

* Journ. N. Y. Prov. Cong., 2 vol., p. 342.

The contumacious conduct of these ladies was reported to the Provincial Convention, which body, as appears by the following extract from their minutes, appointed a committee to investigate the matter:

"A letter from John Sleight, chairman of Kingston, was received and read, stating that women surround the committee chamber, and say that if they cannot have tea their husbands and sons shall fight no more, was received, and referred to the members attending from Ulster county."*

The subsequent records of the convention disclose no further action in this matter; and we are left to infer (what usually attends their course) the triumph of the ladies!

This occurrence, it should be remarked, took place shortly after the Declaration of Independence had been proclaimed by the Continental Congress, but before the formation of the articles of Confederation by the associated states, or the adoption of the constitution by the newly-born state of New York.

Being thus reduced to a state of nature, and in the absence of those written specifications of powers conferred and powers reserved, since become so sacred with the American people, and the important character of which was no doubt fully appreciated by the sagacious females of that day, it may well be questioned, whether, in a matter which so nearly and so deeply affected them, these ladies had not the right of the argument.†

* Journals N. Y. Prov. Cong., 1 Vol., p. 590, 26th Aug., 1776.
† This was not the only case in which the ladies of that day publicly vindicated, if not their constitutional rights, at least the right to use a beverage grateful to their constitutions.
The following, among similar items, appeared in a newspaper of that day: "Aug. 28th, 1776. A few days since about 100 women, inhabitants of Dutchess county, went to the house of Col. Brinkerhoff, at Fishkill, and insisted upon having tea at the lawful price of six shillings per pound, and obliged that gentleman to accommodate them with one chest from his store for that purpose. Shortly after he sold his cargo to some Yorkers, who, for fear of another female attack, forwarded the nefarious stuff to the North river precipitately, where it is now afloat, but the women have placed their guard on each side."

CHAPTER VII.

The surrender of General Burgoyne's army was one of the prominent events of the revolutionary war. It is impossible to conceive what would have been the fate of the United States had the result been different, and a junction of the three Royal armies been affected in 1777. The failure of that scheme for subjugating the colonies determined the political character of thousands who were wavering, and whose politics were fixed by the result.*

The rapid approach of Burgoyne towards Albany, before he had been checked by the defeat at Bennington and the obstructions to his march interposed by General Schuyler; the sudden and unexpected evacuation of Ticonderoga and Mount Independence by the American forces under General St. Clair; and the descent of St. Ledger upon Oswego, and his investiture of Fort Schuyler; with the apprehended ascent of the Hudson river by the British forces at New York, and various other discouraging circumstances, kept the city of Albany, and the surrounding country, for many weeks, in the greatest conceivable state of consternation and alarm. Some of the inhabitants of that city fled to other parts of the country, taking

---

* The SCHOHARIE Committee wrote, on the 17th of July: "The late advantages gained over us by our enemy have such effect upon numbers here that many we thought steady friends to the State seem now to draw back. Our state therefore is deplorable." Col. Vrooman, from that place, also represented, on the 22nd of the last month, that "nearly one half of the people heretofore well disposed have laid down their arms, and propose to side with the enemy."

The Tryon County Committee wrote, on the 18th of July: "The loss of Ticonderoga is a hard stroke to our inhabitants in general, and causeth the number of our disaffected greatly to increase": and again, on the 19th: "The people on these frontiers are in such despondency that a part have taken to flight, and the rest openly declare for submission to the terms the enemy shall propose."

General Schuyler wrote from SARATOGA (whither he had retreated with the army), on the 1st day of August: "I am very apprehensive that a systematical submission will take place in this quarter of the country, for nothing can equal the consternation of the people!"—Jour. N. Y. Pronvin. Con., 1 Vol., p. 1010, 1006, 1019.—2 Vol., p. 507. 518.

with them their most valuable movables, while many of the country people sought refuge in the city. Some buried their valuables, and others removed them to places of greater security.*

Robberies were frequent, and rumored gatherings of the disaffected increased the general consternation. Desertions from the army were most appalling for their extent and character, and could not fail to increase the deep and widespread gloom.†

The lead was taken out of the Dutch windows, to be converted into bullets, and the public records were dispatched, for greater safety, to Kingston, and with the New York records sent to that place the year previous were removed to Rochester in season to escape destruction by the burning of that town. The Albany committee implored the Council of Safety to come to that city, as a measure demanded by the welfare of the state, "in the present distressed situation of the country." In a letter to the Council, bearing date of the eleventh of August, they expressed their apprehensions, in view of "the gloomy prospects to the Northward," that "that city would in a short time be in possession of the enemy." Alarming letters, also, were dispatched by the committee to Berkshire and other parts of the country, and an address was issued by them to the people of the eastern states. Letters of the most desponding kind were received by the Council of Safety from General Schuyler at Fort Edward, and from the committees of Schoharie and Tryon county. The sittings of the Supreme Court, under the new constitution, were repeatedly adjourned by the Council of Safety, without doing any business, in consequence of the public distractions, and the Governor, for the same reason, prorogued the legislature, and repaired to Albany to rouse the drooping spirits of the people.

The signal success of a body of American troops under

---

* An old Kinderhook letter refers to certain papers which were injured in consequence of being "in the iron chest that was under the ground the year Burgoyne came down."

† Schuyler wrote from Fort Edward, on the 5th July, that "it was a melancholy reflection that the militia deserted almost as fast as they came in;" and again, on the 22nd of that month, that about fourteen hundred of the New England troops, principally from Berkshire, had Xnfamously deserted."—Jour. N. Y. Provin. Cong., 1 Vol. 1017.—2 Vol., 514.

General Stark, at Bennington, on the 16th of August, followed
a few days afterward (August 22d) by the retreat of St. Ledger
from before Fort Schuyler; with the successes of Col. Brown,
in General Burgoyne's rear, and in cutting off the facilities for
his retreat, gave a cheering check to the "universal panic,
despair and despondency," which but for these events seemed
likely, for a time, to overwhelm the state. The British general,
after a succession of military movements, which only increased
his perplexities, being finally deprived of all hope of conquest,
was driven to seek his own safety; and a campaign, which had
promised so much to him, and which had so long portended
disaster to the Americans, was finally terminated in glory for
the latter, by the capitulation at Saratoga.

Poetry and song were employed to give vent to the joy
occasioned by so great a deliverance.

The news of Burgoyne's surrender was brought to Kinderhook by Col. Henry Van Rensselaer, on his way from Saratoga
to his residence at Claverack, and its truth confirmed by the
particulars given: that he had dined with the captive General
in General Gates' marque. When the rumor of this event was
mentioned to Peter Van Schaack, he remarked to his informant,
with great emphasis: "If this be true, I pronounce you an
independent nation."

It was among the singular events of the day, to find Whigs,
during the widespread alarm occasioned by Burgoyne's
approach, seeking refuge among those who were classed with
their political opponents.

The newly married lady* of an active Whig, who had been
a law student of Mr. Van Schaack's brother, was conducted
by her husband, from his residence in Albany, to Kinderhook,
and there found an asylum in the family of that gentleman,
who was then residing at his home upon his parole of honor,
taken by the convention of the state of New York in April
previous. The latter gentleman, also, went with his own
conveyance to Kinderhook Landing, and brought thence the
furniture and movables of this lady's father-in-law to the

---

* Mrs. Gansevoort, wife of Leonard Gansevoort, junior.

village, which is five miles distant from the Hudson, to save it from apprehended destruction by the British troops, then rapidly ascending that river. On the following night, was seen in the southern horizon, from the high bank above the Kinderhook creek, a bright light which afterwards proved to be occasioned by the burning of Esopus.

The husband of the lady referred to was, in the next year, secretary of the board of commissioners by whom his former tutor (for whom he ever entertained the highest regard) was perpetually exiled from the scene of these hospitalities, and from his native state. Such are the singular positions in which individuals and personal friends are placed by civil convulsions.

It was provided by the Saratoga articles of capitulation, that "the army under Lieutenant General Burgoyne should march to the Massachusetts Bay by the easiest, most expeditious and most direct route." This route, at that day, was through Kinderhook, and the army encamped on the plains at that village. The captive general, and the other British and Hessian officers, with the American escort, followed the main army on the same or the next day, and dined at the house of David Van Schaack, which is still one of the finest situations in the village.*

An amusing incident occurred at the dinner table. After the cloth was removed, wine was introduced. A glass was handed by one of the company to a little girl then present (an adopted daughter of the gentleman of the house, and her own father being also a loyalist). She was requested to give a toast. Taking the glass into her hand, she turned to the company and archly exclaimed, "GOD SAVE THE KING AND ALL THE ROYAL FAMILY!"†

---

* It has become the property of, and is occupied by, my daughter, a grand-niece of Mr. Van Schaack, Mrs. Aaron J. Vanderpoel; and for substantial architecture is probably not surpassed by many buildings in this country.

† Tradition informs us that Gen. Burgoyne was disturbed by the circumstance ; probably supposing it might be thought that the child was prompted to the act by one of his retinue, and that the occurrence might have an unfavorable influence on his subsequent treatment. The incident, however, was suffered to pass in good humor without stimulating the ire of the republican escort.

As Generals Burgoyne and Phillips were riding on horse-back through Klinekill, a sturdy woman called out and inquired of them, "which of the gentlemen is Mr. General Burgoyne?" The general, removing his beaver from his head and bowing, proceeded on his way.

A considerable portion of the captured army, as is well known, was composed of Germans, many of whom remained in the country. Quite a number of them deserted en route to Boston and took up residences in the vicinity of Kinderhook. Several of them became good and respectable citizens, and acquired property, having their descendants in that community at the present day.

A manuscript written in England, by a loyalist of high respectability, who went to that country at the close of the war, and died there some years afterwards, makes this curious statement: "By the treaty with the German princes for the use of their troops, Great Britain engaged to pay £10 for every dead man, and for every man who should not be returned at the end of the war; and every two wounded men (though ever so slightly) were to go for a dead one. The scratch of a finger in a German was called a wound. He was carried to the hospital and John Bull paid for him as for the half of a dead man."

The capture of Burgoyne gave rise to the coinage of a new word in English lexicography; and the name of that unfortunate general was transmitted from a proper noun substantive into a verb and participle. It was not unusual after that event to say of an individual whose plans had been frustrated by the superior address of another, that he was "burgoyned." We find the word thus used in a letter from Mr. Van Schaack to Theodore Sedgwick in 1785.*

One of the greatest thoroughfares in the colonies at the

* So, in the last canto of Trumbull's McFingal, Cornwallis is said to have been "burgoyned" at Yorktown.

The eloquence which marked General Burgoyne's "masterly pen" (as termed by Chancellor Kent) has frequently been adverted to. Among Mr. Van Schaack's papers was found a manuscript copy, in his hand writing, of a characteristic speech by "Col. Burgoyne" before the King's Bench in 1779, in mitigation of a sentence about to be pronounced against him, upon a conviction for participation in an election riot, at the time he was a candidate for a seat in Parliament. It is a production of great eloquence.

period of the revolution, was the road from Albany to Boston, Hartford, and New York, which then passed through Kinderhook, and was one and the same from Albany to that point. It has been noticed that the Ticonderoga prisoners were conducted through this place en route to Hartford, in May, 1775. Benedict Arnold was also conveyed through this town on his way East, probably to Connecticut, while laboring under the ill effects of the wound he received in the battle at Bemis Heights. This degraded man, then a wounded patriot, stopped over night at Witbeck's tavern. One of the door posts was cut away to admit the litter on which he was borne.

To return to the subject of this sketch, the author has been able to discover but little in regard to his movements from 1777 to January, 1781, when, from a minute made in his almanac, he appears to have arrived in the city of New York. A letter written by him to a friend some years afterwards* sufficiently shows that he experienced, during the revolution, a full share of the trials and sufferings to which the unsettled state of public affairs gave rise.

"I hear our Assembly are not in temper to repeal the Banishing Act. This is in no wise surprising when it is considered that your friend, by these sort of folks, has suffered banishment twice in Connecticut, once in Massachusetts, twice in close confinement in Tory gaol at Albany, twice at Poughkeepsie, once at West Point, five months in gaol in Goshen, and at last removed within the British lines, with my wearing apparel only.

"All those punishments, and thirteen months confinement at Schodack, have I suffered, not for inimical words spoken, but for such as I might utter; not for mischief done, but for the evil I might do; not for using the confessed influence I had among my neighbors, but such as was supposed I should employ; not for thoughts already gendered, but such as the future pollution of the heart might beget."

* Letter to Theodore Sedgwick, 18th April, 1784.

SHEFFIELD, 28th Oct., 1777.

My DEAR SIR: I have sent you a small cask of rum; not so much indeed as you desired, but the cask is the largest could be procured.

The MAJOR can spare none of his spirits. He says he promised none, but on condition of your living in this town. I thank you sincerely for your wine and vinegar, although Burghard has not vouchsafed to send the latter. The wine is just as it should be, except the quantity; but at this time we should be thankful even for the smallest QUANTITY of that heart-cheering, sorrow-forgetting nectaric.

Had heaven so ordered, that you and I had agreed as fully in politics as in those sentiments of generosity and true friendship by which only the generous can be distinguished from the base—the common herd—I should consider it as one of the most fortunate incidents of my life. Had this been the case, I could tell you a story which would be grateful to a Whigish ear. But since this is not the case, I would say nothing which may in any sense be considered ungenerous or insulting.

I cannot, however, avoid reminding you of my prognostication respecting the fate of the INVINCIBLE BURGOYNE; and that events have taken place almost exactly agreeable to my expectations.

Your information that government was to take place here this month was without foundation. The committee, I hear who were appointed by the general court to report the form of a constitution, have made their report, but what its fate is in the House I have not been able to learn.

Yours sincerely,

THEODORE SEDGWICK.

P. S.—As to the threats you mention, I did not design they should ever have reached your ears. Pray, when shall we see you here?

SHEFFIELD, 24th August, 1778.

DEAR SIR: I have but one moment's time to write by the person who will convey this to Mr. Dwight.

I do not despair of seeing you again before you leave the country; but, however, lest the gout or some other cause should prevent, I have enclosed you a letter to my friend Barr, which will procure you, I hope, more than bare civility; with which, as a man of most liberal and enlarged sentiments, I am positive, without any such introduction, he would treat every gentleman whom the misfortunes of the times should put in his power.

I have not the least apprehension that you will be long excluded from your country. Upon the restoration of peace, I am sure than an end must be put to the banishment of all persons who have done no more than in mere opinion to dissent from the rest of the country.

Although perhaps no two men think more differently than we do with respect to the present controversy, yet be assured that no one more ardently wishes your true happiness than I, in everything consistent with (what I imagine) the good of the country.

Give my warmest and most affectionate compliments to your worthy good brother Peter. Tell him, his son Harry appears perfectly contented and happy in his present situation. He has become the favorite of Mrs. Sedgwick. Compliments to David. Wish him in my name felicity and contentment.

God Almighty bless you, dear Harry, and believe me (with compliments to Mrs. Van Schaack) to be your sincere friend.

Farewell!

THEODORE SEDGWICK.

Mrs. Sedgwick's compliments, as due you know, are always of course.

The two letters from Mr. Van Schaack to Mr. Sedgwick, which are given in a subsequent part of this chapter, show that he was at his home in Kinderhook, in September, 1778, and in August, 1780. He was probably removed within the enemies lines at the former, if not at both of those dates, for declining to take the oath prescribed by the Banishing Act.* That oath was in these words:

"I, A— B—, do solemnly, and without any mental reservation or equivocation whatsoever, swear and call God to witness (or, if of the people called Quakers, affirm) that I do believe and acknowledge the state of New York to be of right a

* The Act was passed 30th June, 1778, and entitled "An act more effectually to prevent the mischiefs arising from the influence and example of persons of equivocal and suspected characters, in this state."

free and independent state, and that no authority or power can of right be exercised in or over the said state but what is or shall be granted by or derived from the people thereof. And further, that as a good subject of the said free and independent state of New York, I will, to the best of my knowledge and ability, faithfully do my duty, and as I shall keep or disregard this oath so help and deal with me Almighty God."

The following letter from Goldsbro Banyar, a gentleman of high character, to James Duane, a prominent and well-known champion of the revolution, points out some of the difficulties which those who aimed to be neutral, and conscientiously declined to take part in the revolutionary contest, had in regard to taking this oath.

RED HOOK, 16th September, 1778.

My DEAR SIR: I thank you for your information, and you will be pleased to present my compliments and acknowledgments to Mr. Robert C. Livingston for his attention. We received the baskets he was so kind as to take charge of.

My views are yet what you always supposed them to be, but I never expected to be driven to the present alternative of sacrificing them or violating my conscience. I suppose you have seen the oath; lest you might not, I subjoin a copy.

The Chancellor's construction is that the STATE there means the people; though he acknowledges in the penal clause (declaring it misprision of treason if found afterwards in any part of the state) the state means territory. My impression is where the sense will admit, it means both.

There is some diversity of sentiment whether the state extends beyond or within the lines of the enemy,* and, indeed, it appears more consistent with common sense and the common acceptation of the term, to confine it to those limits; however, the other seems the construction adopted by the legislature.

You know, in construing acts, the construction must be uniform, and if you admit a word or expression in any signification in a particular part, it shall receive the same exposition throughout the law, if the sense will admit of it. You know, also, that oaths are to be understood in the sense of the authority that imposes, not in that of the person who takes them.

* From August, 1776, to the close of the war, the British were in possession of the city and county of New York, of all Long Island and of the greater part of Westchester county.

It must appear I think, to anyone, a matter of great difficulty to swear a country of RIGHT INDEPENDENT while the contest exists, the event of which can only determine whether it shall be so or not. But if he can even digest this, must not his conscience revolt when he is called to swear also that the state or country comprehends places never in their possession, and that no authority can be exercised of right in those places but what is derived from the people of the state, when the fact is, that there is an authority exercised there not by them, and whether of right cannot be doubted, as it may be the same that existed there before the state was formed, or an authority exerted in right of conquest. Can you deny the legality of either, under an opinion which the Chancellor seems to have adopted, that all right is vested in the people, in all governments. Suppose even this a just position in theory, what ought it to avail if counteracted in nineteen instances out of twenty.

I pay great deference to his judgment, and the long conversation we had on the subject confirmed me in the opinion you know I ever entertained of that gentleman. He suggests an expedient, which, as it was a proof of his friendship, I am highly obliged to him for; an explanation of the sense in which I understand the Act; but this, if admitted, is a medicine, in my mind, inadequate to the disease.

I hear the commissioners have, in the cases of Mr. Wickham and Mr. Gabriel Ludlow, delivered their certificate to be signed by at least twelve reputable persons, which, if produced is to excuse the party from taking the oath. I hear also, the same course has been taken with others. If so, I should hope I too might be delivered over to compurgators.

I wish much to see you, but am still so much indisposed as to render it imprudent to travel so far. As soon as I go abroad, expect a visit. I long for that satisfaction. My distress has been great—beyond what I ever felt before, or could have had any apprehension of, at least from this quarter; for who could have expected such a law, in such a country, though even under the most extreme circumstances of distress?

I am, my dear sir, with the best respects of this family to yours and all under the same roof,

Most affectionately yours.

Go. BANYAR.

P. S.—Sept. 25th. I returned last evening from Poughkeepsie, and finding your letter still here I sit down to acquaint you that I obtained the same certificate that had been granted to others. It is too strict to suit the case of one Whig in three, but as I have paid a ready obedience, where the laws have required taxes, horses, carriages or money in lieu of personal service, and have ever been ready to give the government the pledge of my fidelity, contained in an oath of allegiance, I think I am not a dangerous person, and that if the law and the certificate requires more, it ought to be no objection to any reasonable person not at enmity with me, of whom I believe there are few.

Adieu. I shall see you when this disagreeable business is finished.

G. B.*

[TO THEODORE SEDGWICK.]

KINDERHOOK, Sept. 1778.

MY DEAR SIR: I now acknowledge the receipt of your kind and obliging favor of the 20th of the last month. For the inclosed to Col. Burr, you will please receive the warmest acknowledgments, both from myself and brother David. I hope we may be so lucky as to meet at the tents on the highlands, and that we may have him for our conductor to New York.

I am sorry to tell you that our Kinderhook flag is not yet returned, which puts it out of my power to forward the articles my brother was to send from New York for you and Mr. Sedgwick. I have kept the bearer thus long in hopes we might have heard before I sent over.

You will be pleased to send, by my Captain, my brother's son, that we may clothe him, and be enabled to dispose of him agreeable to the directions we may receive from his father. Whether this will be to go to New York, remain here, or procure him schooling in New England, is entirely uncertain. Should it be the latter, will you procure a place for him at Sheffield? or, rather, in more explicit terms, will you take him into your own family? The terms, as you and Mrs. S. shall agree, will be answered. I am sure if my brother is disposed to have him in your family, there is not a man whom he would choose to have him with so soon as with you. Enough of this.

Among the many misfortunes and disappointments that I have met with this last year, I assure you I look upon my not being able to pay your family a visit before I go, not among

---

* Mr. Banyar was an Englishman, and came to America many years previous to the revolution. During the administrations of Lieut. Governor Clarke and Cadwallader Colden, he was secretary of the province, and was distinguished as a gentleman of great courteousness of manners and unsullied character. He resided at Albany a long time, and died there in good old age, leaving a large landed estate. His only son married a daughter of John Jay and died without issue.

the least. But so it is; I am ordered away on Wednesday next. This short notice engrosses my time so much that I am at it night and day (I mean with my pen) so I cannot devote one moment to society. My friends for some days past have been refused admittance. However, I propose to go up next Monday to Albany, to try to have the evil day put off for a fortnight or three weeks longer.

I derive great consolation from that part of your letter where you seem so sanguine we shall not be long gone from this. The shorter, my dear friend, the better. I have no connections among the new folks half so dear as those I leave behind. You may therefore easily imagine that the hour of my returning to this country will be one of the happiest of my life. God grant it may be so.

Apropos. You know I have been often charged with being a monstrous Tory. You may remember that you once told me that much smoke indicated some fire. For once you thought proper to dissent from this opinion. I mean when you saw me at Poughkeepsie before a great public Board.

The last Board I was before, the present commissioners declared publicly that I was charged with no crime; but they were obliged to consider me as coming within the description of the Act as a neutral; and, as they were conscience bound, they were obliged to banish me.

When I am gone, do you do justice to my character. I should be sorry to leave a wounded name behind me. While I lived under the protection of my countrymen, I scrupulously observed the state of conduct void of offence, notwithstanding the provocation I had to act contrary. I shall remember you to my brother when I see him, and I am sure it will be a pleasure to him. We have met with little philanthropy from those of opposite principles. Kindnesses when rare become more valuable. May you never experience under any government, the oppressions and barbarities that we have done. I should blush to own a power that would exercise severities, without a cause. I can boast of punishments, nay of severities having been inflicted on me without the tyrants, plea "necessity." I shall grow gloomy—I shall endeavor to forgive, and I wish I could forget also.

God bless, prosper, and preserve you, in every stage of your life. Every blessing I wish you now; and those I cannot express accompany your dear good wife and Miss Dolly.

Your affectionate and obliged humble servant,

H. VAN. SCHAACK.

[TO THE SAME.]

KINDERHOOK, August 10th, 1780.

DEAR SEDGWICK: We have waited upon the Commissioners, in pursuance of the mandate I showed you when you were here. We were told that the Commissaries of prisoners had requested them to remove us, under the care of a guard, to Fishkill, but out of TENDERNESS to us, and they confiding in our honor that we would fulfil engagements of a milder nature, they thought proper to take a written parole to appear at Fishkill on the 1st of September next. This morning we are honored with another epistle from these gentlemen, wherein they tell us, "THAT IT HAS BEEN REPRESENTED TO THEM THAT THE SERVICE REQUIRES OUR BEING AT FISHKILL AT AN EARLIER DAY THAN THE FIRST OF SEPTEMBER, AND THEREFORE WE MUST GO DOWN BY THE 20TH WITHOUT FAIL."

What all this means I know not. We are not even told whether to New York, or a severe confinement, or what. Thus we jog on in the dark, wholly unprepared for either one or the other.

I shall not animadvert upon this measure. You may comfort and amuse yourself with your own reflections, whatever they may be. I am sure of your good wife's tender pity for the sufferings of her friend.

I suppose you are all in high spirits, as your brethren the while are here, upon the news of Graves and Clinton being driven into New York by the fleet of our good allies. Col. Lewis brought the report here the day before yesterday, so my friend Major Goes says.

May God bless you, and if ever you have masters, may they be milder than mine, is my earnest wish. Tell your wife she is remembered always with the tenderest affection by her

Affectionate, humble servant,

H. VAN SCHAACK.

It will here be proper to speak of the lady to whom the subject of this sketch had been united in marriage, in 1760. Mrs. Van Schaack was a remarkable woman. To a highly cultivated, and indeed a superior mind, for that day, she added an uncommon share of fortitude and decision of character. She was with her husband on several of his journeys to Detroit, immediately after the conquest of Canada from the French, and remained with him nearly a year at that early period, at that remote military port. During a period of about three years of the revolutionary war that her husband was absent from her in New York, she carried on his farm at Kinderhook, superintended the erection of out-buildings and of an addition to her house, and for nearly a year after communication was opened, so that sloops could go down to New York. She also conducted a country store, keeping her own accounts and receiving in barter for merchandise, lumber, grain and other farming productions, which she forwarded six or eight miles to Hudson's river, and there shipped to New York, attending personally in some instances to the shipment.

On one occasion during the war, after undergoing the fatigues and hazards of a land journey from Kinderhook to New Jersey, a distance of about 160 miles, and being disappointed in not meeting her husband at the latter place, this resolute lady rowed herself over alone in a boat from the Jersey shore to Staten Island, determined that neither land nor water should defeat her cherished purpose of seeing her husband then in the city of New York.

[FROM MRS. VAN SCHAACK.]

KINDERHOOK, 10th April, 1781.

MY DEAR HUSBAND: I wrote you on the 8th instant and told you how unhappy Mrs. Goes was with the news of her husband's death, and that it is her wish to have her daughter return to her, but she does not order anything about it until she hears from her first. I forgot to tell you in my last that I had received your letter of the 3rd of March; which, with one of the 19th of February, is all that I have had from you.

How unhappy do these times render us! What havoc has death made with our friends, sent from this place! I tremble to think of what may perhaps happen to either of us. I pray Heaven to grant us once more to meet—not to be separated.

I shall send this letter to Jersey, to be sent to you by the first flag from there. As I trouble myself with no public matters, I hope in whatever hands this may fall, that they will be so kind as to forward it to you.

All friends here are well, and happy to hear of your recovery.

Adieu, my dearest Harry, and believe me to be
Yours,
JANE VAN SCHAACK.

Thus far, there has been no attempt in our historical or biographical annals to perpetuate the trials, anxieties, and sufferings of the wives, daughters and mothers of those of our ancestors who took the unfortunate side in the revolutionary contest. To them, to their virtues, and to a detail of their hardships and adventures, history has to this day been a sealed book; and yet it requires no stretch of imagination to conceive, nor does it impose any great tax upon our credulity to believe, that materials exist in this quarter for the elucidation of female fortitude and heroism, and for the exhibition of strength of character and elevation of mind of the highest order, and such as could not fail to excite our respect, if not love and admiration.

Ancient philosophy has imparted to exile a factitious character—representing it as a blessing and an honor, the reward of the wise and the good.

"A sentence sacred to dreaded eminence."

It was only when ostracism had fallen to the lot of an unworthy individual, that it fell into disuse among the Athenians.

Literature and philosophy have no doubt been indebted to the restraints of banishment and its ally, incarceration, for some of their choicest contributions. But what more melancholy object can be presented to our view, what more trying exhibition to a sensitive heart, than to behold the head of a family —a husband and father—driven from those so nearly allied to him into a long and precarious exile, and leaving the latter to the gloomy incertitude of accident, sickness and death, and to the mercy of political and personal enemies, and all those baneful influences which are so often engendered by a state of civil war. When a considerable population are thus situated, it will readily be believed that occasions would be frequent for the transpiration of thrilling scenes, calling forth our liveliest sympathies, and exhibiting traits of character which would do honor to the most distinguished of our race.

"Few events, indeed, in human life strike the mind more painfully than banishment—a calamity sufficiently disastrous in the most ordinary circumstances, but peculiarly affecting when the banished are brought before us in the narrow circle of a family; a circle, the whole of which the eye can see, and whose sufferings the heart can perfectly realize. Peculiarly is this true, when the family in question is enlightened, polished, amply possessed of enjoyments, tasting them with moderation, and sharing them cheerfully with their friends and neighbors, the stranger, and the poor."*

It is touching to read the letters which passed between the exiled heads of families and those from whom they were thus separated. Expressions such as these we find in them: "May God, in mercy to our country, put an end to this horrid war." "I never expected to see such days." "May the Lord soon restore peace to our land, and may the present distress be the means of humbling us all." "When will this dreadful war have an end? I am tired out of living in this cruel suspense and separation from the only object that can make me happy." "May God bless you and keep you under his protection." "When shall we meet again in our native place? Would to God there was any prospect of it! But I fear, indeed, that our peaceful days are far remote." "What pain and grief does it give me, to see poor mortals imbruing their hands in the blood of their fellow creatures, and to see others (who perhaps have not proceeded so far) harboring resentment, hatred and enmity against each other. How contrary to the meek spirit of the gospel!"

In not a few instances could the inscription be appropriately placed over the tombs of Americans who departed this life while in exile:—"He died of a broken heart."

* Doctor Dwight.

CHAPTER VIII.

In 1781, and a part of 1782, Elizabethtown, in New Jersey, was a place designated for an exchange of flags between the British and American armies.*

Here Mr. Van Schaack was wont, at times, to meet his wife and some of his other friends from Kinderhook, and to commingle with the interesting society at that place. As elsewhere, here also he made a very favorable impression, of which a lively recollection was retained for half a century; forming friendships with persons of opposite political sentiments, and which the latter were solicitous to keep up and did sustain long after the peace.

Among other interesting families then residing at Elizabethtown were those of the reverend Doctor Chandler (who was then in exile) and the Daytons. From the latter, who were prominent champions of the popular cause in New Jersey, Mr. Van Schaack received many civilities.

[FROM JONATHAN DAYTON.]

ELIZABETHTOWN, May 24th, 1782.

DEAR SIR: Your very kind letter of the 8th came safe to hand. I cannot too much thank you for the attention and goodness you have shown in having collected and sent over so speedily the articles contained in the memorandum which I put into your hands upon your departure from us. Your very punctual execution of the orders you were intrusted with, have, I assure you, sir, not only pleased, but laid me under great obligation.

---

* Elizabethtown was a border town alternately in possession of the British and the Americans.

I am exceedingly sorry that the discontinuance of the reception of flags at this place will put it out of my power to render you such favors in return as I could have wished. Liberal and worthy minds will ever command my esteem and veneration. Yourself and your brother (David Van Schaack) may always be assured of my sincerest respect, my best wishes, and my most friendly offices toward you. As an emblem, too, of her esteem, Mrs. Dayton has put up for you a few dozen of eggs of which she expects your worthy brother will partake. They will be delivered to you by Mr. Lenox, who is also charged with several packets from J. Leary.

Your sincere friend,

Jona. Dayton.*

[FROM GOLDSBRO BANYAR.]

Redhook, 8th June, 1782.

My Dear Sir: It is high time to thank you for the papers. Want of opportunity alone prevented my doing it sooner. Continue your goodness especially at the approaching juncture, the most important and critical America has just beheld. The idea of conquest relinquished, the question seems merely who is able longest to maintain the contest. With ample experience to assist her deliberations, God grant she may determine with wisdom, and that happiness may be the future portion of this country.

Anxious to get home, the ladies kept the post road, and deprived us of the pleasure of seeing them. I rejoice, however, that you and your brother David were well while at Elizabethtown. Has Peter† submitted to the operation, or has the disorder abated and superseded the necessity? We cannot flatter ourselves with seeing him during the present troubles. When you write, tender my affectionate regards.

---

* This gentleman was a son of General Elias Dayton, who served through the whole revolutionary war, part of the time as colonel of a regiment, and afterwards as Brigadier General and Commander of the Jersey brigade; was in nearly all the principle engagements, and had three horses shot under him. Jonathan Dayton graduated with honor, at Princeton college, in 1776. Soon after, he entered the army, in which he held the rank of captain. He was the youngest member of the convention that framed the constitution of the United States. He was also speaker of the House of Representatives of the United States from December, 1795 to December, 1799; and was appointed a Brigadier General in the army of 1798. He was also a senator in Congress, from New Jersey, for several years during the administration of Thomas Jefferson. He died in 1824 of disease contracted from fatigue and exposure in attending upon General LaFayette, when the latter made his triumphal visit to the United States.

† Peter Van Schaack.

You often see General DeLancey. Tell him I exist, and so long shall cherish the same attachment to him and my other friends. Early impressions are rarely effaced or lessened by the vicissitudes of life, and years serve as so many rivets to these, as well as to our opinions.

Adieu. God bless you. Commend me to every friend; to David in particular; and believe me as ever, my dear sir,

Yours most sincerely,

Go. BANYAR.

[FROM ELIAS B. DAYTON.]

PHILADELPHIA, Feb. 20th, 1783.

MY DEAR SIR: Your two agreeable letters dated at Elizabethtown came safe to hand. I am very sorry I could not have been in Elizabethtown at the time you were, that I might have had the pleasure of again offering my services to a person I so much esteem.

You mentioned in your last your expectation of immediately taking your departure from E., since which I am informed by our friend I. Davis, that you have actually gone, and taken with you two of my female friends. If they still continue under your protection or jurisdiction when this reaches you, please to present to them my best compliments, and wish them a great deal of happiness in their visit.

It gives me great pleasure to think that the sword is once more to be sheathed, and the olive branch presented, when I make no doubt our countrymen will with open arms receive so innocuous and worthy a man as yourself, and that it may take place, is the sincere wish of

Your real friend,

E. B. DAYTON.*

---

* Also a son of General Elias Dayton. Although too young to enroll himself in the regular army, he was a volunteer "in several dangerous expeditions against the enemy." He was one of a party of thirty or forty men, who, under the command of Capt. (afterwards Gen.) William Crane, the father of Commodore Crane, captured the British gunboats, at Staten Island. These gunboats were lying near the entrance of the Sound from New York Bay, fully manned and equipped, and were to proceed the next morning to cruise off Delaware Bay, for the purpose of intercepting American vessels. The party crossed from Elizabethtown to Staten Island, about twelve o'clock at night, and, after proceeding several miles through the woods, made a sudden descent upon the boats, while most of their crews were carousing at a house a few yards distant; and, quickly overpowering the men who were left on board, they pushed the vessels into the stream, and, by daylight the next morning, had them safely moored at Elizabethtown, having passed a British fort, and two or three armed vessels that were lying in the Sound. Mr. Dayton was the last man who left the

[FROM THEODORE SEDGWICK.]

SHEFFIELD, 24th March, 1783.

MY DEAR SIR: I beg you to be assured that no distance of time, or opposition of political opinions has had the most remote tendency to obliterate those feelings of esteem and affection which I am happy in having entertained for you. Believe me, that I reflect with sensible pleasure and satisfaction on those few characters who have directed their political pursuits not by objects of interest but of principle, and I hitherto have, and sincerely hope I ever shall have, the same regard for such characters whether I can keep them company, or whether destiny or accident has separated me. Such men, however different their principles, will always propose the attainment of the same object—the general happiness of the community with which they are connected.

All political questions are involved in a vast variety of circumstances, and with the utmost attention the most capacious mind can give upon such an important question as the American war, all the assurance that we can obtain that we are right is an opinion that we are so. Hence, minds the most enlarged, possess a degree of liberality from which little ones are excluded. Hence, we find among the former, charity, softness, and mutual forbearance, even with those who most essentially differ, while among the latter, the most inconsiderable difference excites implacable resentment and bitterness, and, were it not that it might be imputed to vanity on my part, I would add, that hence it is, that notwithstanding we have set our faces

---

shore, having cut the fastenings of one of the boats with a sword, which was handed him for the purpose.

"On another occasion, having heard that some of the refugees who infested the county of Bergen slept outside of the fort, he determined to make an attempt to surprise and capture them. Though but eighteen years of age, he was furnished by an officer of the army with a detachment of a dozen men, part of whom were regulars and part militia. He crossed Newark Bay at night, in a boat, and, after a march of some miles, succeeded in making five or six prisoners, and hastened with them toward his boat. The main body of the refugees, however, at the Fort, had become alarmed, and sent a strong detachment to intercept the capturing party. They arrived at the water's edge at about the same time with those of whom they were in pursuit. Mr. Dayton with his men sprang into the boat, taking the prisoners with them; and so sharp was the fire of the enemy from the shore, that but one man beside himself could be persuaded to use an oar. The rest threw themselves upon the bottom of the boat. Before they were able to get out of reach, two or three of the party were killed, and two or three others were wounded; while he and his fellow oarsman (Luther Baldwin, of Newark) though much more exposed, escaped without injury, and arrived before daybreak with their prisoners at Newark."

Mr. Dayton was the father-in-law of Dr. Berrian, rector of Trinity Church. He died in the city of New York, in 1846, in the 84th year of his age.

different ways, in the great question which has so much agitated our country, yet this has not. I flatter myself on your, and I am concious on my part, suspended any social sentiments towards each other.

Since I had the happiness to see you, Mrs. Sedgwick has presented me with two children; the eldest, a fine boy now more than two years old, is playing by my side; the youngest, a sweet girl eight months old, died a fortnight since. Mrs. S. feels this misfortune most sensibly, but you know her equanimity is equal to her tenderness.

Mrs. Van Schaack did us the favor to make us a visit some time since, but I was unfortunately from home at Boston.

To-morrow I am going on business to Claverack, and if I can possibly save the time, I will call on Mrs. V. S. The young gentleman who will hand you this, I have obtained leave for to go to New York on some private business. He is my nephew.

Pray, my dear sir, in your letters to your brother Peter assure him that my affection for him remains unabated. I beg you to inform me of the state of his health, and whether his eye-sight still continues.

Present my compliments to your brother David and let him know that I hope I shall again meet him when there shall be peace, happiness and social intercourse and nothing to disturb these.

Mrs. Sedgwick has particularly desired me to present her compliments to you and to request you to do the same to your brothers. I am, my dear sir, with great regard and esteem,

Your affect., humble servt.,

THEODORE SEDGWICK.

[TO THEODORE SEDGWICK.]

NEW YORK, April 10th, 1783.

MY DEAR SIR: You have given me very great pleasure by the favor of your obliging letter of the 24th of last month. The happiness of hearing from you and Mrs. Sedgwick was enhanced by the opportunity it gave me of making an acquaintance with the agreeable young gentleman who delivered me your letter. The personal accomplishments of Mr. Gould must recommend him everywhere, but his obliging attention to ——, and all the inquiries about you and Mrs. Sedgwick and many other friends made him a most welcome visitor.

I do not know that I have had such an amazing regale for a year back. Lest Mr. Gould should hurry off to-morrow, I have taken time by the forelock, that I may not lose the opportunity so favorable to my wish.

I am surprised that you say nothing about receiving a bundle of newspapers and a number of letters I have at different times sent to you. I hope they have not miscarried, as they were intended as a memento of my affection for and attention to you.

I will felicitate you and Mrs. S. on this new pledge of your love ; but forbear the language of condolence on the loss of the other. You both possess so much good sense as to render the language of condolence unnecessary. I shall always feel for your distress and rejoice in whatever tends to make you happy.

My brother is in health, yet blind with one eye, not having had an operation performed when he wrote last. He remembers you most affectionately in all his letters, and before I conclude this scrawl I will make several extracts from those he wrote me last.*

The liberality of sentiment you entertain for persons under my description, is not more kind in you at this time, than flattering to those who are affected by them ; and I trust the time is accelerating so fast that we shall before long express our friendship in a more feeling manner than we can in an epistolary way. Next June will be three years since Mrs. V. S. and I paid you a visit. Who knows but by the expiration of the last of the three years we shall meet again.

The thought is so pleasing that I will indulge it, and anticipate the pleasure of such a meeting by dwelling often on it.

At length the long wished for hour of peace has come. The animadversion about the goodness or badness of it are topics of no avail to me. Sufficient it is that it is peace. God grant it may be long and lasting, and that it may prove a beneficial one to the United States! The old government being annihilated, those who are not yet members of the new establishment and wish to remain here, have now no ties of honor or scruples of conscience to withhold the most unequivocal allegiance to the American empire. I am among the great number of the English who wish to stay, and propose with all possible speed to quit these lines. I am clear and decided in my opinion that by the 6th of July I ought to be secure in my person, property, and liberty, but I could wish that those who sent me here, would from principle and inclination, wish and invite me back.

---

* These having been published in the "Life of Peter Van Schaack" will not be repeated in this work.

Should the spirit of the treaty be disregarded in the state of New York, I shall direct my course to the east-ward, from whence the wise of old used to come. I hope you think it needless to tell you the county in Massachusetts that has the preference, but this is a matter for future consideration. At present I sit down to write you a long letter on politics, business, etc. We must open our vision to a new era and look FORWARD; and all past animosities should now be sunk in oblivion. No one who wishes the prosperity of the United States on the grand scale, should act from the impulse of passion but the dictates of reason. The sacred nature of the first treaty made by infant states, who must be desirous of laying the corner stones of their governments in justice, clemency and benignity has, I know, spoken to you forcibly, and it will eventually operate strongly upon enlarged minds, whatever jarring there may have been heretofore on the grand political question.

Now is the time in which THOUSANDS of people are agitated with the question to go or to stay. A disposition shown by the American councils to retain these people will eventually prove of the utmost consequence, as a vast number of those who are involved in the question would be as firmly attached to the independency of this country, as heretofore they were to the British government. A dismission of persons will be accompanied with a removal of property, and I suppose, in the plenitude of power and importance, that the wisdom of America will consider population and wealth essential at this time. A man of plain understanding like myself cannot raise his views to that sublimity of speculation which is necessary to impress a belief that the loss of all the Tories with their property from the continent would not be a public loss to this country.

I hope, my dear Sedgwick, that you know and love me too well to harbor a thought that these sentiments I have thrown out are intended as a bait. You will, I am persuaded, think better of me, and consider what has thus hastily slipped my pen, as the pure effusion of the heart.

People here are under apprehensions of a want of security from the disposition manifested upon a late——— in the state of New York. But I hope another spirit will prevail in the hour of prosperity. A gentleman of my acquaintance in Berkshire county (and who you and Mrs. Sedgwick will readily recollect), was sour when Burgoyne was coming down the country so rapidly in 1777, but liberal, cheerful, and benevolent after the Saratoga convention was concluded. This disposition I could wish to prevail generally at this time. If it does, I predict that the happiness and prosperity of the citizens of the United States will be as great as their country is extensive and beautiful. The part of the continent ceded to the thirteen United States has room for millions of souls. Why then should those already here be driven away, when they can have room plenty, and be exceedingly useful in this extended empire, as well as to themselves and families.

I suppose you will be sufficiently tired before you get through this long letter. I will therefore draw to a conclusion, and only add my most affectionate remembrance to Mrs. Sedgwick, Col. Dwight and his lady, and to assure you how much and how sincerely I am

Your aff., humble servant,

H. VAN SCHAACK.

[FROM THOMAS GOLD.]

PITTSFIELD, 30 June, 1783.

SIR: Before this time I was in full expectation of seeing you in the country. But my hopes and expectations are vain. I do not hear that you have made even an attempt to return. Do you, sir, thus keep aloof because we do not invite your return, or do you dread that political frenzy which so greatly prevails in the state of New York? I have long wished to write you on the subject. I have waited to hear what Congress will advise to, and the states comply with. But, as yet, we know nothing of what Congress really intends. As for the states generally, you have no doubt seen and heard their sentiments. Few are wise on the subject. Revenge has inebriated the minds of some, and resentments, ill-directed and wholly incompatible with sound policy, have precipitated others into wretched resolutions.

This crisis is pregnant with a thousand ills and unforeseen dangers; and the few candid and wise are driven to the alternative of either counteracting the dictates of reason or of sacrificing their popularity to that justice and policy which our distracted country so greatly needs, you can in this dilema, figure to yourself the part men of wisdom, candor and popularity will take. Silence seems to be their asylum, or, if necessity drags them forth to speak their sentiments, they must at least connive at what is doing. Popularity upon the modern scale is the hobby-horse of almost every great man, and sacrificing at this altar has at one time or other demanded a sacrifice of real dignity and independence, drawn down on their memories foul disgrace that consigns them over to a righteous oblivion. Those who kindled the flame of war and directed popular zeal through the whole course of it; who have fashioned the sentiments of the people to the varying hour; prepared them to embrace any doctrines, and especially any cause, can, at this period (if they but will), step forth and wipe away the doubts of ignorance, the prejudices of the honest, and moderate the frenzy of the zealous. They enjoy the power, if they want the will, to do good. Theirs is the crime; but the misfortune is general. If, by chance, they are drawn from their inglorious silence, it is but secretly to approve of what is doing, or done by their LORDS, THE PEOPLE.

Thus, each state suffers. Have they not lost their millions by such bigotry? They barter ease and happiness for a sullen gratification of WILL. The great hazard the consequence of unbridled fury, that they may make their PLACES sit easy and secure in their day. But, sir, this state policy will accumulate on their heads the just contempt and righteous resentment of the future race, who will see, not as we see, but dispassionately and wisely.

Soon after I saw you in April last, I was going on the circuit with our Supreme Judical Court, when much of our leisure time was spent in canvassing this subject. Little could be learned, for those in office were rather reserved, except the Attorney-General, Mr. Payne. So far as I could understand him, I verily believe it is the policy of this hemisphere to submit the question to the people, and leave them to decide; and you will know, sir, they will dispatch the business quick, for they have not accustomed themselves to the burden of long, tedious deliberations. I have lately been journeying in Connecticut, and find them much in the same plan. The state of New York is not behind the curtain, but shows what they are. Hampshire, in policy, resembles us, and as for Rhode Island, they at present seem detached from the Union, and much neglected for their conduct respecting the impost.

It appears to me there is but one plan that will facilitate the re-admission of refugees, and secure them a quiet residence, which is to loan Congress a large sum of money. I verily believe and know they are so pressed for money at this time that such an offer would produce the happiest consequences. At this critical moment, money will do wonders; for Europe will afford them no further loan, and very little cash can be obtained at home. Such is our distraction in opinion, that no funds are, or can be formed immediately. Therefore, such an offer must carry with it peculiar merit. But after a while we shall necessarily establish funds, and then Congress can obtain supplies without begging. But, perhaps, while I am writing, the unfortunate refugees are provided for amply, and need not the pity, generosity or justice of their deserted country. Happy if this should be their situation. I hope they will find the fullest resources in the new world; and may success and a series of fortunate events inspire fresh hopes, and gladden all the scene.

.I hope, sir, you are not forming resolutions of leaving the country, in pursuit of uncultivated wilds. I think we have a right to expect your return. Your friends fondly wish it. I cannot, on such an occasion, remain indifferent, but must express the warm wishes of my heart for your happiness and safe return. Before this I presume you have heard from our old friend Mr. Sedgwick. From him you will learn more than is in my power to inform you. He is now at Boston, and one of the honorable Senate, as the papers inform us.

I have now troubled you with a very lengthy letter. It ought to be apologized for; but your civilities to me, and the anxiety I indulge for my friends have protracted it thus.

I am, sir, with the highest esteem and respect,

Your most obedient and humble servant,

THOS. GOLD.

[TO THOMAS GOLD.]

NEW YORK, Water Street, No. 93.
July 26th, 1783.

DEAR SIR: I received your letter of the 30th of June some time ago. It would have been answered long since, but the gentleman who brought down your favor was gone some days when I inquired about him.

I am exceedingly obliged to you for discussing some prevalent points so fully as you have done. You have depicted the times so clearly that I felt the force of every sentence you have written me upon that gloomy subject. I am not a little curious, as well as impatient, to know the effect General Washington's circular letter will have upon the minds of the people at large. As yet I have seen no comments or any kind of reply to it. The magnitude and importance of the subjects he has written upon, will make the ablest pens cautious to reprobate His Excellency's sentiments. If you have not seen it, you may get a printed copy from Mrs. Van Schaack, at

Kinderhook. I beg my best regards to all my Pittsfield friends, and be assured of the esteem with which I am

Your friend and sincere well-wisher,

H. VAN SCHAACK.

[TO THEODORE SEDGWICK.]

NEW YORK, August 13, 1783.

MY DEAR SIR: Orders have come for our evacuation with all possible speed, and I suppose between this and the middle of November, if so long, there will not be a British or German soldier in this place. If you have money to spare you can lay it out to good advantage in all such articles as you may have occasion for. If you will come down with it yourself, I will assist you. Otherwise, send to me your cash and I will be your faithful agent.

I have two letters from my brother* since my last. In the first he says, "Sedgwick has my unabated affection. In him there never existed a circumstance that could create a suspicion. In trouble he was the same man as ever—UNIFORMLY FRIENDLY. I know not how to express myself with SUFFICIENT ENERGY respecting him."

He has not seen you at certain periods as I have or he could not be so broad. But to go on. In his last (16th of June) he says, "I am preparing for my long intended trip to the continent, and mean to take Holland in my way to Paris. To return to America next spring, remains my purpose; but whether it will be at New York or Halifax, will depend on advices I may receive from you. If my friends out of the lines think that I may not be an unworthy member of the community, my native place would be my choice, but if my sins are beyond forgiveness, I will go elsewhere. I have been so long smiled upon and treated with respect, that insult now would be intolerable. I aspire not to any elevation beyond that of a quiet, unmarked citizen. I shall expect the candid advice of Benson and Sedgwick."

The time has now come that people in my situation must determine on the place of their destination. I therefore beg that I may hear from you as early as possible in answer to my letter by Doctor Whiting. Vessels will be offered to the loyalists to go to Europe, Nova Scotia, Canada or the West Indies. To neither of them do I wish to go, if I could help myself. I

* Peter Van Schaack.

am fixed in myself to be a citizen of your state, if it can be done. So is my brother David, and I dare say it will be Peter's wish also. It would give me great satisfaction if business, pleasure or curiosity were to lead you hither at this time, as a personal conference would be of service, and tend to more minute explanations than in this way. I would not risk a refusal for any price. I would rather venture to appear in person, and trust to a *viva voce* determination, and plead my cause before THE PEOPLE, whose voice, you know, is the voice of God, in all events. I beg to hear from you.

No definite treaty yet, and I am pretty sure, from advice I have had from your side, that there will be none for a month or six weeks to come. But this will not retard the embarkation of troops one moment. Nothing is now wanted to send them off but shipping, which, I dare say, will soon arrive.

Farewell. Heaven bless you and Mrs. Sedgwick, and give me opportunities of telling you in the future how faithfully and affectionately I am

Your friend and well-wisher,

H. VAN SCHAACK.

[TO MRS. VAN SCHAACK.]

NEW YORK, August 12th, 1783.

MY DEAREST WIFE: Your letters by Vanderpoel's sloop I have, with the several articles enumerated in them, received. The wool cards herewith sent for Lucas are very good and very dear, too. They are exceedingly scarce indeed, but as I wish to promote industry, I have sent them, lest the looms should stand still for want of yarn.

I am to dine to-day at Mr. Louis'. Our company will be large and agreeable. The old speaker,* his nephew, Henry Cruger,† and two other Bristol gentlemen, Gerard Walton, etc.

I imagine in the course of a fortnight or three weeks Mr. H. Cruger will be at Kinderhook. He has particular directions from my brother Peter to see all his children. Much will be expected of Harry. It is to be hoped and expected he will make exertions in his studies and manners, so as to impress his uncle to give a favorable account of him.

---

* John Cruger, Speaker of the New York House of Assembly for many years before the revolution.

† Henry Cruger, for many years a member of Parliament.

I am anxious to hear how John Stevenson has fared in Great Barrington. It is a matter of so much concern, that I hope you will lose no time in your communication of it. I shall not, you may be sure, venture among you until I can do it publicly.

A mail arrived from England to-day. Orders are at last come for an evacuation, though there is no definitive treaty arrived. Several vessels have come in since Sunday last, and many more are expected momently. I suppose by the middle or latter end of October all will be gone—perhaps it will be the middle of November first. But certain it is, all will go this fall. I shall feel myself happy when I am informed that there is a retreat secured for me. My letters to Sedgwick have an eye to that. I therefore hope care will be taken to have them forwarded by a safe hand. They go by Mr. John Sergeant.

Farewell! Heaven bless you, and believe me,

Ever yours,

H. V. S.

[FROM MRS. VAN SCHAACK.]

BEAVER SWAMP, August 26th, 1783.

MY DEAR HUSBAND: By the inclosed you will find, my dear Harry, that your friend* invites you to come, and that you and your brother must come to his house. He will protect you ; but you must come soon before any more new laws can be made by their Assembly. At present there is no law against you. He means you shall have a trial as soon as you get there, for which purpose he and Mr. Gould are both, as lawyers, retained for you. The judges and prosecutor we mean to prepare with something irresistible ; for which purpose your brother sets off for Sheffield next Monday, where he is to find Mr. Sedgwick at home. Mr. Edward is very liberal and in this matter has given Cornelius very good advice.

Stockbridge encourages your coming, and Pittsfield still more. I am in hopes of getting a permit from the Select-men of Pittsfield for you to come there. If I do I will send it; and lest all these things should fail, I have ordered a friend of ours to apply to Governor Chittenden for a permit for you to go to that state. This I have done without anybody's advice and without your knowledge. I hope you and your brother will not take it amiss that I have taken so much upon myself.

Should it ever after be made use of as a bar to your return-ing to this state, the blame must all be mine. I think such a

---

* Theodore Sedgwick.

pass may be a safeguard in traveling through New England.
The whole of what I now write must be secret. Well would
it be, if you were there and your trial over before it was publicly known here.

Mr. Sedgwick advises you to have a copy of the Banishing
Act with you, and all papers that will show how you have
been persecuted since this war began; you are not to mention
your exchange by any means. He means to have you on a
better footing than the gentlemen at Barrington are. After
the trial, if it is favorable, you will be able to go into any part
of the state unmolested, and about your own affairs.

August 28. Our Captain just returned with a permit from
the Selectmen of Pittsfield. I inclose it with Mr. Gould's
letter. I think it will protect you in your travels and bring
you near to her,

Who is ever your affectionate

JANE VAN SCHAACK.

After reading this to your brother, he tells me I have not
written pressing enough for you to come. He desires me to
tell you to come as soon as possible; that you have nothing to
apprehend in Berkshire, and you must state where you mean
to land, and about what time, and if it be necessary, he will
send a hot Whig to fetch you!

[FROM MRS. VAN SCHAACK.]

BEAVER SWAMP, Sept. 5th, 1783.

MY DEAR HUSBAND: Cornelius returned yesterday from
Mr. Sedgwick's. After writing the inclosed, they have both
agreed that it is best and most desirable for you to come immediately—the sooner the better. The best people out there know it.

I have not forwarded your letter to Savage, as I do not like
your selling off here, and buying six rights in the new States
I cannot think of spending the remainder of my life in that
part of the world. I would much rather go to Canada.

How happy I shall feel myself, when you are safe in Berkshire Indeed, I think, after a while, you may steal in and take
a peep at your farm. I can always see you in a few hours and
you will have it in your power to look over your own affairs,
and settle your books; which last it becomes very necessary,
as the interest is almost as much as the principal. Our barn
is finished, and the house almost in order. I have hurried all
I could, to have as much work out of the way as possible before

you arrive. (To-day Captain has finished with rye.) Next week we plough for wheat; then for getting in corn, and the rest of the fall we shall bestow on the swamp. Please send me two panes of glass 11 x 9.

Have you not a friend that you can recommend to me, after you leave New York, that can do my business, for I shall have wheat to send down, and buy rum, or anything else I may want? I think the shippers are better able to do their own business than mine.

Adieu! God bless you, and may you soon be near

Your ever affectionate

JANE VAN SCHAACK.

[TO THEODORE SEDGWICK.]

NEW YORK, Sept. 8th, 1783.

MY DEAR SIR: I wrote you a day or two ago in a very great hurry, by a person who unexpectedly went to Barrington, but as the opportunity was direct, I could not resist the temptation of saying something to you. Your two friends will leave here by the last of this or the beginning of next month, so that by the 8th or 10th of October they mean to embrace you.

The evacuation of this place goes on rapidly, and I suppose in the course of next month the whole will be off. But I am sorry to inform you, that the wealth and number of inhabitants gone and going is so great, that the effects of it will be felt in this state and the western part of your state greatly. Country produce of every kind is falling in proportion to the emigration. Wheat, which would otherwise be sold for ten shillings a bushel, will hardly fetch 7-6. Boards, staves, etc., are daily lowering and merchandize rising, by the immense quantities shipping off to the new world. I mean Nova Scotia. I give these hints in hopes they may be useful to you, and to your friends in Berkshire.

I suppose not less than a million and a half in specie is gone and going. The emigrants from Long and Staten Islands will carry out not less than three hundred thousand pounds in cash. What a pity it is that the policy of this state had not put a stop to this immense, important frenzy!

I inclose you yesterday's paper, in which you will see an ordinance of the King and Council of Great Britain, very unfriendly to our ideas in America, of being carriers for all the world. Should France and Spain adopt the like policy, we should be at loss what to do with the produce of this country, otherwise than by smuggling, for, surely, we will hardly submit to so humiliating a condition as to let foreign powers carry for us. This matter I should suppose would occasion serious and warm debates in Paris, before the definitive treaty is finished. It is inconsistent with the sense of the American commisioners, I am sure. For I am well informed they would insist upon the following articles before the completion of the treaty:

1st. A free navigation to Europe and the West Indies.

2nd. Liberty on the island of Aux Sables to dry the fish.

3rd. A stipulation that no fortification in future be ordered on the Island of Bermuda.

4th. That the British shall create no —— in the interior country. The reasoning upon these stipulations I shall reserve to a future day, when we meet.

We have reports, and they are believed, that the Queen of Portugal has prohibited American vessels from bringing flour to any part of her dominions.

So much for news and politics. How do you all do? Are you in want of any necessaries, before I leave for CANADA? If so, let me hear from you in time, as I shall not be here long. Having finished the different subjects I had to write about, I now come to a close, which naturally leads me to tell you, my dear Sedgwick, how much I am

Your affectionate and obedient servant,

H. VAN SCHAACK.

P. S.—Remember me with truest affection and regard to Mrs. S. and Miss Dolly. When you go to Barrington tell the Colonel* and his lady that I long to see them with an ardor easier felt than expressed.

[TO THEODORE SEDGWICK.]

NEW YORK, SEPT. 10th, 1783.

MY DEAR SIR: I wrote you yesterday, since which I have been favored with yours of the 2nd instant. Your apology about not writing me more fully was unnecessary, because none of your neglects of me proceed from the HEART. I have to render you a thousand thanks for your generous concern about my present situation, and it gives me pleasure beyond description to find that the result of your present inquiries "is

---

* Colonel Dwight.

THAT NOTHING IS TO BE FEARED." What a happy prospect to meet those friends I have been torn from, and with whom it has been my wish to spend my days! I have only to regret that my departure from here cannot be sooner. I shall adjust matters so as to be in Sheffield immediately after the Barrington court.

You do right to consider yourself as my counsel. You are to be more than my counsel in law. You shall upon all occasions be my mentor. I shall take the liberty of sending your letter to Peter to-morrow, because I am sure it will give him pleasure to find he is so near your heart: and that he has so good a prospect of getting an asylum where, I am convinced, his heart is so much interested. I shall do a little in the way of business when I come to settle, and I know of no place I should like so well as Berkshire, on the score of society. David and I are determined to sell all off at Kinderhook.

My affectionate regards to Mrs. Sedgwick.

Eve yours,

H. VAN SCHAACK.

[FROM HENRY CRUGER.]

PHILADELPHIA 3rd October, 1783.

I take very kind, my dear friend, your obliging letters. I hope to be in New York by the 15th instant. Business of great importance will detain me here till then.

I am glad we at least know where our brother Peter Van S.* is to be found, that a body MAY WRITE TO HIM. He has spent his summer something like Gen. Howe did a few years ago. Nobody knew WHEN he'd go; nor WHERE he'd go; nor HOW he'd go; nor did he know himself, till at length—but I leave GEN. SARATOGA to tell the rest. Give my love to him when you next write, and say I am by no means unmindful of him.

I long much to come to New York and to REASSURE you how much I am

Your aff. and obliged friend,

HEN. CRUGER.

The writer of the foregoing letter is that Henry Cruger who, in 1774, was chosen a member of the British Parliament

* Peter Van Schaack then in England. He married Mr. Cruger's sister.

for the city of Bristol, at the same time with Edmund Burke.
At the date of this letter Mr. Cruger was on a visit to the
United States, having a large number of debts owing to him here,
growing out of his business as a merchant in Bristol, anterior
to the revolution. During his absence from England, at this
time, he was returned to the House of Commons a second
time by his old constituency. He was in the city of New
York at the time of its evacuation by the British, and had
anticipated serious disturbances on that occasion. But on the
30th of November, he wrote this reassuring letter to his
brother-in-law in England:

"Having a few minutes to spare, I must inform you that
the Americans have been in full possession of this town four
days. The 25th inst. the British marched out and embarked,
and the Americans, with General Washington at their head,
marched in and took the post evacuated, and nothing but good
government is discoverable. An old grudge now and then occasions a black eye among blacksmiths, etc., but among the
citizens at large, everything remains PEACEABLE AND QUIET. It
seems the wish of the LEADERS that it should be so, and I am
persuaded it will be so. Governor Clinton, in understanding,
good intentions, and firmness of mind, is worthy of the
high rank he holds in this state. If he is second to the
great Washington, he is certainly behind no other man on the
continent. Hence, we may reasonably expect all the blessings
which usually result from wisdom, integrity and sound policy.
Believe me, my friend, in spite of calumny and disappointed
malice, they have begun well. Freedom, Generosity and
America have shook hands. Stimulated by noble motives and
a DUE SENSE OF THEIR COUNTRY'S GLORY, they mean to lay
the foundation of their future greatness by acts of mercy, justice and honor. Excuse haste, but be assured I am as much
yours as if I wrote volumes. The times, though tranquil, are
rather agitating. Anxiety and inquietude have some affinity."*

---

* In a letter written from New York, 6th February, 1784, Mr. Cruger says: "PHOCION
is said to be written by Col. Hamilton, a brave, GOOD, sensible man. He has laid aside his
regimentals, and now he cuts a figure at the BAR."

[TO PETER SILVESTER.]

NEW YORK, September 18th, 1783.

MY DEAR SIR: When I first entered upon the subject of removing from here I expected to have been gone long before now. At present my detention is influenced by the cause of humanity. The interest of widows and orphans will require my personal attendance in this down to the tenth of October, at least. Without me, they would certainly be sufferers. By my stay it is probable their interest will be promoted. In this situation, my feelings for my own convenience must give way, to promote the interest and welfare of others.

I think you have in one of your letters mentioned an intention of being down here by the middle of October. If I could have any assurances from you on this subject, I would certainly put off my journey a few days, because I am sure I could be useful to you in this noisy place.

The parliament was prorogued the middle of July. No definite treaty then, nor for a fortnight afterwards. I wish that important business was over.

We are alarmed here with reports from Maryland of an epidemical disorder raging there, and that it has even reached Philadelphia, where several persons of note have lately died very suddenly. 'God avert all public and private calamities, pray I most sincerely. When the evacuation will be completed is a matter of doubtful speculation, as there is scarce shipping sufficient to carry off the remaining refugees and other loyalists that wish to remove.

I suppose before now you must have seen Sir Guy Carleton's letter to Congress upon his final orders for leaving this place. If you have not, Mrs. Van Schaack will, I suppose, send the newspaper which contains the letter.

Heaven bless you and yours, and grant me life, that I may personally assure you how much I am

Ever yours,

H. VAN SCHAACK.

[TO MRS. VAN SCHAACK.]

MY DEAREST WIFE: I have written you by C. and by Peter Vosburgh, since which I have not been made happy by any of your favors.

Parson Inglis just now acquainted his audience from the pulpit, that the Disposer of all human events had ordered and

directed matters so that it was probable that this day's administering of the sacrament would be the last by him. This was
followed by some pretty exhortations that moved his hearers
very much. I was greatly affected I assure you. Matters are
drawing to a crisis about the evacuation, and I suppose next
month will be the last of any British power to be exercised in
America. God's will be done. Perhaps it is for the best.

Two of the transports with refugees to Nova Scotia are cast
away. Upwards of one hundred souls perished in the first.
What were lost in the other is not known, perhaps the whole.
Four hundred of the Queen's Rangers, officers and soldiers
were on board. I dread to hear of more disasters from the
Eastward, as the weather of late has been very unfavorable
indeed. I long much for the return of the Kinderhook sloops,
as I wish more and more to be gone. Richmond, I suppose
and hope, will be my portion. Peter Van Dyke carries this,
and he will tell you how I am, but no one can say how very
much, and how very affectionately, I am

Thine own.

H. VAN SCHAACK.

[FROM WILLIAM LAIGHT.]

NEW YORK, December 17, 1783.

DEAR SIR: As yet all has been peace. Newspapers threaten
aloud, and private admonitions speak still more pressingly for
the departure of particular characters. When political opinion
is the only test of merit, a life spent in the exercise of every
social virtue, but deficient in that one point, loses its value
when compared with those who, with no other recommendation, can complete the possession of so capital a qualification.
This sentiment pervades our system. It is the burden of
conversation WITHOUT, and influences our councils WITHIN.
Such measures, however, promote not the good of society; they
gratify private revenge, and of course proportionably disturb
the quiet of communities.

But this is no time for reflection. Your friends are all
well. Those whom you least expect, assure me it is probable
they will see you in your retreat this winter.

Accept the compliments of Fish, Mrs. L., etc., etc., and
the affectionate regards of

Your friend,

W. LAIGHT.

CHAPTER IX.

On the evacuation of the city of New York, Mr. Van Schaack and his brother David repaired to Great Barrington, where, after a judicial examination, they were, upon taking an oath of allegiance, admitted citizens of the Commonwealth of Massachusetts.

The views and feelings with which he resumed his citizenship under the new order of things, are pleasingly indicated by the following correspondence, which furnishes some evidence also of the integrity of his political course during the revolution; for no man would thus write whose conduct had not been dictated by honorable and patriotic motives, however erroneous that conduct may have been.

[TO PETER VAN SCHAACK.*]

RICHMOND, January 10th, 1784.

MY DEAR BROTHER: I wrote you soon after I arrived at Great Barrington. The day following, David and I had our trial before two justices upon the exclusion acts; and I am happy to inform you, that it was adjudged that we did not come within the description of that law, whereupon we took an oath of fidelity to this commonwealth.

As my business lays here, I removed immediately up from the lower part of the country. As soon as I came, the people of all ranks, with a few exceptions, flocked to me, and I can with truth say, that I am now much happier than I have been since the year 1776. All is peace. Decency, order and sobriety seems to prevail as much as if there had been no civil war. I

* Still in exile in England.

never in my life saw any people come so nearly to the morality of Swift's Hounheims as my present townsmen. Fortunately for me, that my character as a trader, and my reputation as a magistrate among them, was universally well spoken of, and, when contrasted with the new men at Kinderhook, it gives me more weight and consequence; and this you will be surprised at, when I tell you, that the greater number of the inhabitants owed me before the war and their accounts stood open when I came here, which I am daily closing, and those who owe me allow interest as cheerfully as if my demands were in bonds and notes.

We have no house-breaking, robberies, cursing, swearing, tavern-haunting, or scarce a scene of immorality. I am entreated by every town where I am acquainted in this country, to take up my residence and engage in trade. Were I about thirty years old, I know of no fairer prospect to accumulate wealth, either in the wholesale or retailing way. But as I need not involve myself again, having got pretty well through my debts, I believe I shall not in a great hurry be indebted in large sums for the future. Besides, my affairs stand much better than I feared they would when I left New York. The patrimonial estate, too, wears a more flattering aspect than I had reason to believe. Be assured, I shall separate the tares from the corn, and take care of the latter for you.

I have put out two hundred pounds lawful of your children's money to the town of Stockbridge; the committee consisting of Elijah Brown, Timothy Edwards and I Woodbridge, esquires. The rest of the money I shall do with, after a little inquiry, as shall seem most beneficial to the children and you, for I can get the best security here for money, and that so as to receive the interest punctually. These considerations will hinder me from remitting any more of the children's money to England, especially as law, order, and good government now universally prevail.

This commonwealth has to boast, what perhaps no people on earth could ever say before, and which is, that they have been the prop of the confederacy in carrying on the war, and after a struggle of seven years, they have established a good government, and never executed a single man for his political principles. When this fact is handed down to posterity, by the faithful pages of history, ages hence, will rank the Massachusetts among the first people of the world. This is a theme I could be copious on, but business forbids it.

Your affectionate brother,

HENRY VAN SCHAACK.

[FROM JOHN DAVIS.]

POUGHKEEPSIE, Jan. 22d, 1784.

DEAR SIR: I now sit down to write this letter to you, but when it will reach you I cannot tell, for I do not know where to find you any more than the Pope does; however, to direct it I shall send it to Mr. Silvester.

Inclosed you have a letter from your brother Peter as I suppose. Mr. Parkinson inclosed it to me. He desires me to tell you, that if you will let him know where to send letters to you, he will for the future take up all letters directed to you which he can meet with, and will take some pains to seek for them when vessels arrive that are likely to bring them. I have not certainly heard from you since you left, only I heard a rumor that you were somewhere in Berkshire.

I stayed in New York during the evacuation and for eight days after, during which time matters were very well conducted; much better than anyone expected, which was very much to the honor of the Americans, and to the great disappointment of the British. I saw several British officers after the evacuation, and they all expressed their surprise at so much regularity and order as was kept up in the city; but I believe there is not so much now, for I hear they are forming committees, and I am apt to think for no good purposes. The town is much in want of bread and fuel. I hear flour is sold for £45 per cwt. and wood for £12. 16. o. per cord, which causes much complaint among the refugees from the country, so as to talk highly of taking those articles which are scarce, from the people they found in town; which, if they are permitted to do, will be cause enough for complaint on the other side, and will, in my opinion, tarnish the honor they have lately acquired.

I hope this will meet you in good health and your brother also. Mrs. D. joins in sincere love to you, your brother and his wife; and be assured, I am, with respect,

Your affectionate friend,

JOHN DAVIS.

[FROM WILLIAM LAIGHT.]

NEW YORK, 5th of August, 1784.

MY VERY GOOD FRIEND: As I cannot plead a want of time, I should have been unpardonable in continuing so long silent, if a better reason could not be urged in my favor. We flattered ourselves that you were interested in our fate. We wished therefore to remove every apprehension which your fears might have occasioned, for in no single instance have we ever received insult, nor has there been a necessity for that extreme caution which once was feared. I long since meant to have told you how unrestrained we lived, and how well the peace of our city was preserved, with a thousand, etc., minutiæ, which it would have given me pleasure to communicate to one whom I know would gladly have received the intelligence.

I should trespass too much if I attempted to communicate the state of politics either here or in Europe. Jay is arrived and so is Mr. Laurens. The Marquis de La Fayette landed last night from France. From neither of them has the public yet received any official information.

As a vestryman, I never RECEIVED, OCCUPIED, INJURED or destroyed the property of an exile, and therefore no suit on the TRESPASS act can be brought against me. This is no uncomfortable reflection to

Your friend,

W. LAIGHT.

[TO JAMES WHITTAKER.]*

RICHMOND, 20th Nov., 1784.

DEAR SIR: I have before me your letter of the 13th instant, wherein you express your approbation of my conduct towards such of my neighbors as live in fellowship with you. Actuated by a sense of justice, it has been my lot to have been an advocate of a number of your people who I conceived were injured ; but, while I was endeavoring to aid them, I flattered myself that common sense, which is strongly connected with the laws of self-preservation, would have dictated to them that they should have used their exertions to support that power on earth from which they derive temporal protection, and not wish me to do that for them which, from scruples of conscience, they refuse to do for themselves.

While I have been laboring for their cause with great anxiety and deep concern, attended with the loss of precious

---

* Mr. Whittaker was a Shaker "Elder," and came to this country from Manchester, England, in 1774, in company with the famous head of that singular sect, Ann Lee. His letter was written from Niskayune, near Albany, where the first Shaker settlement in this state was formed by "Mother Ann," as she was called. A few years afterwards, similar communities were formed at Hancock and New Lebanon, in the immediate vicinity of Mr. Van Schaack's residence.

time to my own affairs, I find them to continue inflexible in absurdity, and that they would hear God's name profaned on Sunday in their places of worship, themselves abused, their women treated with obscenity, rather than make complaints to a magistrate. A question here arises whether any sin results from such application? I answer in the negative; because the complainants do nothing more than hold up their hands, and call God to witness that what they declare is the truth, and nothing but the truth. Does God delight in faithfulness and truth from his creatures? He does, be it declared when it will, especially when it is brought to light for the praiseworthy purpose of suppressing profaneness, vice and immorality. It is to be lamented that many of those who have scruples about a manifestation of truth before the civil power have no hesitation on their minds to call upon the Supreme Being to witness the sincerity of their declarations about a bargain for a sheep, a bushel of wheat, and the like trifling occasions.

A submission to the higher powers is strongly inculated by the great apostle St. Paul, because they are ordained of God and that even under a heathen government. For what purpose? The answer is, for the temporal good of the people on earth. It is admitted St. Paul is right; surely there ought to be no doubt on any GOOD man's mind, not only to submit, but have recourse to this kind of authority, more especially when we seek the magistrate for the laudable purpose of suppressing wickedness.

From such principles I draw these conclusions: That if God's laws are trampled upon, my neighbor abused in his person or property, it is a duty he owes to God, himself, and the community at large, to take the most probable and efficacious means in his power to get the crimes so much spoken of punished; and that if he tamely submits to such enormities, he, in a measure, becomes criminal and an encourager of the very crimes he professes to hate and abhor. The places where I attend public worship are free from outrages of this kind, because we use the means God has given us to suppress such atrocious actions.

We are told by the highest authority "to render unto Cæsar the things which are Cæsars." Hence it is clear: render unto the magistrate your complaints that the powers ordained by God may be enabled to bring public offenders to public justice. If government is ordained by God, God's creatures are bound to promote and support the establishment. If, in the public assemblies of your people, the wickedness complained of is a growing evil, by reason of their forbearance to bring offenders to justice, it is a question whether the magistrate ought not to interpose to prevent such meetings. "By the fruit ye shall know the tree."

I have thrown these hints and observations together for no other purpose but of the probability of their being improved upon to be useful to a number of my neighbors I have an unfeigned regard for, especially for the good man who will put this letter into your hands. If my opinions and conclusions are disapproved of, I hope, nevertheless, a favorable construction will be given to my well-meant intentions.

While I have been laboring on these points, it is with deep concern that I hear an opinion is disseminated, that it is for the glory of God that your people should quit their present possessions and seek for an uncertain residence elsewhere. A sentiment of this sort, sir, from you, I know has great weight here among those who surround me, and on whose behalf I exhort you most earnestly that a matter of such vast importance and so serious in its consequences may have the fullest consideration before it is brought into practice.

In all your just undertakings I wish you prosperity, but in what I have said, I shall continue to bear my testimony.

I am your friend and humble servant,

H. VAN SCHAACK.

[TO PETER VAN SCHAACK.]

RICHMOND, March, 1785.

MY DEAR BROTHER: Your several letters of the 19th and 27th May, 30th June, 10th and 21st July, remain all unanswered, owing to want of time and want of health, and the want of the latter makes writing and reading painful to me in the extreme. I scarce ever take up my pen, but when I am compelled to write, which, by-the-by, is almost every day of my life, and so many concerns have I on my hands, that I can never go abroad for recreation but my amusements are clogged with business of my own, or the paternal estate. Besides this, since the month of May we moved out our effects twice; once to Stockbridge, and since from there to this place. Here I have made an advantageous purchase and live in the midst of those who owe me. I have made some other purchases about me, and I have a number of mortgages in the neighborhood, so that in all probability, I shall be a considerable landholder in a little time.

The farm I live on I bought for four hundred and seventy four pounds York money, and contains eighty-six acres of good land, with a tolerably good house, barn and a young orchard, and a pleasant lake in sight of me. In my lifetime, I never lived among a more civil, obliging people. During my residence in Richmond, I never was a witness to swearing, drunkenness, or a breach of the Sabbath ; or, in short, any flagrant trespass upon morality. A purse of gold hung up in the public streets, would be as safe from our inhabitants as it used to be in the great Alfred's time. Beggars and vagrants we are strangers to, as well of overbearing, purse-proud scoundrels. Provisions we abound in, beef, veal, mutton and lamb; in the spring, summer and fall we buy at 2d. lawful per pound ; in winter, beef and mutton 2-2 and 3d, and everything in proportion and very plenty. I throw out this by way of bait to get you here, and of caution not to determine upon a residence elsewhere.

I have just returned from Vermont. I took your son Harry and F. Silvester in my sleigh, who, as well as myself, were much pleased with the jaunt. We met with agreeable society and very good fare. In Bennington, we lived in a style much beyond what I had any conception of ; and so we did in Manchester, about twenty-five miles farther. We paid our respects, in going and returning, to His Excellency, Governor Chittenden, who is a conversant, pleasant old gentleman, and as much superior to what I had conceived of him as the town of Bennington exceeds Kinderhook in the elegance and taste of building and living. In traveling sixty-four miles and back again, four days out, lived extraordinarily well all the time, and among other things, we dined upon boiled turkey and oyster sauce at Manchester. The whole expense of our bill while we were out (horse-keeping in the bargain), was twenty-six shillings, eight pence, York money, a piece. Add to the advantage of travelling, that your person and property, on the road and in the inns, are perfectly safe.

Murders, robberies, burglaries or petty larcenies are scarce heard of in this country. So perfectly am I satisfied with the manners, customs and laws of this commonwealth, that I would not exchange it for any other I know of in the world.

It will be difficult for you to believe, at so great a distance, that, immediately after the horrors of a civil war, the new government should have force and energy, the morals and religion of the inhabitants apparently as pure and uncorrupt as they were at their best a number of years before the late distractions. It is surprising that no more people in the middle stations of life do not leave the Old World and come hither. It is true the public calamities have brought heavy burdens, but these become lighter and will be more and more so every year. The epitome of human misery (I mean the civil war) in this country has been accompanied with a failure of crops for some years back, which has added to the sufferings of the inhabitants. The last season has been an extraordinary one for the farmers to get their grain in the ground, and thus far everything .promises well, as the ground has been covered with snow since the middle of December last.

If any of your friends wish to migrate, by way of inducement, you may assure them that lands are cheap and good in Berkshire. Building materials of every sort in great plenty. All that I now want in this, my delightful retreat, is a few people of your cast about me. Come over to us, and we will meet with such cordiality, love and friendship that we shall in our brotherly embraces, forget that we ever differed on any single point.

Your affectionate brother.

HENRY VAN SCHAACK.

About this period Mr. Van Schaack received a letter from his friend William Laight, of New York, inclosing one received by that gentleman from Peter Van Schaack, and which the writer characterized as one of "your brother Peter's friendly, REASONING letters."

[PETER VAN SCHAACK TO WILLIAM LAIGHT.]

LONDON, 16th August, 1784.

MY DEAR SIR: I did not write to you in answer to your short though agreeable letter, because I hoped to have had a longer one from you before now; at least, I trust the cause has been removed long since. I have sincerely sympathized with you and my amiable friend Mrs. L. in the calamities you have undergone, but I trust you will both find your fortitude rise in proportion to your trials, which, I thank God, has been my case upon several occasions, of a very affecting kind. We had a report that you had lost you own father also, which I have been happy to have had fully contradicted, though not until after a considerable time.

Next spring, I hope and fully intend, shall put an end to

my exile from my native country, where I doubt not but I shall yet enjoy many happy hours in the society of my old and never-to-be forgotten friends; for no changes shall ever alienate my affections from them.

We are apt, my dear friend, to view our situation in the most unfavorable point of light and to think that a CHANGE of scene would give us that happiness which in the present eludes our grasp; and in this instance we REVERSE what I take to be a just observation of the immortal Shakespeare, applied as he applies it to a FUTURE state, for in the concerns of this world, rather than bear the ills we feel, we fly to others, probably greater ones, which we know not of.

It may be owing to this (but I have endeavored that it should NOT) that I think as I sincerely do, that our own country will be full as happy as THIS is. I mean, there will be as much INDIVIDUAL happiness, taking a view of all the circumstances which contribute to or obstruct it in life; and composed of that, as much in the aggregate, though not formed of the SAME MATERIALS, if I may so express myself. The distress in America arises from the yet unextinguished embers of party and civil war. In the nature of things, the cause will every day grow weaker, and with that the effects also.

You have been in this country, my friend! Let us not be dazzled with the splendor of luxury and wealth. Recollect what numbers we have seen of the houseless children of want. Political security under a mild government, and the execution of wholesome laws may be made the themes of eulogium; but alas, how is humanity shocked by the many, many victims which are every month offered up at the shrine of violated justice. What a black list do the calendars of every session exhibit! How are the streets crowded with the sons and daughters of vice! Can you travel with safety; have you security in your own habitation; can you enjoy in peace the acquisitions of your own industry? Ask the housekeeper in and about the metropolis. Ask the wealthy possessors of the elegant seats which so much attract our admiration. The laws indeed punish; but they cannot prevent where a licentiousness of manners prevails.

All this may be called mere declamation, and may be said to necessarily result from the refinements of a wealthy nation, but in considering the comparative happiness of two countries, with a view of making a choice of the one or the other, we must look to FACTS; the manner of accounting for them is another matter. In my conscience, I believe the depravity in our country is not so general, nor the subjects to shock our feelings so frequent, nor upon the whole (though this is more problematical and admits a copious discussion) personal security or private property more precarious.

What I hear objected to my theory, appears to me to amount to nothing more than to assert what we all know, that there has been a CIVIL WAR. That indeed as long as it lasts is the epitome of all human calamities. This HAPPY country has experienced it, and let its annals, stained with kindred blood, show whether there has happened anything in America of a more enormous kind than might naturally be expected from such a dreadful visitation.

But, my dear sir, when I hear of mobs in America, I cannot help recollecting what I have seen here, where I have been present at two general elections. Whether a man's sign is pulled down and himself tarred and feathered in America because he is a tory, or his windows and doors demolished and his head broken in England because he votes for A and not for B, and because he wears a cockade of blue ribbon only without a mixture of pink, I own to you the frenzy, the injustice, the illiberality and the bigotry appear to me alike, and equally disgrace human nature; and equally prove the imperfection of that society where this happens to be the case.

You have perhaps no idea of the widows and orphans which these contentions have made. Suppose the perpetrators are detected and brought to trial; is it always that JURIES decide without regard to COCKADES? Are fines here always proportioned to the offense? Read the history of Sacheverel's Day among others. Even as to the impotence of the laws in America and the want of energy in their governments; examine the SMUGGLING annals of the coasts of England; read the narratives of bloody actions in the channel between the violators and the executioners of the laws, read of scores of armed horsemen escorting contraband goods to the very environs of the capital, which happens sometimes; at a distance, almost every day (I do not declaim without information) and you will see how imperfect all governments are. You will pardon this harangue, which I began, I assure you, unintentionally; but as I do not often talk so much without some reason or impulse, though perhaps not conscious of it at the time, I find, upon examining myself, that I have been led to it by the friendly MOTIVE of contributing my mite towards reconciling you to your present situation. An ASSURING attempt it may appear, but the rights of friendship will sanction it.

I assure you, I have thought very dispassionately, and as far as I could, like a citizen of the WORLD, upon this subject.

My language is not dictated by chagrin, or a sour temper, for few men are more happy or less discontented than I am. As a traveler, perhaps I could not be so happy anywhere else; but when I think of an ABIDING place, and of closing the "evening of a stormy life" like a rational, benevolent being who feels the noble sentiment, HOMO SUM, HUMANI NIL ALIENUM PUTO, who estimates the happiness of a society not from the overgrown wealth of the few, but from a distribution as much conformable to the natural equality of mankind as is consistent with the general good and the principles of an efficient government. Then, indeed, I examine the subject upon a larger scale.

I shall always be happy to hear from you and of the welfare of you and yours. With my grateful compliments to Mrs. L., believe me,

Your affectionate friend,

P. VAN SCHAACK.

[FROM JOHN C. WYNKOOP.]

KINDERHOOK, Aug. 4th, 1785.

DEAR SIR: The happiness we all experienced on the arrival of Uncle Peter,* is much easier imagined than described. But the peculiar agitation of my mother-in-law† into which her tender weakness threw her, was sufficient to have melted the heart of a man of much less sensibility than Uncle Peter. The tender passions are the most severe, and on this occasion quite unmanned his soul. Here language fails. Let your heart conceive the sequel.

There is a certain something in his deportment, looks and conversation which, in my humble opinion, speaks him an uncommon man. How happy will I be (and I sincerely wish my hopes will not be in vain), to find our new acquaintance ripen into a permanent friendship! With my compliments to aunt, I remain, sir,

Your dutiful nephew,

JOHN C. WYNKOOP.

In the autumn of this year (1784), Mr. Henry Van Schaack removed to Pittsfield, where, having purchased a farm, he

---

* Peter Van Schaack just returned from England.

† Jane Silvester, wife of Peter Silvester, and sister of Peter Van Schaack.

fixed a residence, which he designed to make permanent; about a mile from the present village, on the road to Lenox. Here he devoted himself to agricultural pursuits, and a few years afterwards erected a spacious house (for that day), an undertaking then considered as of momentous importance. Although a door had been opened by a provision contained in an act of the New York legislature, passed the year previous to his removal to Pittsfield, for his return to the state of New York, he was too well pleased with his situation and prospects in Berkshire to avail himself of it. It is not unlikely also, that his feelings had been too much disturbed by the treatment he had received during the revolution, to reconcile him to a residence among persons who so recently had been instrumental in bringing about his proscription.

The act of the New York Legislature above referred to was passed on the 12th day of May, 1784, under the imposing title of "an act to preserve the freedom and independence of this state, and for other purposes." By its provisions, all those who had been unfriendly to the revolutionary movement were disfranchised. They were "forever disqualified and rendered incapable of holding, exercising or enjoying any legislative, judicial, or executive office or place whatsoever within this State;" and they were "disqualified and incapacitated to elect or vote, either by ballot or *viva voce*, at any election to fill any office or place whatsoever within this state."

There was a redeeming section in this act, so far as it respected twenty-seven gentlemen therein named, and it was creditable to Mr. Van Schaack, that his known integrity of character should have been such as in the then high state of political prejudices, and in a statute otherwise of the severest character, to secure a special provision allowing his return to the state, and paving the way for his restoration to his country. The section referred to was in these words,—"WHEREAS a very respectable number of citizens of this state well attached to the freedom and independence thereof, have entreated the legislature to extend mercy to persons hereinafter mentioned, and to restore them to their country:

"III.   Be it therefore enacted by the authority aforesaid,

that Gysbert Marselius, Henry Staats, John Stevenson, Henry
Van Dyck, John Van Alen, Henry Van Schaack, David
Van Schaack, Harman Pruyn, William Rea, Myndret
Viéle, William Lapton, Cadwallader Colden, Walter Dubois,
Cornelius Luyster, Andrew Graham, John Thurman, Samuel Fowler, Joseph Mabbitt, John Green, Dick Van Vleet,
Jost Garrison, John Booth, Rolef Elting, Solomon Elting,
Richard Harison, James Smith and Benjamin Lapham
shall be and every one of them are hereby permitted to
return to and reside within this state without any molestation,
and therein to remain until the end of the next meeting of the
legislature, or until further legislative provision shall be made
in the premises; anything in the act entitled "an act more
effectually to prevent the mischief arising from the influence
and example of persons of equivocal and suspected characters
in this state," passed the thirtieth day of June, 1778 ; to the
contrary thereof in any wise notwithstanding."

At a subsequent session of the legislature held on the fifth
day of May, 1786, a section which, on motion of the speaker,*
had been introduced into "an act for the payment of certain
sums of money, and for the purposes therein mentioned,"
became a law, by which it was provided, that the several
persons mentioned in the third clause, as above recited,
of the "act to preserve the freedom and independence of the
state," together with "Peter Van Schaack, Richard Bartlett,
Theophilus Nelson and Zebulon Walbridge shall be, and they
are hereby respectively restored to all their rights, privileges,
and immunities, as citizens of this state, from and after such
time as the said persons respectively shall, in any court of
record of this state, take the oath of abjuration and allegiance
prescribed by law, anything in any former law contained to
the contrary thereof notwithstanding."

On the enactment of this latter law Mr. Van Schaack had
the satisfaction to receive a letter from his friend General
Schuyler, who was then a member of the New York senate and
had been active in procuring its passage: "As you are now fully

---

* John Lansing, junior, afterwards Chief Justice of the Supreme Court, and still later
Chancellor of the State.

emancipated, I wish you would LAY OUT to reside within the state.   What with compulsory and involuntary exile your absence from it has already been too·long."

CHAPTER X.

The year 1786 was memorable in the history of Massachusetts for the breaking out of that alarming revolt known as
"Shay's rebellion."   Eli Parsons, one of the leaders of that
extensive commotion, was a resident of Berkshire, which county
was one of the principal theatres of the rebellious movement.
Mr. Van Schaack took a decided part, on the side of the Government, in the efforts made to quell the insurrection. He was
indefatigable also in his exertions among the disaffected to
convince them of the impropriety of their conduct, and to
reclaim them from error.   Some of the officers attached to the
army sent out under Major-General Lincoln, in the winter of
1786-7, were quartered in Mr. Van Schaack's family. This circumstance led to the formation of some very interesting friendships, and, among others, with Major Henry Warren, one of
General Lincoln's AIDES-DE-CAMP, a gentleman who, though
Mr. Van Schaack's junior by thirty years, was of a remarkably
congenial spirit, being distinguished for a kindly flow of spirits,
a generous heart and unbounded hospitality; and it was a
remarkable trait in the character of Henry Van Schaack—that
of attaching to himself by such firm bonds of confidence and
intimate friendship his juniors, whilst at the same time the
respect due to seniority of years was in no wise evaded.

Major Warren was the son of General James Warren, well
known in Massachusetts as one of the most active whigs during
the revolutionary contest.   General Warren was for sometime
paymaster of the forces, and upon the death of General Joseph

Warren at Bunker's Hill, was elected President of the Massachusetts Provincial Congress, then sitting at Watertown.*

In the rebellion referred to, the respective parties in Berkshire were distinguished from each other by badges. That of the Shayites consisted of a small sprig, a branch of evergreen (usually cedar, pine or hemlock), generally worn under the hat band, and sometimes in the buttonholes of their coats, or affixed to the front of their persons. The supporters of government, or "government-men," as they were called, wore a white paper in their hats, on the right side, near the top, in the shape of a rose.

These badges are said to have been first adopted when a battle or skirmish was about to take place between the two parties, so that each could distinguish friend from foe when they met in deadly strife. They were worn by young and old, and so far was the matter carried that even little children at school wore their green and white badges, the sentiments of the parents being thus indexed by their children.†

These preliminaries will help to explain the following anecdotes, pertaining to this period, found among Mr. Van Schaack's papers and in his handwriting:

Feb. 14th, 1787.—Having regained the use of my office and thereby the use of my pen, and having got over all my ill humor—by the situation my family has been in since Monday—and having the prospect of sitting down to dinner for the first time since my house and office have been converted into barracks, and above all, my wife so far able as to sit in her chair, I can now inquire with a degree of

* Major Warren was born in Plymouth, Mass., in 1764, and died at that place in 1828. He was a descendant in the sixth generation from Richard Warren, who came over in the Mayflower in 1620, and to whom an assignment of land was made in the first division, in 1621. His mother wrote a history of the American revolution. (She was a sister of the celebrated James Otis.) The present Judge Charles H. Warren of Boston is a son of Major Warren, and possesses some of the leading traits of character for which his father was distinguished. Judge Warren's mother was a Winslow, and a descendant, in the sixth generation, from Governor Winslow, of Mayflower memory. She was also descended from Peregrine White, the first child born in the "old colony," and from Carver, the first Governor of Plymouth.

† The venerable Daniel Burhams, D. D., who at that time taught a school at Lanesboro, informs me he was obliged to interfere, to prohibit his scholars from wearing these badges for fear of evil consequences.

satisfaction how you all are.   I hope Mrs. W.'s spirits and
health are equal to the fatigue she has undergone.

ANECDOTES.

"A judge of the Common Pleas, a deacon and a priest deranged by the love of politics and a desire for farming, were
my guests last Saturday night.   Sunday morning I proposed
to send a servant to inquire if the General had arrived.   My
guests wished to go to town to hear a SERMON.   When we
arrived at the place of worship, instead of going in we paid our
DEVOTION during divine service at headquarters.   On our return home, neglect of Sabbath, etc., were spoken of.   I told
my friends that I had read an epigram which I considered not
altogether inapplicable to them, and that when I could recollect the lines they should hear from me.   The epigram
was written by Swift, on seeing a worthy prelate leave the
church, on the Duke of Dorset's arrival in Ireland in the quality
of Viceroy.   The lines are

> "Lord, I am in the church (could you think it?), kneel'd down;
> When told the Lieutenant was just come to town,
> His station despising, unawed by the PLACE,
> He flies from his God to attend on his Grace;
> To the court it was fitter to pay his DEVOTION,
> Since God has no hand in His Lordship's promotion.'"

" Feb. 15th, 1787.—A gentleman living in Pittsfield proposed yesterday to a clergyman, his friend and guest of a
neighboring town, to visit the prisoners at Mr. Ingersoll's.*
The good man, out of tenderness to their distresses, declined
to accept the proposal, upon which the gentleman observed
that it was well sometimes to go to the ' house of mourning.'
Quoth the priest: 'True, sir; but not to the house of rebels.'
The layman replied pretty quick in his turn: 'The most
proper place in the world for gentlemen of your cloth to go to.
The sin of rebellion is heinous, and a sincere repentance of
consequence to the offenders.' "

* A tavern in Pittsfield at which several Shayites were confined.

[TO DOCTOR ERASTUS SERGEANT.]

PITTSFIELD, 15th Feb., 1787.

DEAR DOCTOR: Upon the subject of the propriety, or rather the necessity, of wearing a piece of paper on my hat, I shall observe that those who first adopted the distinction armed for government. I then considered it neither prudent nor safe for me to wear one. When the danger was over, I declined at the ELEVENTH HOUR to wear the badge. From various quarters I have understood it was in a manner necessary. I have hitherto opposed my own judgment to the opinions of others, well knowing that I can be of more service in delivering opinions and giving advice to the poor, deluded people without, than with a piece of paper. Being at the same time convinced that there is not a man in the county with whom I live on terms of friendship but knows my attachment to the Governor, from the earliest period of my becoming a citizen of this commonwealth, I will close this letter with a true story:

"In the beginning of the struggle for independency, Doctor B., eminently distinguished for his professional knowledge, was, however, wavering in establishing a political opinion. The events of the day directed his conduct. When the American troops took possession of New York the Doctor became more decided, and gave full scope to his abilities to promote the American cause. He settled himself down in New Jersey and erected salt works, borrowed public money to forward his business; in short, became a distinguished Whig.

"The rapid successes soon after of the British troops brought on as rapid a change in the Doctor's political conduct. General Howe's proclamation offering pardon and protection hurried the Doctor from Jersey Shore to New York. After his peace was made he returned to his family at Sandy Hook. He met one of his neighbors, by profession a Quaker, who had, under every trial of distress, adhered to the principles of loyalty he at first adopted. Quoth the Doctor: 'Well, neighbor, I have got it in my pocket; I have got my protection before you, etc.' The honest Quaker (without any visible badge of distinction) put his hand to his HEART and replied: 'Friend B., I had it here before thee.''

Here ends my story. If any of my friends doubt that I have not been before you and others in that trying spot, I will venture boldly to say that I have kept up with those who have been in the front.

Extracts, with their dates, will here be made from letters

written by Mr. Van Schaack from Pittsfield to his brother
Peter at Kinderhook:

"August 21st, 1786.

"My apprehensions about commotions in this government,
when we last conversed, were but too well founded I fear.
Some of the towns in Berkshire call for a county convention to
deliberate about a mode of redress of certain supposed grievances.

"Sept. 18th, 1786.

"I called upon our friend Sedgwick last Friday on my way
home, and took a friendly dinner. I was happy to find that
he did not abscond (as was reported) on the day the court
stopped. In conversing with him I observed that the character
of the people of this county, even in this business, was so
singular that it deserved much admiration. A vast concourse
of people out of twenty-three towns met together with arms in
their hands (did an act in the eye of the law which amounts
to treason), and while at Barrington, and in their way up and
down (some travelling the distance of forty miles), not one act
of private outrage was committed during the whole transaction. Two men at Pittsfield got drunk; those were confined
by their officers lest they should commit irregularities. Does
history exhibit such another transaction as this, and yet every
citizen secure in his person and property? The conduct of the
people at Hampshire and Worcester has been the same with
that of Berkshire folk. The more I see of the New England
States the greater is the room for admiration. The people at
large are for such a reform in the constitution as will give the
administration of this government a very different tone from
the present. Its total subversion, I am persuaded, is not aimed
at by the majority; but what the present measures tend to, time
only can develop.

"Sept. 25th, 1786.

"You have doubtless heard that all the inferior courts which
attempted to sit of late are stopped. The Superior Court of
Worcester met and were protected for a day or so, but the
people opposed prevailed, and have broken it up. It will be

attempted to-morrow at Northampton where, I presume, the opposition will likewise prevail. It appears beyond a doubt that the General Court must abolish the Common Pleas and give up the State Tax, or there can be no accommodation. If this is conceded, government will move on unobstructed. Without this concession the anarchy will continue.

"Jan. 26th, 1787.

"I presume you would wish me to say a few words on the important subject of the present tumults.

"An express arrived from Shay's this afternoon to exhort all his adherents to come to him with all expedition if they wish to preserve their lives, liberty and property. This will occasion great exertions to increase the number of the Insurgents. It is said, and I believe it to be true, that some of those people were lately killed at Springfield in an attempt to seize the public stores.

"The government accounts, which I have pretty direct, are that Lincoln, with upwards of 2,000 foot, 400 horse and five pieces of artillery, is now at Worcester, where the Court sits unmolested. Shepherd, with 1,500 men, occupies advantageous ground at Springfield and is in possession of the Continental magazines. The friends to Government in this country are roused and are making every exertion to give weight and energy to the cause they have embraced. Besides public-spirited associations, they now wear white paper on their hats as a badge of distinction. Green twigs designate the other party. I think both sides get more inflamed, or rather animated; particularly the first.

"You probably will wish me to give you, confidentially, a conjecture of what will be the probable issue of this very unhappy contest. I believe the exertions of Government are so weighty and entrusted in such able hands that it will prevail in spite of all the powerful efforts of the people who are opposed.

"If you are not a very busy man I should think curiosity would lead you to make another visit here next week. The proposed ball I will discountenance. Dancing and fiddling at this time and in this commonwealth might look like the conduct of the wretch who diverted himself with music when the capitol was on fire. So great is my abhorrence of bloodshed, that if this town is to be the theatre for spilling blood you will probably see me in your state soon.

"Jan. 28th, 1787.

"Agreeably to what I wrote you by Tancred I went yesterday to Stockbridge and fetched Betsy's things. I drove down to our friend Sedgwick's, whose house was full of armed associated Government people. Indeed every street on the plain was full of men, who displayed in their conversation as well as their countenances an enthusiastic military ardor, and appeared to be greatly irritated at the obstruction given to the Government they had helped to establish with so much labor. Mr. Sedgwick acts as aid-de-camp to Major-General Patterson, who commands this county's militia. His activity, his zeal and his attentions to the great object he is engaged in made it improper even to mention your memorandum.

"General Lincoln's advance troops were, on the 20th inst., within ten miles of General Shepherd, who, as I told you in my last, was posted at Springfield. Shay, with about 1,100 men, was on that day between the two Government armies. It was thought expedient by him to move to this side of Connecticut river to make a junction with his adherents posted there. The most direct way for the junction was to pass Gen. Shepherd, who, on the approach of the Insurgents, sent out to warn them not to advance within certain limits. No attention was paid to this warning. Upon the near approach of Shay's men a second messenger was sent for a like purpose. This, too, was disregarded, and on their advancing still nearer a piece of cannon was shot over their heads. Like the two other warnings, this too proved ineffectual. Shepherd then advanced, ordered a number of pieces of well-directed ordnance to be discharged, which killed four men upon the spot and wounded upwards of twenty. The Insurgents were broken, scattered, and made off as far as possible. It was some time before the officers could rally and bring the men to order. There is reason to believe that there was no design to attack General Shepherd, but that the Insurgents relied on a belief that Government would not, without greater provocation, proceed to extremities.

"There is nothing now but vigorous preparations for war. Government forces were to march to-day eastward to co-operate with Lincoln and Shepherd, and to intercept the Insurgents in their retreat, for this, it is supposed, must happen. The Insurgents rely upon it that their superiority is such that a junction of the White Cockades with Lincoln and Shepherd cannot be effected. In this melancholy situation what good man does not shudder at the dreadful idea of the kindred blood that will most likely be spilled on this truly unhappy occasion? It is even dreadful in contemplation! How then must it be when we read a catalogue of the dead and wounded?

"I have written General Schuyler an account of what has happened. I wish you to forward my letter by a safe private hand or by the post, as you like. I inclose you the Governor's address on the present alarming occasion. It is much admired here and I think very deservedly. When you and your friends have read it I should be glad if you would forward the paper, with my compliments, to General Schuyler."

[FROM GENERAL SCHUYLER.]

NEW YORK, Feb. 6th, 1787.

DEAR SIR: Only your favors of the 28th and 31st ult. are come to hand. These I received on Monday and were brought by Saturday's post. They contained more minute and regular information than any which had been received here. Indeed, no account had as yet been received of the capture of West Stockbridge but yours. Not knowing how a promulgation of the details under your name might affect you, I thought it prudent to conceal the author, except from General Knox ; to him I made the communication under the seal of secrecy. Mr. Shay seems to me to want a good head. I think he should not have appeared in the vicinity of General Shepherd without having previously concerted with his other leaders a plan of attack. To leave that adjustment to the last moment was injudicious, and with irregular troops it appears to me that he should have attempted to dislodge General Shepherd at the dawn of day ; but *tant mieux pour nous,* for heaven only knows what would have been the consequences if Shay had gained a victory.   The legislature seems to be influenced by more generous and liberal sentiments than any' we have had for some months past.   The restrictive laws, so injurious to our interests and our fame, I believe will be done away.

As your favor of the 31st ult. contains the latest accounts we have of the operations in your quarter, and as those we may receive from others may be very incorrect, shall I entreat you to continue your communications?

I have been pretty severely handled by my old enemy, the gout.   Last week I should have needed an amanuensis to write as much as I have done now.   Be pleased to assure Mrs. Van Schaack of my best wishes and respect.   I entreat you to accept the like from, dear sir,

Yours very sincerely, etc.,

PHILIP SCHUYLER.

Further extracts from Mr. Van Schaack's letters to his brother at this time will here be given:

"February 24th, 1787.

"The General Court has passed an act to enable the Governor to pardon to the 23rd of next month, when the terms of mercy expire.   There is expected out of the pardon such of the Insurgents as were members of the General Court, members of convention, and all persons who have held any place of trust, profit or honor under Government.

"I made my respects at headquarters yesterday.   The General was pleased to show me his orders upon the dismission of his troops, and was polite enough to direct a copy to be made for you, which you have here inclosed.   If you think as well of the orders as I do, you will get them printed in Hudson.

"About three companies are enlisted out of the three regiments that were here.   A number of the inhabitants have embodied, at the General's request, for ten days; by that time it is expected fresh troops from below will arrive."

[GENERAL LINCOLN TO PETER VAN SCHAACK.]

PITTSFIELD, Feb. 18, 1787.

SIR: Should there be any of our deluded men in your neighborhood I will thank you to publish to them that if the non-commissioned officers and privates will come in, surrender their arms, and take and subscribe the oath of allegiance to this commonwealth, they will be recommended for pardon. That they will obtain it I have no doubt.

I remain, sir, with esteem,

Your obedient servant,

B. LINCOLN.

[TO PETER VAN SCHAACK.]

DEAR PETER: In addition to the copies inclosed I can, with truth, inform you, that after the action at Sheffield, the government party improved the advantage they gained so effectually that scarcely a man of the Insurgents escaped. Captain Hamlin and his party, besides plundering at Stockbridge, have disgraced themselves by their conduct in such a manner that all good men on both sides will think with abhorrence and detestation of those proceedings. Some of the prisoners they took at Stockbridge were forced in the front of the battle by which one Gleason, a schoolmaster, lost his life. 'Squire Woodbridge and Captain Jones' sons were also in front, but they have escaped unhurt. This transaction is, I believe, almost the only instance where the Insurgents, since the opposition to the government has taken place, have manifested a premeditated design of cruelty. 'Squire Woodbridge and Major Ashley were among the prisoners who were paroled just before the action. They assured me last evening that Hamlin told them that his orders from his commanding officer were not to take them, and some others he named, alive. Fortunately for Sedgwick he was from home, as the probability is that he would have been put to death.

The supine conduct of your state is the subject generally discussed. Some think your great people defer interfering lest they should lose their popularity. Others say that if New York is for breaking the confederation, let us know it, that then every state may provide for their separate safety. It is not uncommon to hear people say that while the well-affected to government are crushing a dangerous rebellion in this commonwealth, your people are fostering it in view of us. I fear these kinds of jealousies will have no effect. It, however, appears to me that, after mature consideration, your state will act consistently.*

The General dined with me on Wednesday, and I have the pleasure to tell you that he does not give up the idea of his proposed visit to Kinderhook. The more I see of this good man the more I admire and love him. His philanthrophy to the unfortunate and deluded does him honor. I will endeavor to procure you his objections to some parts of the inclosed acts.†

He was pleased at dinner to ask me my opinion. I stated to him my objections, upon which he showed his in writing. I was not a little pleased that my opinion coincided with his. I am now upon such a footing with him that he is to eat and drink with me by his own appointment and not mine. This proposal came from me lest my days for amusement might encroach upon his for business.

You ask me, "Is it true that one of the Light Dragoons was killed the other day, and that Baker was rescued in our state?" A Light Dragoon was killed in Northfield, in the county of Hampshire; he was AMBUSCADED. As to the part of the question relating to Baker, I do not know how to answer, having heard nothing about such a man; but it is true that Adam Wheeler was secured by forty men in your state.

The General did not leave "The Pool‡ precipitately." After he saw suspicious faces he stayed an hour and retired to his quarters leisurely, you may be assured.

My love to you all.

Yours aff.,

H. V. S.

If you want more news from me, you must communicate what you are about in your state.

2nd March, '87.

[TO THE SAME.]

DEAR PETER: In addition to what I wrote you yesterday I can now inform you that the General Court has appointed a special Court of Oyer and Terminer, to be held in the county

---

* On the 24th of Feb., 1787, George Clinton, Governor of New York, at the request of the Governor of Massachusetts, issued his proclamation for the arrest of the four leaders in the rebellion, if to be found in New York state, and enjoining its citizens not to supply the Insurgents with arms, provisions, military stores, or other aid.

† A copy of General Lincoln's views in regard to the Disqualifying Act will be found in Appendix D.

‡ Lebanon Springs, in New York state.

on the third Tuesday in this month. They are unanimous and full of vigor below. It is incredible what energy this Government has, considering how its strength appears to be mutilated in some of the counties.

Our friend Sedgwick would, I believe, have been assassinated if he had been at home last Tuesday. Captain Hamlin told 'Squire Woodbridge that his orders from his commanding officer (whose name I would not mention) were to put him and some others at Stockbridge to death. Adieu.

Yours,   H. V. S.

March 3d, 1787.

Had Captain Hamlin retired with his prisoners into your state, as he at first intended, he would have been pursued over the line. The people here will not be insulted at home nor from abroad—depend upon it. The spirits are exceedingly high indeed. I hope we may not get to quarreling with your state.

[TO THE SAME.]

DEAR PETER: Have you thought of the draft of the address to our great man? We dine together at 'Squire Woodbridge's to-morrow. Yesterday I dined at headquarters.

Part of a regiment of four-months' men arrived to-day from below. Wednesday the other companies will be up. Tuesday, come a fortnight, the Supreme Court will sit at Lenox for the trial of the prisoners. I suppose you will be here.

We have a report that your state have taken decided steps against our Insurgents. What have you done? It seems to me that you ought to write me all that is going on, at this time in particular.

Yours aff.,
H. V. S.

4th March, '87.

There is an intercepted letter published of one Capt. Eli Parsons proposing to his friends in Hampshire county to seize the magazine at Springfield and then to join their friends here to "burgoyne" General Lincoln. He holds a determination to carry his point by fire and carnage. Mr. Parsons is one of the leaders for whom Government have offered one hundred pounds reward. He was, before our present distractions, considered in the light of a WHOLESOME inhabitant. What will not passion make people do! The poor man, despairing of success, a few days ago was seen sixty or seventy miles off, bending his course northward, supposed for Canada. We hear all the principal leaders are gone off. The people in this town who have been most active have generally surrendered themselves, in order to take their trials.

[TO THE SAME.]

PITTSFIELD, March 10th, 1787.

DEAR PETER: General Lincoln left us yesterday for Boston, from whence he is to return next week with the judges of the Superior Court. The General Court have made a flattering resolve, so that the General will not be able to quit his command before the whole business is completed. There is that universal confidence in him throughout the state that whatever he does is always considered as right. I believe that he has recommended nothing to the legislature but what has been punctually complied with. His extensive philanthropy ensures the confidence even of those very people he has subdued by arms and policy.

We are full of troops, inasmuch as that two companies are now on the march for West Stockbridge and another to Williamstown. Two or three companies more are expected soon from the eastward.

I hear a proclamation similar to your Governor's has been issued in Vermont. Everything now is perfectly quiet. We hear of no Insurgents. I hope the poor people will come to a sense of their error, and throw themselves on the justice of the Government, and I am persuaded the justice of it will be tempered with a great deal of mercy.

I accompanied the General four miles on his journey. We hear Capt. Shay has got back to Vermont. This I can easily believe, for I cannot suppose that Lord Dorchester would either admit him as an inhabitant or detain him as a prisoner.

Yours, with truest affection,

H. VAN SCHAACK.

On the 12th of March Mr. Van Schaack wrote to his brother: "When the news of the depredation on Stockbridge arrived in Boston the General Court (under the idea that your state had taken no notice of the representations which had been made about the Insurgents sheltering themselves among you), resolved to send an officer of note with a peremptory demand to have the disturbers of our Government delivered up ; and withal notified your legislature that application had been made to Congress for leave to march troops into other states to suppress the rebellion. Gen. Lincoln's powers were enlarged. The General Court have taken, I hear, a resolution that if the state of Vermont will not deliver up the Insurgents that are harbored there, to ask their leave to admit troops to march for the sole purpose of apprehending our disaffected.

There will be a struggle for the chair this spring. Hancock and Samuel Adams have coalesced a union in this Government as odious as that of Fox and North was in G. B."

[FROM MAJOR HENRY WARREN.]

Six o'clock, 9th March.

MY DEAR SIR: The inclosed, according to promise, is shockingly transcribed : agitated, hurried and confused. It was done between eleven and twelve. I doubt whether you can read it ; but if you do not like to trouble yourself to copy it, I dare say the good Peggy will decipher it and become your fair amanuensis. I am sure, with General Lincoln for compositor and Miss Van Vleck copyist, it will be an essay worthy of a place in your archives. We move eastward in two hours, eight at least sooner than I expected, which deprives me of the two minutes that I intended to have stolen to pay my respects to your good lady and her young friends. Please do it for me, and if you will do it with a grace equal to my feelings I am sure they will be acceptable.*

The General tells me to request you that none but your brother see the inclosed.

I shall do myself the honor to address you immediately on my arrival ; and after saying once more to you and the ladies ADIEU, I am, with perfect respect and esteem for you and them, my dear sir,

Your assured friend and humble servant,

H. WARREN.

The "composition of General Lincoln" referred to in the

---

* Major Warren was quite smitten with one of Mr. Van Schaack's nieces.

foregoing letter was his paper on the Disqualifying Act passed by the General Court, to be found in the appendix.

In a letter to his brother, a few days afterwards, Mr. Van-Schaack says: "The General has come all the way from Boston without any escort but an unarmed servant. He wisely considers the impropriety of an expensive parade at this time, and in this kind of government. As Major-General, he is entitled to a large suite; not less, among other arrangements, than four Aids."

[FROM MAJOR WARREN,]

Boston, March 14, 1787.

MY DEAR SIR: I have the vanity to flatter myself that it will give you one spark of pleasure to hear of MY safe arrival in this town on Sunday evening, in high health and spirits, and found my good friends all well. This will be honored by my good General, who leaves us early to-morrow for Berkshire; and I do assure you I regret the necessity which obliges me to stay behind. I feel myself attached to him—to the army, and to THE agreeable family to which I had the honor of being introduced, and by which I was treated with an unremitted attention and complaisance which merits my sincerest thanks, and which I beg you to accept.

Our General returns to you in the double capacity of Commander-in-Chief and Commissioner, etc. The nature and extent of his commission will be best explained by the practice, which will be conformable to the feelings of humanity, the dignity of government and the good of the commonwealth. I am happy that government discovers a disposition to pardon every one of these deluded wretches that they can, consistently with the public safety.

I return to-morrow to the business and employments of civil life. I shall fix down at Plymouth and often recollect the happy little circle at Pittsfield. Will you, my dear sir, present my best respects to Mrs. Van Schaack. Tell her I feel a weight of obligation for her many friendly attentions which I know not how to discharge; but the benevolence of her own mind will be a sufficient compensation, when she recollects that the retrospect is to me a constant source of pleasure and gratification.

Will you be good enough to sacrifice some few of your leisure moments to tell me what is going forward in Berkshire? I shall feel much honored by such a flattering token of your friendship.

I have the honor to be, with the most perfect respect and esteem, my dear sir,

Your assured friend and obedient servant,

HENRY WARREN.

[FROM WILLIAM WILLIAMS.]*

DALTON, 25th April, 1787.

DEAR SIR: You will recollect that when, in our late short interviews you requested me to give you a copy of the list of grievances which were laid before the first county convention by this town, together with my motives for assisting the town in stating them, I told you it would be a lengthy matter, because, in order to explain them clearly, a detail of my conduct relative to the late insurrection would be necessary. The request, I have no doubt, was influenced by benevolent views. If the satisfaction you may receive as you go along with me should not relieve your patience, and in some measure compensate for the trouble I shall give you, you will please, for the present, to give me a place among your poor debtors. Whenever a fit opportunity presents, you may expect my acknowledgments for the balance.

---

* This gentleman was of "an ancient and honorable family," in the county of Hampshire, and clerk of that county before the revolution came on, from which he was ejected on account of the political part which he took, and then left the county, settling on a farm in the town of Dalton, adjoining Pittsfield, and never, as I have understood, took any ACTIVE PART against the revolution, although his father did, and for which HIS name has been handed down to immortality in the pages of Mr. Fingal, in two lines, which may be found there, the first of which has escaped my memory, the last line of the couplet being, 'Nor smok'd old Williams to a Whig;' alluding to his having been shut up in a smoke-house for his recusancy by the zealous Whigs of his town.

"Mr. Williams acquired and retained the confidence and good will of the people where he resided and spent the residue of his life. He was a very grave and religious man, a deacon of the church, and for some time a member of the senate of Massachusetts from Berkshire and dying at the age of ninety-four years, left a considerably numerous and respectable family."

JOHN CHANDLER WILLIAMS was a branch of the same family, though younger than the preceding one. He was a lawyer of respectable standing and practice, and frequently represented his town in the state Legislature. He was a man of integrity and great assiduity and method in all his pursuits, exceedingly quick and zealous in his temperament, in which he was countenanced and sustained by his wife, who was a cousin of the same family, and rather a remarkable woman. She, too, gloried much in her ANCIENT TORYISM and that of her family till the day of her death, of which there are many amusing anecdotes told. For instance: "When toward the close of her life she was about taking leave of a young friend, then going on a visit to 'Old England,' her parting request was, that he would give her best respects to His Majesty, George the Fourth, and assure him that CHANDLER WILLIAMS AND WIFE were still as good and staunch Tories as they ever were."—Letter to the author from the Hon. Ezekiel Bacon, of Utica, who was a native of Berkshire county.

The first start that Dalton took was in July. We had occasion for a meeting to settle some town matters toward the
end of that month.   Previous to the meeting, and after the
warrant was made (relative to which, I suppose, a pinto was
consulted), I had a message from Captain Cleavland in which
his wishes were expressed that I would exert myself.   As I
knew his warm make, and had before received some hints that
the people intended something which, I believe, was not then
fully determined, I was prepared to meet with this clause,
which I found at the close of the warrant, viz:"To act upon any
other business that shall be thought proper."

When we had gone through with the business of the meeting I called upon the select-men to explain the design of inserting that clause.   None of them could tell the meaning of it.
I pressed an explanation.   They said they did not know but
there might be other business which had escaped their attention at the time they made their warrant, and, in case it should
so happen, it might be taken up under that clause.   I told
them it would not support any vote that might be taken upon
it.   It was too general;   and added, there must have been some
"design in inserting it, and since you, gentlemen, decline
explaining yourselves, I will take the liberty to conjecture
your meaning."   For several times I missed the mark; but at
last hit upon this, that it was intended to give the people
opportunity to express their feelings and wishes relative to
matters of government.   They then confessed, and I further
objected against doing anything upon a clause too general and
indeterminate regularly to ground a vote, and told the people
if they felt grievances it appeared to me most regular and
advisable to call a county convention and state such grievances
as the county should be agreed in, and petition for redress.
More was said ; I mean only to epitomize.

Soon after this the Partridgefield mandate, which absurdly
purported itself to be a statement of public grievances which
required the consideration of a county convention, was handed
to our select-men.   They brought it to me to peruse.   I found
it filled with Deacon K. (a character with which I was but too
well acquainted in 1774), and calculated to do mischief. They
wanted my opinion as to the expediency of calling the town
together.   At this time I conversed several hours with them.
I found them loaded with grievances: that government did
nothing well ; that they should be ruined unless vigorous and
decisive measures should be immediately pursued by the
people for their preservation ; in a word, that the frenzy had

got to such a pitch that they could think of nothing less than breaking up government.

Upon this occasion I fairly stated to them the utter impropriety and irregularity, as well as folly and absurdity, of attempting to overturn the government; pointed out the danger of the attempt; assured them they would fail; that government would make the most vigorous efforts to suppress the people and do the business, and in the end they would get themselves into halters; or, in case the opposition should become more general than appeared probable to me, they might land themselves where they did not wish to land—in Great Britain, and unconditionally.

I told them, at the same time, they had no grievances, and challenged them to state one to me. That what they considered as grievances were unavoidable burdens, and much less than they had agreed to submit to. In short, I said all I could to bring them from their mad purpose to overthrow government. I found, however, that all attempts to convince them they had no real grievances would be fruitless.

What was the Deacon's opinion about a meeting? I told the gentlemen there would be danger in it, the minds of the people were so fired; but they might be blamed if they should neglect to do it. I was at a loss what would be the best. On the whole, it appeared to me best to encourage it, and a warrant was prepared accordingly. Stopping the courts was the object. This folly I determined, if possible, to prevent the people of Dalton from committing. How was it to be done? The answer to this question furnishes the general motive of my conduct in this matter. The people could not state their grievances to convention without my assistance, and if by affording it I could buy them off from their purpose to stop the courts in this county the acquisition would be valuable. With this view I prepared the draught herewith sent you. I mentioned my purpose to Mrs. Williams. She thought opposition to them would get me a broken skull. I told her I could not justify to myself the neglecting it, and I would risk the consequences.

When I came to the meeting I found very few persons there except those who were under the influence of the infatuation which at this time had become pretty general in the county. I waited some time to see the operation of the frenzy. Nothing of moment was said by any one. I called upon the meeting to proceed to business. One said, "We don't know what to do; we wait for you to tell us."

This gave me the opportunity I wished for. Having mentioned what I conceived was the intention of the people, viz:

the breaking up of the courts of law, I explained to them the unjustifiable nature and irregularity of such a measure; told them they had in the constitution prescribed to themselves a very different line of conduct in case they felt, or supposed they felt, public grievances. Such a measure, therefore, must be a violation of their own covenant. I pointed out the absurdity of it, and assured them, if it was pursued, they would meet with disappointment and most probably fail of obtaining their professed object or a redress of their grievances. I told them they might rely upon it government would exert itself to suppress them, and would probably do it, and, in that case, they must expect serious consequences; that a civil war, the probable consequence of their exertions against government, must in every view be shocking, and particularly as it must add to burdens they complained had already become insupportable, and possibly might land them in Great Britain without condition—an event which, for myself, I wished might not take place.

This, in substance, is what I said to the meeting. Your good sense will easily supply some things I have omitted which might make the several parts appear more consistent. I closed what I had to say in these words: "Gentlemen, if you will agree" (I had before proposed a note for it) "not to stop the courts, I will assist in stating your grievances, if not, I will have nothing further to do with you."

They appeared like so many mum-chauses for a few minutes. At length two persons came forward and said they had no objection against the town passing a vote not to stop the courts, but they should not hold themselves bound by it. The rest appeared to be convinced of the impropriety and irregularity of the measure (stopping the courts), and probably would have come into the proposed vote if it had been judged necessary to further urge it then.

It was then moved that the select-men might be a committee to state the public grievances and report, etc., and they were chosen accordingly. I was also nominated. I declined, but told the meeting I would assist the committee agreeably to my promise, and accordingly withdrew with them. I read and distinctly explained to them what I had prepared; mentioned those things in the draft which might possibly give offense, and told them that although I had written it, if they should sign and report it, it would be theirs and not mine, and they must be accountable, etc. Lest they might have failed of getting the sense of it, I erad and explained it to them a second time with the like caution. The gentlemen signed and reported, and the town accepted it.

Not contented wholly to lose sight of their dear object, a warm debate immediately ensued respecting the courts of law.

How should they be prevented doing business till grievances should be redressed? was the question. While the people were debating the matter I drew the concluding vote. The word "suspend" was objected to as insufficient. I told them it occurred to me while writing, but if they did not approve of it I wished them to suit themselves with a better. A jealousy of my integrity was hinted upon the occasion. However, after the matter had been sufficiently canvassed they agreed to let SUSPEND stand. I then brought on my motion again for a vote not to stop the courts. It was replied to it that the vote we had last taken implied it. I felt the weight of the reply and dropped the motion.

It has been said the Dalton grievances are spiced. I do not deny it. As the matter had been conducted (and the whole plan was settled when they were prepared) justice required that their feelings should be truly and fully expressed.

By doing this, with obvious and natural remarks intermixed, the real situation of the government would be best discovered; and consequences have made it evident that the portrait was not over animated.

You now have, my dear sir, the general and particular motives of my conduct in this affair. To support my character with you (did it need support) I could give you a further detail of my exertions against the measures of the people both in our public meetings and in private conversation; and with the same view I might mention repeated private applications, or rather proposals, made to me to join with them, together with my constant and peremptory refusal, accompanied always with a declared opinion that they were wrong. But I persuade myself there is no occasion for it.

I will not deny to you that I have all along conducted with more or less of that prudence which fear suggests. It was impossible to foresee to what lengths the infatuation might carry the people, or what mischiefs they might do. I was therefore ever careful in my opposition to the people to keep full possession of myself, and never to use any weapons but those which truth and reason furnished. Besides, the constitutional importance of the people lays a foundation for such claims of honor and consideration as to render the precise degree of respect due to them a point of very nice decision. And, if I do not mistake the import of some late arrangements,

I am not alone in this opinion. But with respect to the late insurrection this uncertainty would not operate. Their measures were clearly and confessedly wrong, and no good citizen could entertain a moment's doubt as to his duty.

I am sufficiently sensible that I have lost, by Dalton grievances, the good opinion of some gentlemen in the county through whose influence I might have been brought out of my present obscurity. On this account the loss occasions me no great pain. Constitution, habit, circumstances and philosophy unite their influence to make me believe that domestic pleasures and enjoyments are the best the world affords. Were it not so, persons of my character are too much suspected to be useful, however well disposed. Other reasons, and of more weight, concur to make me desire you would consider this letter confidential. If I can secure the good opinion of a few friends whose feelings do not change with times and seasons, whose esteem is my pride and honor, I have all my wishes as to men. You may place to the score of stupidity or philosophy, as you may judge it merits. And believe me to be, with sincere esteem, dear sir,

Your most obedient servant,

WM. WILLIAMS.

At the general state election in April, 1787, Mr. Van Schaack was chosen a representative for the town of Pittsfield in the state Legislature, known as the General Court. As it was his uniform practice to exert his best energies in whatever he undertook, we now find him seeking prime information among his constituents in regard to their condition, wants and grievances, whereby he might be enabled to act understandingly and usefully in the new position to which he was called.

[FROM WILLIAM WILLIAMS.]

DALTON, May 18, 1787.

DEAR SIR: The late choice is respectful, and, your short residence in the town of Pittsfield considered, I think does you much honor. I congratulate you upon it. It gives me pleasure on two accounts especially, as it brings into view a long-injured character in a conspicuous manner, and promises real advantage to the town and community at large.

I am now possessed of the piece I mentioned in my late letter, and, being permitted to do it, inclose you a copy of it. It was intended, when first written, to have been published, but the writer afterwards altered his mind and it has not seen the light. There are some things in it which merit attention, and, though too late to be advantageously published, may give you some ideas of which you may make some use. I must beg the favor of receiving the copy again after your return from Boston.*

My very respectful compliments to Mrs. Van Schaack, and permit me to request your polite communication of this idea to her, that similarity and identity are not the same. The wig, the bow, the great coat and the pied horse may be the same, or very like, and the rider not so.

I should have been inexcusable to have passed your house at any time, but especially at this time. Be assured, I have not done it. It must have been parson Collins.

I wish you a prosperous journey, an agreeable session and safe return.

I am your obliged and most obedient servant,

WM. WILLIAMS.

[TO JOHN HANCOCK.]

PITTSFIELD, Aug., 1787.

SIR: The ardent love your excellency has for your country and my own desires to promote so much of its happiness in the narrow sphere I move in, I trust will apologize for the freedom of this letter.

Very soon after my arrival here numbers of the better people of this town, particularly such as have been tinctured with a spirit that prevailed to oppose government, called on me to know the proceedings of the General Court in the late session, which I detailed as well as my memory would let me; and it is with a degree of satisfaction that I have it in my power to assure your excellency that if the resolve of the 13th of June last had comprehended persons under indictments or smaller offences, the inhabitants at large of the town of Pittsfield would have been entirely satisfied. Major Oliver Root, Capt. Daniel Sackett, Lieut. Aaron Noble and Constable Moses Wood are of this class of men, and were among those

---

* The paper here referred to is a document of very decided historical interest, vide appendix C.

who, in an early stage of the insurrection returned to a sense
of their duty and have ever since demeaned themselves as
faithful citizens. They feel exceedingly chagrined that they
should be under degrading disqualifications, while those who
have committed high-handed offences against the public have
returned to the bosom of their country without punishment. I
felt the force of this when a reconsideration of the above
resolve was brought forward in the House, and I have much
satisfaction in reflecting that I voted with the majority, so as
to make the terms of reconciliation as extensive as possible
under an unhappy embarrassment.

A few days before I left Boston, I presented, through Mr.
Secretary Avery, petitions from the persons that are mentioned
above, addressed to your excellency and the council. As those
petitions were sent forward before the resolve of the 13th was
known in this country, they, from that circumstance, in my
opinion, have the more merit. Several of the friends to
government of unequivocal political character are decidedly
in opinion with me, that the benefits which would result to
government by immediately complying with the prayers of the
petitions, would have a happy tendency to quiet effectually
the minds of our townsmen. The more I contemplate this
subject the more I am convinced that the public good will be
better promoted by pardoning them than by exacting a paltry
fine in one instance, and the still more trifling consideration of
the costs which have accrued in prosecuting these people.

Actuated by principles entirely independent, and from a
thorough knowledge of the characters and dispositions of those
in whose behalf I write, I take freedom to beseech your excellency's early, as well as favorable, attention to the petitions.
The respectability of those people as citizens, and their extensive influence among their townsmen, together with a proposal
two of them made last evening to me of calling a town meeting for the purpose of entering into an association to suppress
any combinations that may be formed to molest the peaceable
inhabitants (and this mode they consider more efficacious for
THIS TOWN than the protection of troops), are facts worthy of
consideration.

I am extremely happy in having it in my power to
acquaint your excellency that we have had no plundering in
the county since the enormities which were committed at
Egremont upon the Rev. Mr. Steel; and this I am induced to
attribute to the very spirited and decided part your excellency
has taken to promote the government, and the disapprobation
shown to those unpardonable offences by the better sort of the

citizens who have been in opposition to the government, and who have returned to their allegiance. I must here observe that I hope our policy should make a wide distinction between those who have erred from political opinion and such as have been actuated by the degrading notion of living upon the industry of others by taking their property in the dead of night.

Governor Clinton's visit to our neighborhood has contributed not a little to the quieting the minds of the people in that part of the state of New York and discouraging our Insurgents that had shelter there. If your excellency's health would admit of an excursion into the western counties it would not only be productive of much public good, but it would be highly gratifying to the people of all descriptions. In that case it would give me an opportunity of personally testifying the great consideration with which I am, sir,

Your Excellency's ob't serv.,

H. VAN SCHAACK.

[FROM AARON DEXTER.]

BOSTON, Aug. 30th, 1787.

MY DEAR SIR: I received your favor by Major Larned with much satisfaction. I fully believe in your system of politics, and that the government and council ought by all means to grant a remission of fines to all the small offenders, but those convicted of high treason in Hampshire and Middlesex are old and bold offenders, and ought to be made examples of. It might have a happy effect in future to prevent insurrections. Shattuck was proved to have been one of the chief heads in the opposition to law, and it was not the first time with him. I do not expect our present administration will suffer one of them to be executed. They have conducted in every other respect agreeable to what I conceive best. I wish the governor would pay a visit to the western counties this fall, but I do not expect that his health will admit of it.

The people in this part of the state are quiet, enjoying the good things that heaven has sent them this summer in abundance. We have in this port a French fleet, to pass away the hurricane months and return to the West Indies. Mrs. Loring has five of the officers, who are all civil, clever fellows. They are not, like our old friends the British officers, drunk every day.

I most sincerely congratulate you on your fine crops of wheat, flax, barley, etc. When the farming interest prevails, and has that influence in government that it ought to have, you will rank in that place which merit deserves, and in my opinion it will be more conspicuous than law, physic or divinity. As to merchants, they ought to be mere servants to farmers and manufacturers; they are and must be the nobility of the country. It is at present a great misfortune that more attention is not paid by them to obtain philosophical information.

I executed with pleasure your commands in a former letter in saying what I pleased to your friends in this town. I have repeated the same since receiving the last. As to Eustis, I showed him the paragraph and he declares himself free from imputation that he is immaculate with respect to moral and religious belief. I always make my religious opinion suit my company or am quiet on the subject. I am happy to hear that Mrs. Van S. is so well pleased with your representation of the savages of the east; but you must take care not to raise her expectations too high for fear she should be disappointed. Remember, female imagination is not easily confined. Make my particular regards to her and Harry. All our friends here are well and wish much to see your honor.

There has been a little newspaper war about a letter supposed to have been written by S. Higginson to G. Lincoln last winter. It is now over and all parties are quiet. You want the history of Tristram Shandy. I refer you to Yorick.

Adieu. I am, with esteem,

Yours sincerely,

A. DEXTER.

[FROM PATRICK JEFFREY.]

BOSTON, Aug. 30th, 1787.

MY DEAR SIR: Doctor Dexter did me the favor of delivering me your obliging letter of the 21st, and for which I pray you to accept my thanks.

That amidst the various revolutions of life I should have it in my power to show any the least attention to an old acquaintance, who, amidst the convulsions of the worst of times, thought for himself, and who acted consonantly to those thoughts, will on every occasion be matter of thankfulness to me, although the merit of intention is all I claim, for you permitted little more.

Since the receipt of yours I have not had an opportunity of seeing the Governor, who is now something better, but has been extremely ill. Whether that gentleman will be able to visit the western counties appears to me at least extremely problematical. I wish it, however, because I think it will tend to good, and if by any means in my power will certainly promote it. I at the same time thank you for your wishes, which I believe most perfectly cordial, but there is no chance of our being of the party supposing it to take place. In all such cases a certain degree of ceremony and parade ought and certainly would take place, all of which is highly averse to my feelings, for without much vanity I may be allowed to say that I am arrived at that period of life which should teach me, and to that situation which should induce me, to appreciate happiness by my own feelings and not by the estimation of others; and (between ourselves) while I am as I am, AN IDLE SPECTATOR, I do not wish to swell the train of any man in existence.

As a sincere well-wisher, and deeply interested in the happiness and prosperity of this country, you give me much satisfaction by the hopes you entertain and the favorable prospect you draw of returning industry and frugality. I ardently hope we may soon see that true independence prevail, of every man enjoying the luxury of living within his own income, which I have frequent and melancholy proof is not always the case.

However, my friend Van, I beg you may accept my most humble congratulations. You exceed much some of my debtors. You not only acknowledge the debt but confirm a claim of which I had neither proof nor recollection ; and, depend upon it, like a true miser, at our next meeting I will do my utmost to double the debt.

The Chinese gentlemen and ladies whom you saw at Boston (the young ones I mean) have either been distributed or more accurately discussed since you left us—gone, I believe, to embellish higher scenes, for sure I am there is sufficient proof of the Pythagorian system, that princes, potentates and powers, are in general more of PIGS than their fellow mortals. But seriously, in about a month there is a breed which will be fit for travel, and one of each sex is, I assure you, reserved for you.

My good friend, farewell. I shall be happy in often hearing from you; and more so if you put it in my power to render you the least service, and I pray you do not be frightened at the length of this letter, for I promise you I am not often guilty of these offences.

With sincere esteem,

Your very obedient servant,

PATRICK JEFFREY.

CHAPTER XI.

The people of the commonwealth of Massachusetts had scarcely recovered from the shock occasioned by Shay's rebellion when they were called upon to perform their part in the great contest, which agitated and distracted all parts of the confederation to an extent of which the generation of the present day has but little conception. The question of the adoption of the federal constitution engrossed the attention and feelings of all, and occasioned a degree of anxiety and solicitude which it would be impossible justly to describe. Mr. Van Schaack's feelings and efforts were deeply enlisted in favor of the constitution.

The Massachusetts ratifying convention met at Boston in January, 1788, and, after a session of twenty-nine days, adopted the constitution by a majority of nineteen out of 355 votes. It was a delightful spectacle, after such great conflicts of opinion, to see many of the prominent opposers of the constitution, after the vote was taken, rising in their places and solemnly pledging themselves to an honest support of that instrument.

Some selections from Mr. Van Schaack's correspondence, at this interesting crisis, will here be introduced, commencing with a letter from General Schuyler, containing many bold and original views entertained by that distinguished man at an early period.

[FROM PHILIP SCHUYLER.*]

NEW YORK, March 13th, 1787.

DEAR SIR: I have many thanks to return you for your interesting favor of the 3rd and 5th instant, and for a

* Schuyler was at this time a member of the New York senate.

former one, which I declined answering for reasons which I stated to your brother, and of which you are probably advised before this.

As you have seen Governor Clinton, and (I suppose) the powers he was clothed with by the legislature, it may be needless to enter into a minute detail on that subject. Let it suffice to observe that in both branches of the legislature the members were unanimous on the occasion. It is, however, probable (and I believe) they were not at all actuated by the same motives. Principles of a good will and a regard for the government of Massachusetts undoubtedly influenced many, whilst others, who invariably oppose every measure that tends to give more energy to the federal head, might, and I think were, led by apprehensions of local consequences, should they not have discountenanced your insurgents and our abettors of them.

Previous to the recommendations of Congress to the states to appoint delegates to meet in convention for the purpose of revising and amending the confederation and reporting thereon, several members of Congress expressed an anxious wish that some state should instruct its delegates to move in Congress for such a recommendation as now exists. Those of our legislature who have ever held in abhorrence the interested policy of this state, so injurious to, and so justly reprehended by, its neighbors, embraced the idea with alacrity. A favorable opportunity offered to propose it. Col. Hamilton's speech on the impost bill, although it carried no convictions to minds determined not to be convinced, had such an effect on the numerous and respectable audience that indignation was strongly marked on their countenances, when a majority, without a single syllable having been said in answer to Hamilton, rejected the bill. Severe animadversions were made on the conduct of the majority in every company, and such of them as had been led to vote against the bill by promises and the influence of a certain great man, were ashamed of their conduct and wished an opportunity to make some atonement.

Whilst this impression influenced these people, it was conceived the proper time to bring instructions forward, and it was accordingly introduced into the Assembly violently oppossed by the ——s friends; but as many of those who are at his beck had committed themselves too far in private conversation, they voted (though perhaps) reluctantly for it.

In Senate Mr. Abraham Yates took the lead in opposition to it. Aristocracy, king, despot, unlimited power, sword and purse fell from him in all the confusion of unintelligible jar-

gon. In short, he was outrageous, and had the mortification
to fail of success. The resolution was carried and transmitted
to our delegates.

The recommendatory resolve to the states was then moved
in Congress, carried, and, without delay, communicated to the
states. It was too late to retract, and they acquiesced with
chagrin in a resolution for the appointment of delegates to the
convention.

Inadvertently, the friends to the measure had acceded to a
resolution so worded as that the appointment should be by
joint ballot of both Houses. This would have afforded the
opponents an opportunity to commit the delegation to
creatures of their own complexion. I moved a rejection of
the resolution on the specious and well-founded reason that
the senate would be deprived of the proper share of influence
in the appointment. Yates soon perceived the true cause of
my objection, but dared not avow it. He stickled, however,
most strenuously for adopting the resolution as it then stood.
My motion, however, prevailed by a small majority.

I then moved a resolution in substance as to the powers
and number of the delegates, the same as that which came
from the Assembly, but directing the like mode of appointment as is used in the nominating delegates to Congress.
Abraham attempted to shackle this, but without success. He
then moved a reduction of the number of delegates from five
to three. In this he prevailed. This was followed by proposed amendments, on his part, to the powers to be exercised
by the delegates, which, if carried, would have rendered their
mission absolutely useless. Long conversations ensued in
support of and against the amendments. The latter were successful, and the resolution was sent to the Assembly, concurred
in, and delegates were appointed. Judge Gates, Col. Hamilton and John Lansing, jr., esq., are the men.

"What will our state do—will they prefer temporary
advantages to lasting good?" This is your question. It is
almost decidedly answered by the rejection of the impost bill.
But we have decided for a convention to amend the confederation, and this you may think augurs well. It will doubtless
appear so to those who are unacquainted with the political
system which prevails with a certain junto, the principles of
which are a state impost, no direct taxation, keep all power in
the hands of the legislature, give none to Congress, which
may destroy our influence and cast a shade over that plenitude of power which we now enjoy. Since we could not prevent a convention, let it meet; alterations will be proposed con-

ferring additional powers on Congress. We will propagate that
every additional power conferred on that body will be destructive of liberty, may induce a king, an aristocracy or a despot; the
people will be alarmed, and their representatives will be
deterred from affording their assent; besides, a variety of pre-
tenses may turn up for not acceding.

This I am fully persuaded is the reasoning of this selfish
junto, which, under the present distracted state of the federal
government, is increasing in influence—an influence which there
is too much reason to believe will soon become as extensive as
that of the British minister in the House of Commons, but
directed to infinitely less laudable and honest purposes.

But will not these people carry their principles too far for
their own views? I think they will, and that whilst their
powers may become annihilated the state may be lost, for I
believe it must be decidedly evident to every discerning mind
capable of combining causes and effects, that unless such
energy is bestowed on the federal government as shall enable
it to compel all the parts of the union to contribute to the weal of
the whole, that union must inevitably dissolve, and very
soon. That event taking place, it would be the quintessence
of folly to suppose that New Jersey, Connecticut and Massachusetts will suffer themselves to be taxed through our custom
house. It may perhaps, too, occur to these states, if we even
had no custom house, that a very considerable portion of the
profits of their agricultural and other produce would eventually
CENTER in this state, and such considerations may induce them
to wish that there was no such state as New York. The wish
once formed, and no confederation existing, the thing is done.

Will this be an evil or a good to the citizens of New York
is a question that involves such a variety of combinations that
I am at a loss which way to conclude.

I will, however, venture to say that in some respects it
would be extremely prejudicial, whilst in others it might be
eligible ; but on which side the balance would preponderate I
must leave to those who are capable of seeing further into
futurity than I can.

But short-sighted as I am it is no encomium on my penetra-
tion if I declare that, having attentively considered the present
confederation soon after it was promulgated, it struck me as
totally inadequate to its object. The observations I made in
the progress of the late war, and the opportunities I had, in my
public character, of experiencing its weakness, confirmed and
strengthened the opinion I had formed of its inefficacy. I
was seriously alarmed. I feared lest the dissolution during

the war would have enabled Britain to subjugate this country. This apprehension became infinitely painful to my mind. I resolved on expedients to prevent the direful calamity. I beheld with chagrin that the politicians of this state seldom if ever drew with those of the eastern states. I wished to eradicate the injurious jealousy which prevailed between them and us. Impelled by these sentiments, I proposed in 1781 that a convention should be held, the ostensible object of which would be to devise more efficient means for prosecuting the war, but the real one to form such a tacit compact as has long subsisted between what we called the New England States. I avowed my motive and expressed it by a variety of observations, having previously prepared myself to combat the objections which might be made. But my plan was too bold to meet with success from timid politicians and such as still regarded with jealous suspicion the people of New England. In short, I failed.

Methinks I see you smile and wish to know what was the ultimate object of this visionary being, as I was then called by some, and which epithet you may probably also bestow when I detail it, as I did in part to the senate at the period above mentioned.

I proposed that, in a candid explanation of the causes which had been productive of the jealousy which prevailed between us and our neighbors, we should convince each other not only how futile they were but how infinitely injurious to both; that a perfect reconcilliation should be established ; that offices of mutual kindness should constantly prevail; and that we should in all things consider ourselves as a people whose true interests could not be separated without injury to both ; that having attained this great end, a broad basis of security would be formed; if the confederation should dissolve, that we should insensibly and without convulsion slide into a more perfect republican government, which, from a similarity of manners introduced by the great increase of citizens from the eastward, would set easy on all; that fourteen states, covering an immense extent of country varying in climate and produce, and the manners of whose citizens were exceedingly different, could never be governed by one directing council, whose constituent parts had local prejudices and views; that the people to the eastward of the Delaware did not differ in any considerable degree from each other in manners—the climate nearly alike in every part, and the products such as could cause no competition between the northern and eastern states; that these ought to confederate; that if a good government was established, the states to the eastward of the Delaware would have more force than if connected with the rest.

But what this government was I did not venture to detail. The minds of men were not sufficiently prepared to receive it. But as the calamities we now experience will soon bring about a revolution in government of some kind, and, I believe, by general consent, I will venture to hint the outline of the plan which I had then in contemplation. And although you may laugh at it and conclude me a visionary schemer, yet, so strongly am I impressed with the idea, you can only reason me out of it, and perhaps, too, not without considerable pains. I wished that all the states to the eastward of the Delaware should be governed by an executive, triennially appointed by a Senate and Assembly, the seats of one-third of each annually to become vacant; the executive as well as representatives in Senate and Assembly to be re-eligible; this legislature to legislate for all the states, under one common appellation, as, for instance, the state of Columbia; leaving to the several states, or rather provinces forming the state of Columbia, their legislatures for the purpose of making road acts, and others for the more orderly government of their interior affairs; and allowing to each a judicial to preside in the courts for trying causes between MEUM ET TUUM, but all taxes and all laws to be in the legislature of Columbia. In short, that the legislature of Columbia should be to these eastern states what the British parliament is to the counties in England.

I conceive that if any federal government is established with less stability and power than this, it will be inadequate not only to oppose an enemy but to prevent internal commotions, and if so, must sooner or later give way to perhaps a chance government which may be a despotism, arbitrary monarchy, aristocracy, or, what is still worse, an oligarchy.

I dread a dissolution of all union. Immediate quarrels between the states will ensue. These quarrels will beget armies, these armies a conqueror, and this conqueror may give us such a government as prevails at Constantinople.

Certainly, in such a case, we cannot hope for a better than that France groans under. Let us, therefore, seriously strive to obtain such a government as will secure to us that degree of liberty which is consistent with the social state, not that degree which empowers part of the community, uncontrolled, to injure the whole. That is licentiousness.

I believe you will not insist on a postscript. Your patience is already exhausted. Adieu. You stand well here in the estimation of those whose esteem is worth having.

Hamilton and his wife join me in best wishes to you and Mrs. Van Schaack. He has requested me to assure you that he feels your politeness and thanks you.

I am, dear sir, very sincerely,

Your obedient, humble servant,

P. SCHUYLER.

HENRY VAN SCHAACK, ESQ.

[TO CALEB STRONG.*]

PITTSFIELD, Oct. 10th, 1787.

MY DEAR SIR: I have just finished my letter of recommendation in favor of my colleague to our friend Parsons. I now take the liberty of introducing Capt. Bush to your particular acquaintance. He will endeavor to do what is right. Tender laws, paper emissions, etc., he abhors. He will, I doubt not, endeavor to do that which seems right to him. If he is as independent in his principles as he is in his circumstances, the Captain will make a very good member indeed, He is a cautious man and will be at a loss what course to steer in his new business. But I confide in you and others, my friends, that you will guide him safe to the haven of public tranquility. My friend will look up to you for political instruction.

I hope my bar friends will not be too zealous. I mean not show themselves so in favor of the new federal arrangements. Great precautions should be taken in the appointment of convention gentlemen. Cool, temperate but firm men ought to be held up, and such withal as possess the confidence of the people. Who are they? you will ask. That I submit to you and others who are better acquainted than I am in the commonwealth.

I hear J. B. of Stockbridge is opposed to the new constitution. For that reason I should be glad he was appointed a member of the convention. If you should consider this strange reasoning at first, upon a little reflection it will not appear to you to be absurd.

---

* Mr. Strong, who at this time was a member of the General Court, was in the public service through the whole revolution. He was a member of the convention which formed the federal constitution, and of that which adopted it in Massachusetts. On the organization of the federal government he was elected to a seat in the senate of the United States. He was afterwards repeatedly chosen Governor of Massachusetts, and exerted a commanding influence in that commonwealth for more than thirty years. He died at Northampton 7th Nov., 1819, aged 75 years.

When matters are getting to maturity in the legislature I shall be glad of a line from you pointing out what is most proper to be done on the present occasion of political danger. This subject engages my whole attention as well as abundance of anxiety. I shall wish myself, during the present session, a thousand times with you. But you know, from what I said last night, that there is an impropriety in it. God prosper you and land you safe.

I remain, with respect, esteem and affection, my dear sir,
Yours,

H. VAN SCHAACK.

[FROM MAJOR WARREN.]

PLYMOUTH, Nov. 2d, 1787.

MY DEAR SIR: I had the honor to address you under date of Sept. 20th, in answer to yours of August 26th, in which I inclosed duplicate of mine of Sept. 3d, to Mrs. Van Schaack, that I might evince my attention to her very much esteemed favors.

The FEDERAL CONSTITUTION engages the attention and conversation of all parties. You express your wishes that my father may be in favor of its adoption. He does not oppose it; but no personal object whatsoever will ever lead him to swerve from any political system which he adopts, for, however he may be mistaken in any of his opinions, he will act from the purest principles of patriotism and integrity. You will pardon me for saying this much. But there is a paragraph in your last that I do not fully understand, but I guess its meaning.

You will see by the public papers that a convention is to be held in January. If they view the want of power, energy, and consistency in the present government on one side, they will adopt the federal constitution. If, on the other hand, their jealousy might lead them to suppose a dereliction of the extensive privileges and unshackled freedom of the people— a relinquishment of that power which is difficult to acquire and harder to resign—they will reject it. But power is necessary to be lodged somewhere for the government of a great people, and its resting in the body of that people for a long duration is, in my opinion, ideal. They must voluntarily give it up, or it will be usurped; and as usurpation generally is connected with, or leads to, despotism, it would be the policy of a wise nation and the best security to their happiness to delegate part of their power and privileges to preserve the remainder.

I, with you, dread the consequences of a rejection of the proposed system. But are we to dread nothing from its adoption? Suppose, for a moment, should Massachusetts, Virginia, Connecticut and New Hampshire reject, will the other nine states dare attempt to enforce it? But every person who wishes the peace and tranquility of his country will cordially wish that it may be swallowed without opposition.

Forgive me, my dear sir, for venturing thus far on the quicksands of politics, in which I may be engulfed, and will therefore be off immediately.

You have so many friends in the capital, the seat of politics and news, who will no doubt give you every information and every paper, that I, who am so far distant from both, will not attempt so great a gratification to myself as affording a spark of amusement to a gentleman I so highly respect.

I have the honor to be, my dear sir, with perfect esteem,

Your obedient servant,

HENRY WARREN.

[TO DAVID VAN SCHAACK.]

PITTSFIELD, Oct., 1787.

DEAR DAVID: How goes it with your new constitution? We have not a word about it here from Boston as yet, but it is generally believed our legislature will agree to a convention ; and from the appearance of things I believe it will go down. I am called upon to meet the people of other towns to give my sense of it, and which I have vanity to believe will have some weight, as the people in general think well of me. They are doubtless mistaken in my abilities, but they are not about the rectitude of my heart. In this important critical time I will advise with candor and moderation for an acceptance of the new system as the only means to secure political quiet.

Unless it is adopted God only knows where the evil will end. I hope and trust that my brothers are all for it, and that you will (if I am right in my conjecture) express yourself in favor of it. Peter's approbation will have great weight among the better part of the yeomanry of this country. Some gentlemen have puffed him up so that he is spoken of as to rank with the first characters in the country for political knowledge. I therefore hope that, when people from this county converse with him upon this important subject, he will spend some time to explain to them his views on this great question.

Adieu.   God bless you all, and secure to us public tranquility.

Yours,   H. V. S.

[FROM ANTHONY PAINE.]

WORCESTER, Feb. 6th, 1788.

DEAR SIR: Yesterday being the day for the great question to be put in the convention whether they would ratify the constitution or not, the anti-federalists were not for having the question put, but wanted to have the convention adjourned. They could not get a majority to adjourn.   The question was then put and passed by a majority of nineteen in favor of the constitution.   This, I think, is good news for honest men.

Inclosed I send some magazines for your perusal.

In haste, I am

Your friend and humble servant,

ANTHONY PAINE.

N. B.—We have not heard all the particulars or I should write you more fully upon the subject.   Mr. Williams desired me to send a person on purpose to inform you.   This will be handed you by a son of Mr. Pease, to whom I have agreed to pay ten dollars for going.

[TO PETER VAN SCHAACK.]

PITTSFIELD, June 21, 1788.

DEAR PETER: How goes on your convention?   We are federal more than three to one now to what we were last winter.   Indeed federalism has gained so amazingly that the constitution is not even opposed in private conversation.   The tender law is done and all goes on smooth and easy.   Every part of our government is perfectly calm, and a general wish is prevailing to promote the public good.

Before the expiration of the tender law I wrote Deacon Nash that if Stoddard did not pay his bond you would put it in suit.   I send you and David some papers which I wish to have returned by Captain.

Our joint love to David, C., etc.,

Yours aff.,

H. V. S.

KINDERHOOK, June 22nd, 1788.

DEAR BROTHER: The inclosed will speak for themselves. Return them and you shall have a continuation ; though late, you shall be rewarded for your former communications.   Virginia !   Virginia ! !   If she adopts all will be well, and I believe she will.   The new government organized, a lucky incident or two will give it stability.   You see what a figure our   antis make discussing the constitution by paragraphs and so dispassionately after all their clamor against it as RADICALLY wrong. Your commonwealth is my sheet anchor, and happy am I to see them move with such propriety.

I have garbled your papers of the Governor's speech and the address of the House.   Both please me very highly; also the little piece about the extent of the lakes and the exhortation to the consideration of our national importance.   I own I begin to find the revival of those pleasing expectations with which I left Europe, of the rising importance of our country. God grant we may not be deceived.   I really think our prospects brighten after the cloud they have been under for some time.   The perseverance of our commonwealth in the principles of the speech and address above mentioned will give a tone to us.

Yours affectionately,

PETER VAN SCHAACK.

NORTHAMPTON, Dec. 5th, 1788.

Laus Deo! my dear Harry! for thou wast dead and art alive.   Yes, on the 15th of November last, my dear Harry lived, and he lived to purpose, for he lived to write to his long neglected friend.   Yes, I am not mistaken.   'Tis his handwriting.   My dear, pray bring me one of Mr. Van Schaack's former letters, and let me compare it with this.   Oh, 'tis the same! the very same hand! He lives! He lives! Blessed be God! He lives! My much loved friend, my invaluable friend is again restored to the correspondence, to the bosom of his friend Henshaw. What a cordial to my soul! Language cannot express, but the feeling heart may possibly conceive the ineffable pleasure communicated by your last, most precious letter. Think, oh think! my dear Van Schaack, how long your pen has slept in total silence! Think, that I have written you three long and labored epistles, like St. Paul to the Romans and the Corinthians, without receiving one syllable from you; and that therefore I was necessitated to drop my pen, and draw one of those melancholy conclusions, viz: that you were either really dead, or that your ideas—your brains— were so deranged on account of your not obtaining the suffrages of Pittsfield for their representative,* that you were in fact dead to all the refined pleasures of social life—to all the delights resulting from friendly intercourse with your quondam acquaintance.

But happy I am that you have awoke, and that as soon as you have recovered your wonted vigor and social feelings you recognized your long-forgotten Northampton friend. Glorious resurrection ! May you live and flourish in immortal youth ; and may you never again be thrown into such a situation by the antis† in Pittsfield as to deprive me of the pleasure of your correspondence.

Having thus expressed my joy at your reanimation, and believing you are again on the theatre of life, and are able and willing to serve your friends, I must beseech you to use your influence in Berkshire, that our friend Sedgwick may be chosen to represent our district in Congress.

We have had here a large and respectable meeting of gentlemen and were unanimous for Mr. Sedgwick, and have written letters to our friends in all parts of this county and to some in yours, to make every exertion in his favor.

My "rib" rejoices most heartily at your revival. She had thoughts of sending a note of thanks to the great congregation the Sabbath after we received your letter, but I thought it would be rather too orthodox for you.

I have the honor to be, my dear sir,

Your affectionate friend,

S. Henshaw.

---

* A majority of the electors in Pittsfield were opposed to the federal constitution, and their delegate in the state convention voted against its adoption.

† Anti-federalists, or opposers of the federal constitution.

CHAPTER XII.

One of the most interesting features in our revolutionary story is that which presents to our view a picture of the re-union in restored confidence and friendship, after the struggle, of old friends who had been thereby separated for a series of years, in consequence of opposite views of public duty and from honest differences of political sentiments. The correspondence of John Jay and Gouverneur Morris with Peter Van Schaack, as preserved in the published lives of those three gentlemen, constitute, perhaps, the most pleasing illustrations of this matter which have thus far appeared. Into this circle of pure-minded and generous spirits could with great propriety also be introduced the name of their mutually cherished friend, Egbert Benson, a full biography of whose honorable and most useful career remains yet to be written.

The Colonel William S. Smith referred to in the two following letters was a son-in-law of John Adams, having married a sister of John Quincy Adams. In the year 1785 he was secretary of the American legation at the court of London, and having other public business in England, Benson and Jay gave him the following letters of introduction to their old friend, Peter Van Schaack, still in London, not having returned from his exile.

[FROM EGBERT BENSON.]

DEAR SIR: Permit me to introduce to you my worthy friend, Colonel Smith. I have flattered myself that you would have a confidence in my choice of a friend, and, therefore, that on my recommendation Colonel Smith would, in the first

instance, receive your attention. He will himself soon convince you that he merits it.

With great esteem, I am

Yours sincerely,

EGBERT BENSON.

NEW YORK, April 14th, 1785.
PETER VAN SCHAACK, ESQ., London.

[FROM JOHN JAY.]

NEW YORK, April 13th, 1785.

DEAR SIR: This will be delivered to you by Col. Wm. J.
Smith, formerly one of General Washington's aids, now secretary to the American legation at the court of London. He is
a gentleman of merit. Permit me to introduce and recommend him to you. The agents for managing the controversy
(on the part of New York) with Massachusetts, have committed
some business to his management, which he will explain to you.
You will oblige the agents by affording him your aid and
advice.

I am, dear sir,

Your affectionate friend and servant,

JOHN JAY.

PETER VAN SCHAACK, ESQ.

As this work must derive much of its interest from its
being the biography of one who took the unsuccessful side in
the revolutionary contest, no apology will be deemed necessary for introducing into it further correspondence throwing
light upon that class of persons.

Isaac Law, the writer of the two first of the following
letters, was a prominent and opulent merchant in the city of
New York when the revolution broke out. He owned large
real estate situate in the country as well as in the city. He
was chairman of the first committee of correspondence, chosen
in May, 1774, and of the subsequent committee of one hundred. He was a member of the first general congress, which
met at Philadelphia in September, 1774, and in the ensuing
spring was chosen a member of the provincial congress called
to appoint members to the second general congress, but did
not take his seat in this latter body. In May, 1775, he was

elected to a seat in the second provincial congress, and on the
arrival of Washington at New York, on his way to Cambridge,
was associated with Gouverneur Morris as a committee of that
body to ascertain from the Commander-in-chief when he would
be waited on to receive their address. From about this period
he seems to have withdrawn from participation in the public
measures. He was attainted, and his estate confiscated by the
act of April, 1779, and at the close of the war he went to
England.

The first of the two following letters is addressed to Mr.
Van Schaack's brother on the return of the latter gentleman
from his exile in England, and both of them become interesting, not only from what they impart in regard to the feelings
and sentiments of the writer, but from what they reflect of the
cheerful character of the letters from Mr. Van Schaack and his
brother, to which they are answers.

[ISAAC LOW TO PETER VAN SCHAACK.]

MORTLAKE, Sept. 5th, 1786.

DEAR SIR: I return you many thanks for your kind
favor. Be assured, I attribute your not having written me
sooner to the very causes you assign for the omission; and I
should be happy if I could get off so well with you, for having
so long deferred giving you an answer. That I am not what
I was, or ever shall be again, I have the mortification to feel
every day in many more instances besides the common-
unavoidable one of growing older. I used to be fond of scrib-
bling. I now hate to take up a pen upon almost any occasion
If ever I am to write to a friend, and know it ought and must
be done, I threaten for weeks, even months, before I can bring
myself to set about it, and then I am more embarrassed to
make an apology for neglect than I should have been at first
to make out a letter.

Are you satisfied, or must I rack my invention for more
excuses? I will only add, that although you have become a
subject of a republican government, and have been so gracious-
ly received by all the demagogues, you stand as high as ever
in my esteem and regard, and that, you must acknowledge,
knowing my prejudices, is saying a great deal. I only cannot
account how or by what magic you retain so many friends on

both sides. It has been my misfortune to have incurred the opposite fact, as I am cursed on the other, and not thanked on this side the water, for all my jealous and unwearied exertions to prevent the separation of the two countries, as the greatest political misfortune that could possibly happen to either of them. I have seen no reason yet to alter my opinion as to the one I always wished the best, and can therefore only deplore that so much blood and treasure have been wasted to so bad a purpose. I had otherwise ended my days in peace and happiness, which probably must now pass away in sorrow and mourning; for, in spite of philosophy and a good conscience, human nature cannot but sorrow and mourn for the loss of a good estate. I really thought I had a very valuable one, antecedent to its confiscation, and so I believe did you, as you saw it upon paper in this country; but well may you say that English differ widely from American ideas about the value of land there. The word unproductive is sufficient to cancel all other pretensions.

The first payment assigned me is only £1700 sterling, which is little more than thirty percent of the cash paid from time to time for my houses in the city of New York only, and from the land in Kyaderoseras, being upwards of fourteen thousand acres, as alone sufficient to absorb nearly as much as in their idea my whole real estate is worth. I am remonstrating against so very inadequate a liquidation, but I am afraid it will be as hard to induce them to retract their errors, as my prejudices against republican governments, and then I may whistle for redress.

Like a good Catholic, however, who is indefatigable in gaining proselytes, I shall stick to their skirts and not silently acquiesce under so injurious a report of my losses.

I have furnished my brother with materials to vindicate my claim with Mr. Anstill, and I kindly accept the friendly offices you are so obliging as to make me a tender of with that gentleman. I have no idea that his powers would have been so extensive, or his investigations so minute, or I should have bespoken your friendship sooner upon that occasion.

I desired my brother sometime ago to notify you that the memorial and claims for supplies to the British troops were referred to the auditors of public accounts, to be taken into consideration in turn—that is, *ad referendum* forever.

My brother was also instructed to desire you to let me know how the money you received from Col. Skene, for account of Isaac Law and others, had been disposed of. Can I illustrate by a stronger proof my declared antipathy to writing?

I must not forget before I fill my paper to desire Mr. Low's, Mr. Isaac's, and my best respects as well to you as to your brothers Henry and David, the Waltons, Bach, and such others only as you know will be equally glad to hear from, dear sir,

Yours affectionately,

ISAAC LOW.

[FROM ISAAC LOW TO HENRY VAN SCHAACK.]

LONDON, Gower-st., Bedford Square,

April 24th, 1788.

DEAR SIR: Be assured, your kind and much-esteemed favor of the 15th of September was the first and last I have had the pleasure of receiving from you since my expulsion from New York. I intended answering it much sooner, but when once we put off till to-morrow what ought to be done to-day procrastination becomes habitual, and it is not easy to set about a work which begun is generally half ended, and I already feel that I have got through the most arduous part of the business by having at length mustered resolution enough to begin.

The kind reception you met with in Connecticut and Massachusetts does great honor to those states; and, although no more than what good policy might naturally have suggested, could not but have excited the warmest feeling of a grateful heart, and, like a good painter, you have exhibited the leading features of your piece in the most striking point of view. Their having made choice of you afterward to represent your town in the great and General Court does equal honor to their discernment and liberty. Your talents and address always commanded attention and respect in the largest circles under a monarchy, and it had been extraordinary indeed if they were overlooked and not called forth into action under a republic. Equally extraordinary were it in me if, after having suffered so much for speaking plain truth, I should conceal my real sentiments when writing to an old friend.

Confidence begets confidence, and I am extremely happy to learn that, from this and other agreeable combining circumstances, your and Mrs. Van Schaack's situation is rendered so eligible as to afford a fair prospect of being anchored for life. That nothing extraordinary may again happen to ruffle or disturb it is our most ardent wish.

As to myself, I am far from being able yet to confirm the good news you have heard of my being able to go into a prosper-o'ıs line of business, but I cherish the hope of being able to. earn a subsistence in this country, and have therefore now as little desire to leave it as I once had New York, the place of places I had seen or heard of in the world where I wished to live and end my days; and I am certain there could not have been a more happy or contented man in it than myself, but I never could, or can yet, bear the idea of bartering British for congressional liberty, and my implacable aversion to a republican government was such that I declared in the first congress (as I clearly discerned their drift) I would rather become a subject of the most despotic government upon earth than of the best republic history recorded, or I had an idea wisdom could form. I have felt the consequences of my obstinacy, but I still retain the same opinion, your grateful eulogisms in favor of Connecticut and Massachusetts notwithstanding.

You say you have passed an act of government to comply with the treaty of peace. When you can tell me there is so much energy in the laws of any of the states as to compel the payment of just debts, without depreciation, I shall think they begin to see the necessity of adopting the good old maxim, that "honesty is the best policy" in public as well as private life, but until they give that evidence of reducing theory into practice, that there are, as before, in the United States of America, too many whom the best judges of human nature pronounce of old to be scribes, pharisees, hypocrites—appellations peculiarly characteristic (ENTRE NOUS) as far as my little experience has extended, of Jews and New England-men.

I have, too, imbibed the same opinion of many others since I left you. Would you believe, that among my numerous debtors, some of them my particular friends, I have not yet been able to boast of one who has had principle enough to pay me, or my brothers for me, a single shilling! They know too well I cannot compel them to, and yet they pass for what I always before took many of them to be—honorable, honest men. My good old father used to exclaim with rapture, "An honest man is the noblest work of God." I little then thought they were so uncommon, as it has been my peculiar misfortune to find them.

I trust, however, I have seen my worst days, and although the scene of past actions closed very differently from what I expected when it commenced, I reflect with pleasure on the part I acted in it. I have still the consolation to be what I always consider my highest political felicity, a real British subject, and I now have the extreme satisfaction, resulting from a consciousness of having dared to do my duty in the worst times, and after all my persecution and peregrination I have the happiness to find myself settled under a neat and comfortable, though not so large a roof, as at New York, in Gower street, Bedford square, as pleasant a situation, in my opinion, as any in or out of London. Accident has thrown me into a little good business in New York, and I have resumed at Loya's coffee house the business of an underwriter, and am honored with a distinguished appellation there of a good man. From these sources I hope to derive a decent subsistence, and my ambitions aspire no higher.

I freely own to you that it administers no less to my pride than happiness to find myself yet enabled, after having been so shamefully robbed and despoiled by my countrymen, not only to hold my head well above water, but to have become a respected member of, I believe I may, without exaggeration, venture to call it, the greatest as well as the most opulent commercial city in the world. We mix, too, as we used to do at New York, in many of the polite circles of this wonderful metropolis, so that we do not feel ourselves at all degraded by our expulsion from our native country, but have the happiness still to possess a situation much more to be envied than pitied. Indeed I would not (although my enemies may laugh and cry sour grapes) change birth with the most prosperous who, either from necessity or choice, remain behind us; and contentment is wealth; therefore you and I are as rich as Crœsus.

So far, I grant, we are upon an equal footing, but you would not take it kind if I did not mention our son, and it were the highest ingratitude to the beneficient donor if we did not own that portion of our treasure to be inestimable. He really is a most amiable, promising youth and everything hitherto we could wish. Our partiality delineates him to our minds as near perfection as can fall to the share of human nature at his age; and thus possessed of heaven's choicest gift, we ought to be thankful for that, and the many other good things we have received in this world, and not repine and make ourselves miserable about our other comparatively small, though great, losses in America. We are now at the eve of receiving the residue of what they call here compensation for them, as the minister says he means to propose it to the present session of parliament, and although it will be very trifling according to the ideas we have formed of the value of our confiscated real estates (bonds, mortgages and book debts not being yet, and I am afraid never will, be comprehended in the liquidation), I shall regard it as so much clear gain saved out of the general wreck, and bless my fortunate stars that I happened to have a large portion of real estate to lose, as many others, much richer men, are in the contrary predicament.

I must not conclude without some answer relative to the claims of our friends at Bergen, and therefore must encroach on another sheet.

It is considered here that the treaty of peace gave an option to all who had deported themselves as loyal British subjects to continue such at all hazards, or to transfer their allegiance to another government, as might be most consistent with their feelings or interest. Here I confess they had at best but a choice of difficulties, but having made their election they must abide by the consequences, which, in my construction of the laws of nations, exclude every idea of compensation for their losses from any other government than their own, and how they may meet with success there I must submit to your better judgment; but I am afraid they must, like the subjects of their late most gracious ally, be content with a shrug of the shoulders and attribute the unjustifiable destruction of their property to *fortune la guerre*. This will appear less hard when even British subjects, who have lost so much other property, have not yet obtained any satisfaction for similar wanton destruction of it.

How to avail myself of your very kind, and I am certain sincere, offer of your services, I do not know, unless you can recommend me to some of your friends who wish to have their cash laid out to the best advantage for the merchandise of this country. You may confidently assure all such that a trial will produce the same effect as of the spring celebrated in the song, that "They who bathe therein but once will wish to bathe again, will wish to bathe again," or unless you can make interest for me with any of the owners of your Indiamen to let me effect their insurances. I will do it without charging any commission, as their having so much to give to underwriters will procure me so many policies in return as amply to compensate my trouble.

If you, or Mrs. Van Schaack, can point out how Mrs. Low or I can render services for yourselves or friends in this country, be assured it will be a high gratification to our feelings to receive and execute your commands. Mrs. Law is allowed to possess a good taste for any of the European fineries, which you say it is impossible to cure the ladies from hankering after, and there is no person she will take more pleasure in endeavoring to please than her beloved friend, your better half. We shall always be happy to hear of the health and prosperity of both of you, and wish you most ardently a long succession of those blessings.

Isaac desires to join us in kindest regards, and you will not omit them to any of our old friends to whom you know they would be acceptable.

I am, dear sir, your affectionate friend and most humble, obedient servant,

ISAAC LOW.

[FROM CADWALLADER D. COLDEN.*]

KINDERHOOK, January 4th, 1790.

MY DEAR SIR: I cannot say how sensibly the sentiments which you express for your friend, my father, have touched my feelings ; and I pray that my conduct through life may be such as to induce you to transfer to the son a regard like that you entertained for my parent. I do indeed esteem myself fortunate in having gained such a perceptor as your brother, and if I should succeed in my endeavors to make him my friend, I shall think myself highly rewarded for the sacrifices I now make by thus abandoning for a time my connections and happiness.

I will with great pleasure, sir, answer your inquiry respecting our family. Since you knew it, the tyranny of man has paved the way for a much more despotic though not more cruel tyrant. Death has left but a small remnant of that flock that you used to see surrounding our happy parents. But

---

* This then young gentleman was the grandson of Lieut.-Gov. Colden and the only son of David Colden, a gentleman of retired habits, high intelligence and great moral worth, who resided at Flushing on Long Island, and whose large estate was confiscated and he attainted by an act of the New York Legislature. Being thus driven into exile he went to England at the close of the revolutionary war, leaving his family in America. Domestic afflictions in his absence were superadded to the sorrows and trials of exile, and this accumulation of misfortunes inducing melancholy, he died in London in 1784, as is stated, "of a broken heart." He was probably one of that class of persons attainted by the act above referred to, whom John Jay, in his remarks condemnatory of the confiscation act, alluded to as having been "perfectly inoffensive."

At the date of the above letter young Colden was studying law at Kinderhook, in the office of Peter Van Schaack, who, from a regard for "the memory of his ancestors," and at very considerable inconvenience, was induced, at a time when his office was filled with clerks, to take his young friend, then an orphan, under his charge. It will be needless to say that the young gentleman found in his tutor a "friend who endeavored to promote his instruction and to advance him in character," and the latter had the high satisfaction to see his former pupil, for whom his sympathies had been so deeply enlisted, rise to the highest eminence as a lawyer, a philanthropist, a writer and a statesman. He died in 1834, a truly great man.

four of their children are living. On my arrival in this country in March last, when I impatiently opened the door of an
apartment where I expected to embrace my sister, I learned
that she was dead, from seeing it occupied by her mourning
friends.   My sister Mary has made a valuable connection with
the youngest son of Mr. Nicholas Hoffman, a young man of
the first character and of professional reputation. They are most
happily settled in New York, where, sir, be assured, my sister
will be rejoiced to see you, and will take every opportunity of
acknowledging herself indebted to you for the attention you
have shown to me. My sister Eliza lives with her cousin,
Mrs. Thomas Colden, whom you must recollect. She could
have been but a child when you were near the family. But
she is now a dear little girl whose amiable disposition, sweet-
ness of manners and vivacity win the affection of all who know
her. My youngest sister Kate is in New York for her education.

Our fortune has been much injured by the war. Hitherto
we have been able to get from the British government no
more than £3000 sterling for my father's estate. We think
this proceeds from want of proper representation, therefore
hope something more from the new application which we have
made. We have been allowed, by this state, to purchase a
part of the confiscated lands of my father, with certificates, by
which means we are able to save something from the wreck.
My uncle lives perfectly retired on his old place near New
Windsor. He seems to have taken a disgust to all parties and
politics, and endeavors to make himself contented by finding
employment on his farm. However, he cannot forget his disappointment. His spirits are low and I think he breaks very
fast, but when he can meet with an old friend you may see
what he has been.

It will make me happy, sir, whenever I shall have it in my
power to accept of your kind invitation. I shall certainly see
you in the course of the winter. I am sorry to give you the
trouble of reading so long a letter, but I knew not how to
make my acknowledgments for the favor you have done me
and to comply with your request in fewer words. I beg you,
my dear sir, to believe that I am, with great respect, very truly
Your obliged, affectionate servant,

CADWR. D. COLDEN.

[FROM COL. CADWALLADER COLDEN.]

COLDENHAM, June 13th, 1790.
MY DEAR, GOOD FRIEND: The receipt of your letter of

the 20th of January (I am almost ashamed to mention the date), though late in coming to hand, was not unlike the meeting with an old and beloved friend in a manner given up for lost. It afforded me inexpressible pleasure to hear of your welfare and that you had not forgotten me. I was determined immediately to have answered it, and stuck it up in my room, in full view, so as not to forget it. But so it is, that what might be done to-morrow as well as to-day is often too long neglected, and that most commonly when we have the least to do—but do not think from this that I am altogether idle. No, I am as industrious, active and stirring as ever I was in my life. I have had, as it were, the world to begin anew again.

But alas! the day is so far spent that I much fear that I shall not retrieve the time and losses occasioned by that (I had almost said cursed) rebellion, now called glorious revolution, as I sincerely wish it may ever prove to be, though I cannot yet help thinking that we might have been happy at this day had we remained as we were. But as, in the nature of things, we could not expect always to remain in that happy state, perhaps the change could not have taken place in a better time, if not for us, for our posterity. Such great events are brought about by an overruling power, who sees further than we do, and often makes use of bad men and wicked designs to bring about good purposes; that is, though He does not turn their hearts, yet He makes their wicked deeds subservient to good ends. Witness the treatment that Joseph of old met with from his brothers.

But where am I wandering? I did not wish to touch upon this disagreeable subject, which brings things to my mind which I wish to be forgotten. I sat down to answer your kind inquiries after the welfare of my family.

Know then that in body and mind I am well; Mrs. Colden much the same as usual—sometimes complaining and ill, but always about the house. Jennie is Jennie still; the same good girl—too good to part with. Thomas has become a notable farmer; he delights in nothing else; and Ann makes as good a farmer's wife. They appear both to be happy with their situation. Their house is in sight of mine, a fine, elevated prospect, with a quantity of fine mowing ground around it. It is capable of being made a beautiful place and I hope not unprofitable. The only increase of family (except in the kitchen) is the adoption of one of my brother David's daughters, the youngest but one. You must remember her, Betsy, the father's favorite, who had the misfortune of having her thigh broken soon after he went to England, the account of which I believe helped to shorten his days. She is a fine, sweet girl of uncommon talents (as indeed they all are), and she cannot be happier than with her cousin, who is exceedingly fond of her.

Thus far in answer to your particular inquiry. The rest of my family you are not acquainted with, but as you say A SHEET OR TWO FULL on the subject will give you pleasure (for which I shall ever be happy to do) I shall go on in giving you an account of the rest of my TRIBE, as you call them.

My eldest son, Cadwallader, I believe you know, got his second wife (a Miss Griffeth, cousin to Mrs. Marshall) while we were in town. He has three sons by her, and three sons and one daughter by his former wife. He got tired of the farm that I had given him, which was that his grandfather had lived upon for many years. He sold part of it and bought a set of the best mills in the country, three pair or run of stones, saw mill and fulling mill, standing on the great falls in the Walkill, about five miles west of me, where I hope he may do well. I suppose you knew my daughter Peggy, in time of the war, in my absence at New York, married Peter Fell, a son of Judge Fell of Jersey, a violent partisan who now pays dear for it. He used to command a party of the militia and lay out at night on the cold ground, which subjected him to the rheumatism, and at length he lost the use of his limbs, so that he has not been able to stand alone these three years, nor move a foot or even a toe when he sits. She (poor girl !) proves one of the best and tenderest of wives. They wishing to live near me also, have left his father and mother, who have no other children, and are now settling within two miles of me, where they are building a good brick house and will have a pretty farm, also part of Coldenham. They have three children. My sons, Alexander and David, two bachelors, I am going to turn out of my house to oblige them to get wives. One is to go into the house that Mr. Fell moves out of, which is on the left hand of me, and takes charge of part of my farm and stock ; the other, about as far to the right hand of me, takes my mills, part of my farm and stock. I will keep sufficient in the middle for my own cultivation and amusement.

Thus have I got my children all around me, and we are a social society of our own; nay, a little congregation, which has induced me to look out for a minister of the church of OLD England to settle among us, and I believe we have been happy in meeting with the most agreeable man for the purpose, an Irish gentleman, a perfect scholar and an agreeable man, who has the art of pleasing and is an excellent orator in the pulpit.

He had been two years at Amboy, in Jersey, where he was very well liked, but not seeing a prospect of a growing congregation he chose to settle in a more extensive country, where his abilities might prove of more general use. He has now got possession of a valuable glebe at Newburgh, being a tract of 500 acres of land given by charter formally for the support of a minister of the Church of England and a school, where he proposes to open an academy, for which he is perfectly qualified, and I think no place on the Hudson river is better situated for an institution of that kind. If any proposal for public encouragement of this seminary of learning should reach you, I hope you will countenance it.

In the account I have given you of "my tribe" I have omitted saying anything of my two granddaughters, the Antils. They are two fine girls, though the youngest of them has been afflicted for two months past with what is called St. Vitus's dance, of which I now hope she is getting the better.

As for my brother David's children, who were for some time of my family, and for whom you express so great a regard, I need say nothing of them, as you say that Cadwallader (the son) has given you an account in detail of the surviving part of them.

Now, my dear friend, do you not believe that I think you sincere in your profession of friendship for me and my connections? Yes, I do, and I wish I could give as good proofs of mine for you and yours. However, I think these friendly communications are the best proofs of a reciprocal friendship. I regret that there has been so long silence between us, who were mutual sufferers and always of one mind under our sufferings, which I feared you had forgotten when you had become a STATESMAN. I hope next to hear that you are a representative in Congress. However, I am now as good a citizen as you or any other man can be. I wish no more changes less we should be still changing for the worse. God bless you. I have not room to say more, but that is sufficient from a sincere friend, as is

CADWALLADER COLDEN.

[FROM THE REV. ELIJAH PARSONS.]

EAST HADDAM, June 15th, 1790.

DEAR SIR: Your letter of January 27th has come safely to hand. I had before heard the contents, but did not think it prudent to handle and peruse it in its original state. The

letter, sir, was infected with the smallpox. Mr. Mosely's
infant child, which he had with him on his journey last
winter, broke out with that contagious distemper upon their
arrival at Catskill. Mrs. Mosely had the letter in her pocket
until after the child's recovery, and, although she had taken
the pains to smoke and air it, the risk of delivering it to me on
their arrival here was thought to be too great to be hazarded.
I therefore took my position at a convenient distance while
Mr. Mosely read it with a loud and distinct voice. At the
same time he promised to give me a copy whenever I should·
have a direct opportunity of conveyance. That time has now
come. Mr. Dwight of Haddam is going directly to Pittsfield,
and I have the copy of your letter before me.

Very often, sir, both while our public dissensions lasted 'and
since the establishment of peace, I have inquired after you and
always rejoiced to hear of your safety in the time of war and
your happy settlement and prosperity at Pittsfield since quiet
and independence have been given to our country. Anecdotes
of you and Dr. Munro are often recurring to my mind. I
never ride by the pond but I think of the many hours you
passed there in fishing. I have often recollected the full satisfaction you gave Capt. Percival on the subject of your refusal
to fight ; and when I consider the good humor and cheerfulness you have always manifested while with us, I am persuaded
you enjoyed yourself with more ease and contentment than
almost any other gentleman under the same predicament
would have done. This was owing to a certain original
cast of mind which you inherit from nature, and must
always be a source of happiness to him who possesses it in any
reverse of fortune.

We believe, sir, that all the affairs of our world are under
the direction of an all-wise Providence, and that in the final
issue good will in some way or other be the consequence and
effect of evil. When we SEE this happy effect produced from
so unlikely a cause, it affords us present joy, and helps us to
predict favorably concerning all other evils the issue of which
would otherwise be more precarious in our natural estimation
of things. To infer general conclusions from particular premises, I know, sir, is not logical reasoning ; but when we see
things which once wore a gloomy aspect brought to a happy
issue, and behold the good of which evil in some instances
has been productive, we learn from experience the possibility
that what has taken place in one instance may in all others,
and can more easily believe that under the government of
almighty power and perfect wisdom, happiness—increased

happiness—shall be the result of all adverse events, and that even "the wrath of man shall surely praise HIM."

We at present see only a part—a small part. When the whole shall be disclosed to our sight, what joy will animate us, in a retrospective view of all the particular circumstances of our lives, and of all the events which shall have taken place.

One happy effect which has risen from the late war is the diffusion of a liberal philanthropic spirit. The inhabitants of this country have made more improvement in those social and political virtues which are the basis of good government, which improve and happify human life, in the course of a few years of convulsion, than they would have made in an age of profound peace.

In regard to myself, sir, I often look back to the time when you lived here with regret and self-condemnation for the narrow spirit which had too much influence over me, and instead of assuming any merit for my attention to you, I am sorry that it was not doubled, and I am sure it would be were the same scene to be acted over again.

I thank you, sir, for your desire to perpetuate our acquaintance. I am sure, were I to come within twenty miles of your dwelling, I should be anxious to give myself the pleasure of visiting you.

The persons with whom you were wont to associate when here are many of them in their graves. The neighborhood has almost shifted its inhabitants.

Mr. Dwight, the bearer of this, is a fellow townsman of mine, a native of Northampton, a practitioner in the law at Hadden. He is a nephew to Mr. Edwards, of Stockbridge, and is a gentleman of good information and real merit. I beg leave to commend him, sir, to your attention and hospitality.

I am, dear sir, with sentiments of esteem and friendship,

Your obedient and humble servant,

ELIJAH PARSONS.

CHAPTER XIII.

Mr. Van Schaack was, in a high degree, public spirited, and took a deep and lively interest in whatever was calculated to benefit the public and improve the condition of the society in which he resided. The cause of education, improvements in agriculture and domestic manufactures, and increased facilities for inter-communication by means of new roads, turnpikes and more convenient public conveyances, found in him a warm and steady promoter and advocate. In the midst of the advantages and the perfected state of these matters which are now enjoyed by the present generation, we can scarcely appreciate how much remained to be accomplished in the latter part of the last and the early part of the present century.

The first domestic carpeting manufactured in Berkshire county was made under the direction of Mrs. Van Schaack, and a parcel forwarded to the secretary of the treasury. The first Lombardy poplars introduced into that country were brought by Mr. Van Schaack in his saddle-bags from Hartford. "Sir," said a gentleman to him, when placing the shoots in the ground, "do you ever expect to see those twigs grow up into trees?" "Did I not expect to see them run up to the sky like lightning rods, I could not look upon my situation with dry eyes," was the reply. He did live to see them become tall and majestic trees, and the dwelling he erected in 1785 is now one of the most substantial edifices in Pittsfield, occupying a position of commanding interest and beauty.

[FROM ALEXANDER HAMILTON.]

TREASURY DEPARTMENT, April 20th, 1792.

SIR: I received your letter of the first of February shortly after its date, and have duly noticed the remarks i

contained on the subject of manufactures, which will not fail
to recur when the legislature shall have time to go into the
consideration of the proposed arrangements. The business
yet to be transacted will not admit of their further attention to
my report than the giving such modification to the ways and
means recently required as will encourage this interesting
branch of national industry. The bill has nearly made its
progress through the House of Representatives in a form
calculated as well to produce that effect as the necessary
supplies.

The specimens of carpeting, which were very acceptable,
were immediately placed in the committee-room of the House
of Representatives, among a collection of specimens of American manufactures, transmitted to the treasury from several of
the states.

I am, sir, with great consideration and esteem,

Your most obedient servant,

A. HAMILTON.

Mr. Van Schaack took an early and active interest in the
"free school" incorporated at Williamstown, in 1791, and on
its erection into a college two years afterwards he was chosen
one of the first board of trustees. Of this body he continued
to be a prominent and efficient member for upwards of twenty
years. At a late period of his life, and when nearly eighty
years old, he used to travel from Kinderhook to Williamstown,
over rough and mountainous roads, to attend the meetings of
the corporation.*

He was a justice of the peace in Pittsfield for fourteen
years, having received his first appointment to that office in
1793, from John Hancock, then governor of the state, and on
its expiration in 1801 he was reappointed by Governor Strong.

* In further proof of Mr. Van Schaack's disposition to become a useful citizen, we find
him, in 1787, using special exertions to secure subscribers for a volume on husbandry entitled
"The New England Farmer and Geological Dictionary," published under the patronage of the
American Academy of Arts and Sciences. In 1788 he interested himself in the distribution of
the debates of the Massachusetts convention, which adopted the federal constitution. We
afterwards find him circulating the useful publications of the Rev. Jeremiah Belknap, the
historian and biographer, and various newspapers calculated to enlighten the public mind.
In 1792 he became a member of the "Massachusetts Society for Promoting Agriculture,"
and he took great pains to advance the mechanical arts and to encourage new inventions.
His services in the matters referred to were always rendered gratuitously.

[FROM DUDLEY A. TYNG.]

NEWBERRY PORT, Oct. 14th, 1790.

SIR: I have the honor of inclosing for your perusal a copy of the constitution lately agreed on by a convention of the Episcopal church, holden at Salem. You will please to make such communication of the inclosed as you shall think proper.

I am, sir, very respectfully,

Your most obedient servant,

DUDLEY A. TYNG.

H. VAN SCHAACK, ESQ.

[TO DUDLEY A. TYNG.]

PITTSFIELD, January 6th, 1781.

SIR: Your favor of the 14th October last I did not receive until the 4th instant. Had I received it before, the subject of your letter should have had an earlier attention. I have, with great pleasure, perused the copy of the constitution you were pleased to inclose, and shall with equal satisfaction make such communications as I conceive will be useful.

I have long thought that some plan for our church government was necessary in America, and more so since the independency of our civil government has been acknowledged by Great Britain. The mode proposed for its operation will, I hope, have an extensive, beneficial influence to fix the Episcopal church upon a footing of equality. This appears the more necessary in this quarter, at this time, because an intolerent spirit has lately made its appearance to establish, by town votes, a control over different sects of Christians in favor of one denomination only. This claim appears to be founded in injustice, and contrary to the letter and spirit of the constitution of the commonwealth. It has therefore been warmly opposed, and I trust the opposition we have given to it will eventually prove successful.

I have the honor to be, with sentiments of the most perfect respect, sir,

Your most obedient and humble servant,

H. VAN SCHAACK.

About the year 1790 Mr. Van Schaack became an active and prominent champion, in Massachusetts, for freedom of opinion in religion as invaded by the state, in his own person.

Before introducing several from a large number of sympathizing letters, written to him by clergymen and other citizens, I will quote from a modern historian a statement of Mr. Van Schaack's case:*

"The contest for freedom of opinion in religion in Pittsfield began in opposition to the rate levied for the building of a new meeting-house, authorized November, 1789. The right to tax all property for the building a meeting-house, and the support of a public teacher of morality and religion, were given by the laws of the commonwealth at that time to the majority of voters in a town meeting, and dissent from that decision for conscience's sake had to be discussed in a town meeting and there determined.

"The Churchmen in Pittsfield at this time were probably not many, but among them were six tax payers, four of them being prominent and wealthy men. Col. Henry Van Schaack, formerly a member of the Dutch Reformed communion and a Churchman by study and conviction, who was highly esteemed in his town, was the champion of all the dissenters from Congregationalism. After the crying of the first tax for the new meeting-house, a protest was presented to the town meeting in August, 1790, signed by the Baptists, Shakers, Churchmen and others who were property holders, and claiming that such a tax was contrary to the constitution of the commonwealth. No notice was taken of it. Mr. Van Schaack commenced a suit against the assessors and protested to the selectmen in December, 1791; and March, 1792, against the assignment of a seat to him in the new meeting-house. He says that he supports his own mode of worship in a neighboring town, Lenox, and considers that to compel him to maintain that of another denomination bears an aspect too unfriendly to the sacred rights of conscience secured to him by the constitution, and therefore is an imposition not to be submitted to.' "

In March, 1792, Mr. Van Schaack's vigorous protests

---

* History of the Episcopal Church in Berkshire County, Mass., by Rev. Joseph Hooper, printed in 1885.

began to be heeded, and a committee to ascertain the dissenters in November, 1789, was appointed by the town.   They reported in April, and we find in the list these six Churchmen (although Stephen Jewett was declared a sufficiently good Congregationalist to be taxed), Jonathan Hubby, James Heard, Henry Van Schaack, Esq., Eleazer Russell, Titus Grant and Stephen Jewett.   At the same meeting the collection of the taxes of the dissenters was suspended for 'three weeks, that they might deposit with the treasurer a written request to order the collector to pay the sums assessed to them for the support of their chosen religious teachers.   As this was not entirely satisfactory, although the fairest disposition that could be made as regards taxation for it did not touch one chief ground of complaint—the appropriation of the common land of the town for a benefit of only a part of the inhabitants. Mr. Van Schaack continued his suit for the benefit of only a part of the inhabitants, and received letters commending his course from Bishop Seabury, of Connecticut, Dr. Parker, of Trinity church, Boston, afterwards bishop of Massachusetts, Rev. Dr. Stillman, of Boston, a well known Baptist minister, Gov. William Eustis and others.   He was non-suited in the Common Pleas and laughed out of court, but acting upon the advice of Dr. Parker, that, "in spite of the horse laugh of Judge Paine," the court of final resort would be decided in his favor, he appealed to the Supreme Court October, 1792.   The Supreme Court sustained Mr. Van Schaack's appeal and the battle for religious freedom in Berkshire was won.

[FROM REV. SAMUEL STILLMAN, D.D.*]

BOSTON, Jan. 2d, 1792.

DEAR SIR: Your several letters came safe by Judge Wendell.   I have read them repeatedly, and, as far as my time will permit, shall reply to their contents.

I conjecture from your writing that you have not been an inhabitant of this commonwealth long.   The scene is new to

---

* An able and eloquent clergyman of the Baptist denomination, settled in Boston for nearly half a century.

you but not to me.   Though all denominations in Boston are
perfectly free, the Episcopalians and Baptists have not been so
in the country.   Repeatedly have I been called upon by our
brethren in different parts of the state for assistance, and much
have I been obliged to exert myself, but never could obtain a
radical cure of the evil.   In the days of Sir Francis Bernard
the court made a law by which the inhabitants of the town of
Ashfield taxed all denominations to BUILD AND REPAIR THE
MEETING-HOUSE, SETTLE AND SUPPORT THE MINISTER, ETC.
By virtue of which the Baptists had their lands and even
burying ground sold.   We applied to government but could
obtain no redress.   At length Governor Hutchinson (Bernard
had gone to England), IN CONFIDENCE, assured me that as the
Ashfield law was unjust, he would write to Sir Francis Bernard
if I would write by the same ship to my friend in London on
this subject, and have it laid before the King and council.
We did so and soon had an order by which said law was
repealed.

Several, yes INNUMERABLE, instances of like opposition we
have had among our denomination.   We, therefore, as a religious body, have a standing committee who are chosen annually,
by the churches in convention, to whom the oppressed in every
part of the commonwealth may apply for assistance or advice.

When I first saw the third article in our bill of rights I
disapproved of it because ambiguous, and that it put too much
power into the hands of the civil magistrate in matters of conscience.   I therefore wrote against it for many weeks in the
Boston Gazette, and was answered by Mr. West, of Dartmouth,
under the signature of *Irenæus;* and when the town of Boston
acted upon it I was obliged openly to oppose it.   But the
majority carried it as it is, and from it we experienced great
oppressions.   Even the judges of our own Superior Court, you
see, have given such a sense of it as perplexes the matter.   We
may all be taxed, they say, but each man shall have his money
for his own minister.   But how shall he obtain his money?   Only
by a tedious law suit.

Your remarks on the third article in the bill of rights agree
with my own judgment, as well as what you say relative to
the opinion of the judges, that the civil magistrate may tax all,
etc.   We first (in a case of the Baptists in Cambridge) sued
the assessors of the town for our money, as taken from us unjust-
ly; but we lost the case.   Then it was that we asked Judge Sulli-
van's advice, who appears to me to be the real friend to the
rights of conscience.   Necessity obliged us to pursue the methods he pointed out, and we have been successful in every trial

we have had.   The towns that have been cast in this way let us alone, being unwilling to collect our moneys for us.   At present we are determined to pursue it when taxed by the other denomination, not because we approve of it, but because it is the best we have at present.

You are sensible, sir, that Episcopalians and Baptists are in a disagreeable predicament, being the minority.   Judges, jury, etc., are in general of the Congregational persuasion.   Hence the good men are liable to be under a wrong influence.   I cannot think, however, that should you lose your case at an INFERIOR you will lose it also at a SUPERIOR court, to which I am of opinion you would do well to appeal if necessary.

I wish you would furnish me with a paper that contains the Connecticut law, or repeal of that law, that obliged Baptists, etc., to give certificates.

If you will write on this subject in your paper I believe I can have it republished here.   Should you visit Boston I shall think myself happy in a personal interview.   Dr. Parker and I are on good terms.   I will converse with him on the subject of our correspondence.

You ask what I think of a petition to the General Court. I have no inclination for it, believing such application would answer no valuable purpose, because they would refer us to the laws in being.

With every sentiment of respect I remain, sir,

Your very humble servant,

SAML. STILLMAN.

N. B.—You see I have written without reserve, and shall continue to do so as the business shall require it.   That there are certain persons among us who wish to have the pre-eminence I have long known, but I hope heaven will disappoint them.   You remember the saying of LUTHER: "Every man is born with a pope in his belly."   Let us, my dear sir, stand fast in the liberty wherewith Christ hath made us free.   It is shocking that these oppressions should be known among us in this age of liberty and refinement.

[FROM WILLIAM EUSTIS.*]

BOSTON, Jan. 15th, 1792.

DEAR SIR: I had great pleasure in your two letters,

---

* This gentleman was at this time, and for a number of years afterward, a member of the General Court. He was surgeon-general in the American army during the whole revolution.

malgre the length of one of them, though the subject would have been less interesting to me if your interest had been less concerned in it.

The principle is certainly with you. The other day a man in black, in that dark and narrow pass which chills expectation and separates the upper from the lower House (you know the avenues to the Great and General Court), whose wig and phiz determined me at first blush that he was a Baptist preacher, was asking protection and assistance from a very influential character in the House. On inquiry I found his complaints similar to that of my friend, rather that it comprehended your subject. He was promised EVERYTHING, which you know is easy there and usual, and I think it not improbable the question will come before the House.

Dr. J. is perfectly in sentiment with you; and I must think every man who is friendly to the rights of conscience, independent of every little consideration, will allow his neighbor the privilege which he values and enjoys for himself.

Pardon me this hasty scrawl, for I have neither time nor knife to mend it. My best regards for your good lady and daughter, and may the blessing of health abide in your habitation.

Your friend,

W. EUSTIS.

[FROM THE SAME.]

BOSTON, Feb. 1st, 1792.

DEAR SIR: I have the pleasure of your letters. Your memorial, that inimitable piece of composition, has been read and committed to a committee previously appointed to consider the most eligible mode of supporting teachers of piety, religion and morality, who, I am informed, have it in contemplation to report a bill which will embrace all the Episcopalians, Baptists and every other species of HERETIC in the commonwealth.

I am a bachelor, as you know, houseless, homeless, and of

ary war, and received his professional education from Gen. Warren, who fell at Bunker Hill. He was also surgeon in the army sent out under Gen. Lincoln to quell the Shay insurrection. It was probably at that time that Mr. Van Schaack made his acquaintance, which was naturally cherished by both, on account of the urbane and social qualities for which they were alike distinguished. Dr. Eustis served several terms in Congress. In 1809 he was appointed Secretary of War under the administration of President Madison. In 1815 he was sent as ambassador to Holland. He was afterward chosen governor of Massachusetts. He died in Boston in February, 1825, in the 72d year of his age.

course not a good judge of these things. I do not, however, believe there is a good boarding school in the whole town; I mean such a one as I would send to or recommend. My idea would be that the young lady should board in some genteel family, and go to a school kept by a Master and Mrs. Dearborn, who, I am told, are justly celebrated; but if you take the young lady with you, you know a choice can be made of any situation in this or a neighboring town, as you shall prefer.

If your letters had anything for their subject except your cursed dispute with your petition, and rights of conscience, and RIGHTS OF MAN, there might be some fun in the perusal of them; but I had rather take a small dose of tartar emetic than see the rights of man in a letter from a friend. They exclude forever the social pleasures of man, and whenever you see those two words you see (as a learned member expresses it) Pandora's box opened, and all manner of toil and trouble wearying the eye and tiring the imagination; so, if you please, no more of that.

My friend Mr. Jeffery, I wrote you, had gone to Maderia for his health. Since this we have not heard. The old lady is in good health and spirits, and, thank God, we, the others, are in tolerable countenance with the world, bad as it is, and however disposed to tyranize over the Episcopalians. Consider you were all a pack of vile old tories, and that circumstance, like original sin, is sufficient to d—n you to eternity.

If my friend Mr. Sedgwick is with you, I acknowledge his favor and wish to live in his remembrance.

Adieu, and God bless you.

W. EUSTIS.

COMMONWEALTH OF MASSACHUSETTS,
IN THE HOUSE OF REPRESENTATIVES,
FEBRUARY, 1792.

Whereas—It has been asserted to H. Van Schaack, Esq., that there in no boarding school, etc. Now, my friend, I find on recollection and conversation that Mrs. Law is everything you can desire in that line, and I say this from my own and the authority of your friends, Mrs. Jeffrey and General Jackson and others.

I am, in haste,

Yours,

W. EUSTIS.

[FROM THE REV. SAMUEL PARKER.*]

BOSTON, January 17th, 1792.

MY DEAR SIR: Your several letters of the 20th and 26th of December and those of an earlier date have come to hand. I am very glad to find you so firm and indefatigable in the cause in which you are embarked, and think you deserve the thanks of the whole Episcopal church, and beg leave to assure you of all the support which can be given by Episcopalians in this quarter. I purpose to set some machines in motion here to have the laws of 1742 repealed and a new one framed agreeably to the third article in the bill of rights. If this is not affected during the present session of the General Court I will move in our next state convention, which will be held in May, to petition for it by the whole church in this state, in which we shall doubtless be joined by the Baptists.

I think there can be no doubt that you will have a verdict in your favor at the Supreme Judicial Court, if you can get your cause before their tribunal, notwithstanding Judge Paine's "horse laugh." Their credit and reputation is at stake and they will be ashamed to suffer their private prejudices to get the better of law and equity.

I am very sorry the multiplicity of my avocations will not permit me time to enlarge, being closely engaged with the General Court upon business of the late treasurer's estate. I send you a pamphlet of Mr. Ogden's, occasioned by the publication of a private correspondence between him and his opponent respecting the Bishop's sermon and one of the sermons.

Mr. Ogden does not write with so much connection or prudence as I wish he did ; but he has told some very serious truths in these letters, and as it seems to coincide with your situation it may prove of some service to you.

I hope you will not be teased into a compromise of this nefarious business, but carry it through.

I am, sir, with respect,

Your most obedient and very humble servant,

S. PARKER.

H. VAN SCHAACK, ESQ.

[TO THE HONORABLE JUDGE DANA.]

PITTSFIELD, October 7, 1793.

SIR: The great desire I have of standing well in the opinion of the respectable characters who compose the Supreme

---

* Afterward elected bishop of the eastern diocese.

Judicial Court, will, I flatter myself, be sufficient apology for the freedom of this letter.

It is, I think, about two years ago, in an intemperate, desultory conversation (at Mr. Eggleston's dinner table*) that I had the extreme mortification to hear from you, sir, "that I must pay somewhere ; " meaning that I must pay somewhere towards the support of public worship. The disagreeable AGITATION which HAD TAKEN PLACE prevented a reply then, and considerations since of a delicate nature have dissuaded me from writing or speaking to you on the subject. But as the question, whether a town vote to build a place of public worship, for the sole use of one persuasion, is compulsory on other Christian denominations to contribute towards a building in that predicament, has been solemnly determined by the court a day or two ago, I now feel myself unembarrassed to resume the subject of the conversation alluded to.

When, sir, that mortifying sentence, "you must pay somewhere," was pronounced, I felt instantly that a certain indiscreet detractor of reputations had represented me as one of those loose, detestable characters who shift their attendance of worship to evade paying towards any form of public worship.

If through misrepresentation or from any other cause you should for a moment have entertained an opinion so degrading to me as a citizen of this commonwealth, so repugnant to my feeling as a man, and so injurious to the stand I have taken in society, I trust and hope that the facts admitted by the pleadings will sufficiently falsify the foul aspersions which may have been thrown on my character, and obliterate the odium from your memory forever.

When it is considered that I have, from an early period of my life, regarded religious institutions as having powerful effects in the community to instil piety, to promote morality, to meliorate the manners, and to inspire principles of good government in the people, it could not but be grating to my feelings in my declining days, to be driven by a spirit of persecution to produce CERTIFICATES of where I worshiped and where I paid, in a government which secures to the individuals who compose it the power of enjoying in safety and tranquility their natural rights, and at a time that it was as well known where I attended public worship by those who were the agents in this wicked business as any local fact whatever in Pittsfield.

* Mr. Eggleston kept a boarding house in Lenox, at which the judges and lawyer usually stopped.

As my letter is sufficiently long, I shall reserve to myself
a fuller explanation when I shall have an opportunity of doing
it personally.

I have the honor to be, sir,

Your obedient, humble servant,

H. VAN SCHAACK.

[TO PETER VAN SCHAACK.]

PITTSFIELD, April 2nd, 1793.

MY DEAR BROTHER: Isaac just now delivered me your
letter of the 1st instant. I was not a little surprised to find
that you had not sent the deed I transmitted to you.

    *   *   *   *

I have long considered the general government as the
sheet anchor of our political safety. I take unwearied pains
with every individual I come across to impress them with
the necessity of its existence and that the present prosperous
state of the community is entirely owing to this new fabric.
The yeomanry throughout the commonwealth, I have no doubt,
are friendly to it. The rapid rise of land and country produce are too generally felt not to satisfy the public mind. We
have a few croakers in and about the metropolis. The rejoic-
ings on the French successes at Boston were not, I believe, set
a-foot by the real federalists, but they went with the stream.
They have been so completely ridiculed in the Connecticut
papers that I believe we shall hear very little more of this
kind of folly. I am pleased to find that the enormities in
Paris are generally condemned in the eastern states. Poor
Louis is as sincerely lamented here as Charles the First was by
the royalists.

The opposition in Congress to the measures of government
was a matter of serious alarm. The dead set at the secretary
clearly showed a design to put down all the fiscal arrangements. Thank God, the wicked designs of the party have
ended in their own disgrace. I hope our young relations know
by this time that the promoters of our civil feasts are not those
who are the real friends and supporters of the constitution.

Lord Grenville's note to the Frenchman breathes a manly
spirit, and I sincerely hope that England will not recede an
iota from what has been declared. After all that has been
said against that government, I believe it the best in the

world, except our own, provided it can be preserved in its present purity.

Instead of annexing French Flanders to the Belgian power, I presume the French mean to join all the countries they over-run to their own commonwealth. I suppose their new prin-ciples must lose ground wherever their armies go, for they exact such heavy contributions that the people feel more bad effects from them than good ones, from the theory of liberty and equality. The people in Canada greedily embraced the doctrine of American liberty ; but when they felt the effects of war in their own country, they were ready enough to part with their new friends.

I have seen a very sensible remonstrance in one of the papers to General Custine, from the commonalty of one of the German cities, stating that exacting contributions from the wealthy affected them equally.

I have seen the decree of the 19th Nov., and the moment I read it my mind was satisfied that the object was universal rebellion in every country. Paine's doctrines and himself are detested by those in New England whom I consider as builders up of our government.

Good night.

Yours affectionately,

H. V. S.

When Peter Van Schaack went as an exile to Boston, in February, 1777, upon an order of a committee of the New York convention, for refusing to take the oath of allegiance, he experienced very liberal and gentlemanly treatment from Oliver Wendell,* one of the leading patriots of the MASSACHU-SETTS BAY.

---

* Oliver Wendell was born in Boston in 1734. He was the son of Jacob Wendell, who came to that town from Albany in the early part of the last century, and about the year 1720. His mother was a member of the well-known family of Schuyler at Albany, and is referred to in Mrs. Grant's interesting "Memoirs of an American Lady." Young Wendell graduated at Harvard University in 1753, and afterward engaged in business in Boston as a merchant.

He was a prominent and active Whig during the revolutoin and a member of one or more of the popular committees. Although very decided in his political principles he was yet noted for his liberality toward those who differed from him in sentiment, insomuch that he was characterized by his friends as being "fierce for moderation."

After the revolution he was appointed judge of the Court of Probate for Suffolk county; the duties of which office he discharged with great faithfulness and general satisfaction for a long time. He was for many years one of the Governor's council and also a member of the corporation of Harvard College. In 1808 he removed to Cambridge, where he closed an honorable and virtuous life in January, 1818, at the age of eighty-four years. Dr. Oliver W. Holmes of Boston is his grandson.

This gentleman evidently discovered that, in the person of the council referred to, no common character had been sent to the "selectmen of the town of Boston"; while the latter was duly impressed by the consideration and humanity exhibited towards him—a perfect stranger to the place, its inhabitants and public authorities—and with naught to recommend him but his own frank, elevated and gentlemanly appearance and conversation during a few days' stay in the town. It was an acquaintance formed under such forbidding circumstances, that gave rise to the interesting correspondence of which a portion has been published.*

The first time the subject of this sketch went to Boston after becoming a citizen of Massachusetts, he made it a point to call upon Judge Wendell, with no other introduction than his own personal representation, that he called to return his thanks for Mr. Wendell's humane and gentlemanly conduct to his "brother Peter" when exiled to Boston in 1777. In this manner was an acquaintance formed, which immediately ripened into a close and lasting friendship, and they became intimate correspondents for a great number of years.

[TO OLIVER WENDELL.]

PITTSFIELD, December 14th, 1794.

MY DEAR SIR: It is only a few days ago that I was favored with yours of the 28th of last month. It gives Mrs. Van Schaack and me much pleasure to be informed that you got home safe and so expeditiously as you state in your letter. After the electioneering bustle in your absence it must have given you great satisfaction to have found your townsmen tranquil and composed. The choice of Mr. Ames being effected, I suppose our friends feel tolerably well.

The speech of the President is such as to merit the approbation of all those who love the government, and so is the address of the Senate. That from the other House I do not so well relish. It is, however, the best which could be obtained with any degree of unanimity. I fear that we have too many timid friends in Congress. There has been too much opposi-

---

* Life of Peter Van Schaack, LL. D., page 375.

tion to "self-created societies." It was the President's duty to state to Congress the causes of the insurrection, and as he conceived these club gentry had given weight to the opposition against the laws, in the western part of Pennsylvania, he did right to mention these odious associations in the terms he made use of, and, until due submission to the members of Congress, they were wrong in not re-echoing back the "self-created societies." However, all will go well, I trust, for I find the government's friends have found it less difficult to obtain a military force in the rebellious counties than we did in 1787 to facilitate a military check upon our insurgents.

A friend of mine in Congress says: "I will relate to you an occurrence, because I am sure it will give you pleasure. The committee who were appointed to wait on the President, to know when and where it would be agreeable to him to receive the address, were Madison, Scott and myself. Madison was chairman. The President* received us with that solemn gravity which so becomes him and he so well knows how to assume. It had always been usual with him to answer the committee without perusing the address; but on this occasion he received the copy and attentively read it without saying a word. He then rose, and, turning from Madison to me, he said (it was on Friday) that it was more agreeable to him to meet the House on the next day, provided the arrangement would not oblige the House to meet contrary to its inclination. He added: "I wish, sir, you would give me your opinion on this subject." I waited a little time for an answer from Madison, but perceiving I was not to expect any, I said that this was a question on which we had received no instructions from the House, and could therefore express only an individual opinion, which, for myself, was a preference of the next day. Mr. Madison then said he concurred with me, and Mr. Scott added, "and I likewise." The President then, addressing me, said: "You, sir, will have the goodness to inform the House that I shall expect to receive them to-morrow at the usual place."

I think we may conclude from the peculiarity of the President's manner that he did not feel over well towards two of the committee, on account of the part they had taken in the debates, to clog the address with disgusting embarrassments. Thus much for your amusement.

This is my eleventh letter this evening, and as it grows late you will please to excuse BREVITY and accept of the most

---

* Washington.

friendly assurances of regard from Mrs. Van S. and me for you
and your family.

I am always, my dear sir, with sentiments of friendship
and respect,

Your most obedient servant,

H. VAN SCHAACK.

P. S.—A good story against myself. It has happened,
from many causes unnecessary to enumerate for my present
purpose, that my store swine are the most miserable, lean, ill-
looking creatures in the country. A few days ago a wretched-
looking fellow, ill clad, and by his looks still worse fed, saun-
tering in the road stopped at my barn and bravely told my hired
man that "the owner of the house would do well to put some
of the expenses of his buildings on his lean hogs!" The sarcasm
was so well timed that I would have given the greasy rogue
his dinner for the justness of his satire.

[FROM VAN POLANEN.*]

NEW YORK, Feb. 27th, 1796.

SIR: Not before yesterday had I the pleasure to receive
your very polite letter of the 2nd instant. The accounts given
me by our worthy friend, Mr. de Bormechose, of you and your
family, and the friendly manner he has been received at your
house, has caused in me a wish for the honor of your acquaintance, and I receive your approbation of it with gratitude. I
have expected since a long time, and am still waiting, for the
arrival of a vessel from Amsterdam, and with it some letters of
importance to me. These being received, will probably oblige
me to repair to Philadelphia and necessitate my staying there
till after the rising of Congress, and this circumstance especially
makes it impossible for me to form any determination about
the time of executing my intended journey through the New
England states, and having the pleasure of seeing you at Pittsfield; perhaps it will not be before the next summer.

The present situation of affairs in Europe and of my native
country will most probably, what may be the event of it, necessitate many families to seek into this happy country a shelter from
persecution or disappointment. Wishing to serve my countrymen thus situated, without any regard to their political princi-
ciples, whom choice or necessity should bring over to America,

* Minister to the United States from Holland.

I should wish to be more particularly acquainted with the resources the eastern states may offer them, according to their means or former situation in life. A five years' residence in America and much traveling have convinced me, and it is the opinion of all Europeans who have traveled with observation and reflection through this country, that the New England states are that part of the United States where, for many reasons, a European may settle himself with more convenience and satisfaction than elsewhere. There it is where an attentive observer discovers the formation of a national American character, instead of a ridiculous and disgraceful attempt to imitate not only the customs and foibles of a foreign nation, but even the follies, the prejudice and the vices of it.

With great regard and esteem, I have the honor to be, sir,

Your most obedient servant,

VAN POLANEN.

[FROM JOHN JAY.]

NEW YORK, Aug. 15th, 1796.

DEAR SIR: Accept my thanks for your friendly letter of the 3rd instant, which I had the pleasure of receiving this morning. I regret that it is not in my power to accept your kind invitation, for I believe it to be no less cordial than it is friendly, and it is one which it would really give me pleasure to accept.

Mrs. Jay writes to me in strong terms of her kind reception at Kinderhook, and of your friendly visit to her at Lebanon. I am certain she will be pleased with Mrs. Van Schaack, for I have heard of none who know her that are not.

It is pleasant to visit those whom we esteem and are pleased with, but so am I circumstanced, my good friend, that I must deny myself the satisfaction of seeing either Mrs. Jay at Lebanon, or your amiable family at Kinderhook and Pittsfield, this season. They who accept offices must do the duties of them.*

When you see Mr. Sedgwick be pleased to remember me to him. He is a sensible, worthy man.

With the best wishes for your and Mrs. Van Schaack's health and happiness,

I am, dear sir,

Your most obedient servant,

JOHN JAY.

---

* Mr. Jay was at this time Governor of the state.

[FROM OLIVER WENDELL.]

PITTSFIELD, Jan. 13th, 1799.

MY DEAR SIR: Luce handed me your favor in due time.
He also brought me a very fine codfish—as good as ever I
tasted.   It has afforded two meals and there is enough for
another dinner.   Before I close this letter you will have a little
more of fresh codfish.   In the meantime I proceed to matters
more relative.

The European news of late, through the Boston papers, has
regaled me more by far than anything which has come across
the Atlantic for a long time past.   It has been the source of
unspeakable joy to me, as well it affects Great Britain as
ourselves.   I now console myself that the faction of this
country have, by the losses the French marine has sustained,
lost their sheet anchor to keep up turbulence and discontent in
the United States.

· I have written my friend Col. Wadsworth that if the weather
will admit of it, and no unforeseen impediment intervene, I shall
set off next Saturday for Hartford.   It is as yet undetermined
whether I shall proceed with Miss Jane from thence to Boston.
I wish there was provision made by the public to make it as
much my interest to go to the capital as it is my inclination to be
there, and then you may be sure my visits should not be
annual, but at least semi-annual.   Such are my wishes and
inclination, but alas! the means!— I must break off to take up
Russell's "Centennial"—not piping hot from the press, but cold
and wet.   Now for news of the destruction of Bonaparte and
his army and his transports, and the capture of all Bonaparte's
Brest squadron.   Adieu, for the present.   I return from the
"Centennial" disappointed.   It contains nothing new to me, ·
except the strictures on General Health and another address to
Jefferson.   I fear the severity of your writers at Boston will
throw the General on the compassionate list, and thereby make
him appear as an abused patriot.

You see, the American patriots begin to excite my compas-
sion.   Of late, I abound in charity towards the opposition.   In
revolving some part of my own life, I have worked myself at
times to a strange belief of absurdities.   It is not uncommon
for men who are in the habit of hearing, or rather conversing,
with their friends who talk in one stream, to get in the habit
of believing the most preposterous things.   During the American war, conversing principally with men who thought as I
did, I got in the habit of disbelieving everything that was made
against the side I had taken, and believing everything, how-

ever absurd, that favored my wishes. Even in eating and drinking men deceive themselves. Grog drinkers persuade themselves that rum and water is the best liquor in the world, and they therefore prefer it to good wine, punch, cider, etc. The good people of Boston, from habit, have taken it in their heads, contrary to the opinion of the rest of mankind, to prefer DRY cod to a FRESH one. This, to be sure, is monstrous! Now, my friend, if we see those strange absurdities among ourselves, why not have a little charity for the Jacobins, who have so long admired the enormities in France that murder and disorganization has been a pleasing theme to them, and they have arrived to a stage of belief that to destroy the blessings of society is all right. This is the first apology for the Jacobin race I have ever made, and I declare it shall be the last, until they take a different course from the one they have steered seven or eight years back.

In looking back I find that I have imperceptibly trespassed unreasonably on your patience. I confess it a fault, that when I take up my pen to write a friend and when no business interferes, I know not when to stop. I often think of my absent friends with pleasure, and when I cannot communicate with them *viva voce* I consider it time well spent to converse with them on paper.

I have seen with great regret that the Retaliation is taken by the Sansculottes, but with infinitely more concern, the impressment of five sailors belonging to the Baltimore sloop of war, by a Captain Loring of the British navy. If the statement is correct, it is my earnest wish that Loring may be broke. I am truly glad to find that the government has taken this matter up in a serious point of view. However WE may deplore those two untoward events, I believe the Jacobin prints will exult in both.

I beg of you to consider this lengthy epistle as a New Year's gift, and that I expect *quid pro quo*.

I am ever and very sincerely, my dear sir,

Your affectionate, humble servant,

H. VAN SCHAACK.

P.S.—A word or two more and I positively have done. When you see our Governor I beg of you to present him with my respectful compliments, and tell him that it is MY opinion that HE OUGHT next fall to review our militia in this part of the commonwealth. The last general review in October it appeared to me that there was a great falling off. Perhaps the presence of the chief magistrate would excite emulation.

[FROM OLIVER WENDELL.]

BOSTON, Dec. 23d, 1799.

DEAR SIR: By my tenant, Mr. Luce, I received your several favors—liquid, literal and POLITICAL. The two first gave me more pleasure than the last, though an important document. However, one of the ill effects intended by the publication maliciously made by T. C. is defeated by the death of the great and good Washington, which was this day announced in this town by the mournful tolling of all the bells, and closing the doors of all the stores and shops, although the town was more thronged with sleds and teams from all parts of the interior STATES than ever I have known it. All classes seem to unite in deploring the loss of this BELOVED AMERICAN. *Sic transit gloria mundi.*

Mrs. Wendell, with her daughter and myself, are sorry to hear Mrs. Van Schaack is out of health, and present our affectionate regards, with half a dozen oranges, not forgetting the young lady whom we expect to see you with at Boston. Accept our esteem.

O. W.

Having sent for an oration of Mr. Kirkland for Mrs. Van Schaack to Mr. Jackson, who had it not, he directs me to say for him, he hopes to see you at his fireside this winter, when he will endeavor to make up the HASH of politics to your mutual liking—for in essentials he knows you to agree.

[TO OLIVER WENDELL.]

PITTSFIELD, January 10th, 1800.

MY DEAR FRIEND: In compliance with an impulse to hold intercourse with absent friends, I seated myself at my writing table the other evening and scribbled a letter to you, in expectation of its getting to you long before now. I am, however, disappointed. To allude to anything I said in that letter is impossible, for I really do not recollect the subject that incited me to write. If it contains anything wrong, you (who have often had nearly charity enough to excuse the errors of the head in evil doers) will readily forgive the blunders of a friend. Here I rest my cause.

I bow to the good people of Boston with sentiments of great respect for the honors they have shown, and still continue to show, to the memory of the greatest and most important

man this country has ever produced. When shall WE—but
this is out of the question—when shall posterity see a second
Washington ? B. Russell does well to continue his paper in
mourning.*

I find by the last papers from below that Citizen Nicholas,
of the ancient dominion, has brought forward a resolution
pregnant with evil views, as many evils as Pandora's box
contained, without any prospect of good at the bottom of the
Virginia box. To quit metaphor, and to speak intelligibly
and promptly, it appears to me that the mover of the resolution and the supporters of this nefarious measure contemplate
nothing short of prostrating this country to the views of a
foreign power ; but I hope and trust that there is a majority
in Congress who will, with energy and spirit, oppose a project
so highly impregnated with ingredients which lead to the
subversion of all social order. But if my hopes on this all-
important occasion are vague and unfounded, I shall be nearly
in a state of despair. I take for granted that if the opposition
is strong enough to carry the reduction of the military establishment at THIS time, that they will proceed farther and cripple
our naval forces to a mere skeleton of inaction. Do you, my
friend, strike a balance between my fears and hopes? Since
this measure of the opposition was designed, I am glad it has
come out so early in the session. Had this band of Jacobins
kept the resolution back until they could have heard the
soothing language at Paris to our envoys, it probably would
have aided them in carrying into effect their vile projects. I
pray for adverse winds, that we may hear nothing from the
envoys until Congress adjourns. The sooner that takes place
the better, after the prominent measures have been completed
by the national legislature.

So much about my hopes and fears about our political situation; and now a word or two about my hopes and fears on
another interesting subject, on which I am sure you do not
feel indifferent, namely, Mrs. Van Schaack's health. My fears
are much abated of late. She is gaining strength daily, and I
feel pretty confident that she will be restored to a tolerable

---

* In his letter of January 1st Mr. Van Schaack wrote: "Will you tell Major Russell that
he is not correct in his last paper when he says 'every paper we receive from towns which
have heard of Washington's death are enveloped in mourning?' This may be true as it
respects Massachusetts. If he meant to extend the observation beyond the commonwealth it
is not true, for I have now the Philadelphia 'Aurora' of 21st December, which has not a
scratch of mourning about it. In spite of all the Jacobins can say, do or print, the great
Washington lies deep in the bosom of the great body of the people, and the.enmity shown to
his memory by the 'Aurora' man and others will tend more to bring their papers into disre-
pute than anything else."

share of health. An object so long wished for, exhilarates my spirits, *malgre* the clouded horizon and whirlwinds that threaten our political situation; and yet, if we do not despond, but foster a spirit of energy and exertion, I am full of hope that we shall land on good ground.

I am ever faithfully and affectionately yours,

H. VAN SCHAACK.

[TO OLIVER WENDELL.]

PITTSFIELD, March 22d, 1801.

DEAR SIR: The bearer, Mr. Bush, has some business at Cambridge and will do me the favor of proceeding to Boston. So good an opportunity I will not suffer to pass by, without a friendly salutation from me and my family to you and yours.

And so we have got a new President, to the joy of the Democrats, and I hope his administration will embrace the general interests of the country and not pull down from office our friend Jackson* and other good men. The speech is very conciliatory and breathes good-will to Republican federalists and federal Republicans.* In a word, if the administration comports with the language of the speech, we shall have four years of political halcyon days, for I take for granted that the federalists will be quiet and easy if the government is administered upon the principles on which it has hitherto been conducted; and why not four years more? Good citizens should be content if public credit is supported and individuals are secured in their person and property. I, as an individual, ask no more, provided we are not unnecessarily entangled with foreign nations, against which we have the assurances of the CHIEF WHO NOW COMMANDS.

I am sorry Mr. Adams left the seat of government before paying his compliments of congratulation to his successor. There may be good reasons for not doing it, but those are not yet discovered by us, THE PEOPLE AT A DISTANCE. Other motives are ascribed for leaving Washington at four o'clock a. m., on the morning of the 4th. My fears begin to subside of his being a candidate for our state chair, because the antis

---

* Jonathan Jackson, Marshal, residing at Newburyport.

* The allusion is to that clause in Jefferson's inaugural address: "Every difference of opinion is not a difference of principle. We have been called by different names, brethren of the same principles. We are all Republicans, all Federalists."

are already vociferous about Gerry, and pronounce his exalta-
tion with as much confidence as if he was already Governor.
They are intoxicated with their late success, and look up with
a degree of certainty to be successful in all their electioneering
projects.   Their power, in this part of the commonwealth, has
certainly increased much of late, and unless a change takes
place before the first Monday in April, a decided majority will
be given against Governor Strong.   The bulk of mankind are
apt to flock to the successful standard.

The leaders of the opposition have disseminated a spurious
pamphlet dubbed "The Rush Light," which has set the
passions of many of the electors afloat, and implanted belief
that General Washington, Mr. Adams, and the federalists
generally, have been combined to introduce monarchy.   It is
strange that this shameful production should have been known
for many months in Boston and remain without detection.
While the federalists viewed it with contempt and neglect, the
Jacobins have been industrious to disseminate it among the
uninformed.   From the moment I saw the thing I sounded the
alarm at Albany, to my friends there, who are at length
aroused and have come out in the "Albany Centennial" to
repel its audacious slanders.   Here I am exposing it with my
feeble pen from over the signatures of "Regulus" and "Fair
Play."   My pieces are at the printing office.   It is yet ques-
tionable whether the printer will give them admission.   If not,
a system of exposure will be commenced in other papers
against our editor.   And so we will rest the matter, as it is
near bed time.   I have touched on this subject a week or two
ago to Mr. Ames,* in hopes of his taking up the club to knock
down this feeble monster, which he can easily do with his
powerful weapon.   Good night to you.

I am ever yours,

H. VAN SCHAACK.

[TO PETER VAN SCHAACK,]

PITTSFIELD, Oct. 8th, 1802.

MY DEAR BROTHER: Our friend Benson passed through
here (after dinner) on Wednesday last.   The postmaster, to
whose care your letter was sent from Albany, met the Judge
between my house and town, and delivered the letter.

Judge Washington passed my house on Monday evening.

---

* Fisher Ames.

The next morning he sent Mr. Wolcott's letter, with an apology for not calling.

General Hamilton, according to Benson's message to me, is to spend a day or two with me, on his way from Connecticut to Albany.

President Dwight passed Wednesday with me. So you see my house has been a rendezvous for the great. If such visitors could make me as rich as it does great, I should have double satisfaction. By-the-by, Dr. Dwight told me that Judge Washington has sold the copyright of the history of General Washington for $150,000—one-half of this enormous sum to himself, the other half to Chief Justice Marshall, the writer of the history.

Our best regards to you all, big and small.

Yours affectionately

H. VAN SCHAACK.

[FROM OLIVER WOLCOTT.*]

LITCHFIELD, March 8th, 1802.

MY DEAR SIR: We have experienced a more severe storm of snow, rain and hail than is recollected by our oldest persons, in consequence of which your letters of the 10th, 12th, 13th, 17th and 23rd of February did not reach me till the close of last week. I have not, therefore, been quite so neglectful of your favors as appearances would indicate.

My letters from Washington mention that in addition to the courts and internal revenues, we may expect the abolition of the navy department, the mint, the commissioners of loans, and the office of accountant to the war department. In short, to use the words of the "Aurora," "all the establishments of THE FACTION will be tumbled down, one after another," or in federal language, THE GOVERNMENT IS TO BE PROSTRATED.

I am not wise enough to foresee all the consequences which will result from the measures of the present administration, but it is certain that the men who now govern will soon lose, if they have not already lost, the public confidence. Messrs. Jefferson, Lincoln and Granger are already arraigned "at the bar of public reason," and they will soon be convicted of having criminally calumniated the former administration, and of having foolishly supposed that their fame can result from the disgrace

* Successor to Alexander Hamilton as Secretary of the Treasury.

of others, and not from their own virtuous and meritorious conduct.

Notwithstanding the assertion of these gentlemen, I affirm that during the whole time I was in office, persons of both parties were indiscriminately consulted respecting appointments to office, and that a large portion of the men who were in office, when Mr. Jefferson was elected President, were recommended by persons who were opposed to the system of measures pursued by the Presidents Washington and Adams, and who are now of Mr. Jefferson's party.

It is remarkable that but few exchanges have been made in the southern states, although the charge of INTOLERANCE is general and unqualified, and though the prevailing interest was there ANTI-FEDERAL, as in the northern states it was FEDERAL.

I will mention to you a few instances of many appointments which were made on the recommendations of persons in opposition to the former administration, taking care to mention none of which any party can be ashamed.

Mr. Habersham, late postmaster-general, was recommended by Mr. Jackson and Mr. Baldwin, new senators from Georgia; Mr. Clay, district judge of Georgia, by Mr. Baldwin; Mr. Wall, naval officer, by Mr. Jones and Mr. Tatnall; and Mr. Maxwell, surveyor, by Mr. Jackson. Mr. Jones and Mr. Baldwin recommended two persons to be collector of Savannah, and Mr. Powell, one of them, was appointed.

In South Carolina, the appointments were admitted by the Democrats to have been impartially made. I do not know what is now said, but I have heard of no changes.

In North Carolina, the officers are popular men. Mr. Bloodworth and Mr. Martin were often consulted. The collector of Newbern was appointed not long before Mr. Adams retired, on the recommendation of Mr. Spaight. An inspector of one of the surveys was an active and conspicuous partisan of Mr. Jefferson's election.

No changes have been made in the revenue department in Virginia that I have heard of. Men of both parties were consulted, and have often admitted to me that the appointments were satisfactory.

The supervisor of Tennessee was recommended by Mr. Orr and Mr. Greenup, representatives for Kentucky; and the supervisor of Kentucky by Mr. Brown, the present senator.

The supervisor of Maryland was recommended by Judge Duval; the collector of Havre de Grace by Mr. Christie; the surveyor of Baltimore by General Smith. No officers of the revenue have been removed in Maryland.

I might extend the list much further, but deem it unnecessary. The instances which have been cited, prove Mr. Jefferson's declaration to the merchants of New Haven to be untrue.

I do not wish to have this letter published in newspapers, or copies circulated. The people are not yet cool enough to listen to the truth; but you may report the facts I have stated, or give my name as the author when necessary.

May I ask the favor of you to inquire for a sober, honest, good-natured man who understands farming and driving teams and horses, who can be hired by the year and come by the first of April?

The roads are so bad that we have hardly moved out of the house. Mrs. Wolcott and myself will probably take advantage of your obliging invitation next summer, perhaps sooner. She joins me in respectful compliments to your family.

I am, dear sir, with great esteem,

Your obedient servant,

OLIVER WOLCOTT.

HENRY VAN SCHAACK, ESQ.

[TO THEODORE SEDGWICK.]

PITTSFIELD, Oct. 20th, 1805.

When I reflect, my dear friend, on the many pleasant hours I have spent with you in the SHORT period of nearly FORTY YEARS! when I revolve over, that in all this time the friendship between us has been uninterrupted ; when I recollect that in the revolutionary storm you stood a colossus between me and a mob, at the risk of your popularity, and when others preferred to relinquish the friend to retain the favor of the PEOPLE—what was then called so—under such circumstances, every word you utter, and every line you write me, is evidence that the long standing of our intimacy and the subsisting and long-existing friendship between us remains unimpaired, is grateful to my feelings. As such I received yours of yesterday announcing your wish that I should be with you on Tuesday. Mentally, I am at Stockbridge already ; corporeally, I intend to be with you if it is God's will that mind and body keep together, and if a horse can be had for love or money.

I find by your letter that you have mustered a great stock

of patience since you have been a judge. You tell me that you will wait patiently for the result of what may have taken place on the other side of the water. Not so am I, for I am impatient enough at times to throw me into a fever. I cannot be calm when I reflect that the repose of the world is at stake, and that this important hazard rests on the exertions of Great Britain alone. What has our degraded country to boast of when our existence depends on that magnanimous people? They fight with ardor for their altars, their liberty, their wives and children. God send them success. I presume you will join in responding, Amen!

If you call this a long, dull letter, be it so; but you will allow that we can have chit-chat upon paper as well as orally. Hang philosophy! It has introduced too much mischief into the world to be noticed by honest men.

Can you give me an account, when you see me, what this RAILWAY is which enabled a single horse to draw 15 tons, 6w., 2qs, at a rate of four miles an hour, or is it all a hum? It is a story that goes beyond the marvelous.

Please remember me to all the parlor folks in your house, and believe me to be

Your unalterable friend,

H. V. S.

CHAPTER XIV.

Mr. Van Schaack was a resident of Pittsfield for about twenty-three years. It had been his fixed design, on becoming a citizen of Massachusetts, to live in retirement, although ready and anxious to become a good and useful citizen, and to discharge all the duties which should devolve on him as such. The quiet and peace of domestic life, after the turmoils of the revolution, were desired by both Mrs. Van Schaack and himself, without any wish to extend the number of their acquaintances or to form new friendships.

Circumstances, however, beyond his control, soon arose to defeat these deliberate intentions, which continued to be frustrated by a succession of exciting causes operating upon a warm constitutional temperament. The insurrection in 1786-7, as has been observed, brought him into intercourse with many new and conspicuous characters, and this was greatly extended among the distinguished men of Massachusetts on his election to the General Court.

The discussions which preceded the adoption of the federal constitution next enlisted all his sympathies, and his most active exertions were directed to secure the ratification of that instrument. The organizing of the federal government and its leading departments, with the various administrative, financial and legislative measures deemed necessary for the successful operation of the new system by the advocates and friends of the constitution, and which were violently opposed by the anti-Federalists; the exciting elections, both state and national, to secure the success of candidates who were friendly to the new constitution, and who would carry out the intentions of its framers; the sanguinary revolutionary movements in France, leading, in their consequences, to a *quasi* war with the United States; the opposition to Jay's treaty, and various other exciting events, followed in rapid succession and had their effect upon one who took a lively interest in public matters, and whose pen was much employed, in newspapers and correspondence, on these absorbing themes.

But, in the absence of these disturbing causes, his own good qualities and natural activity of mind, and social and hospitable disposition, could not have been restrained for any length of time in comparative reserve and obscurity; and probably the residence of no private individual in the country was more highly or more frequently favored by visits from the great and good men of the land than was his fireside during his residence in Pittsfield.

Here might be met, at different times, Philip Schuyler, Egbert Benson, Theodore Sedgwick, John Jay, Jeremiah Wadsworth, Caleb Strong, Oliver Ellsworth, Alexander Hamilton, Fisher Ames, John Worthington, Jonathan Trumbull, Benjamin Lincoln, Oliver Wendell, William Eustis, Bushrod Washington, Oliver Wolcott, Daniel Dewey, Stephen Van Rensslaer, and a long list of others of the same class whose names it will be superfluous to mention. Many of these interesting men met at Mr. Van Schaack's residence at the same time, by previous appointment, and into the bright circle was often introduced his pure-minded brother-in-law, Peter Silvester, and his brother, Peter Van Schaack, whose bland and classical converse was the delight of all who knew him.

Nearly all of these individuals were revolutionary characters; and what a constellation of talent, genius, eloquence, dignity, simplicity, integrity and patriotism is here presented! In each of these distinguished characters there is a volume worthy of study. The bare mention of them in one array is sufficient to kindle in the bosom of every patriot the highest veneration for the age in which they lived, while he asserts with pride, "these were my countrymen!"

The mind delights to dwell on the intellectual picture here exhibited, and to invoke the associations which it is calculated to inspire. How interesting must have been the interviews of these choice spirits! How instructive their conversations! How rich in revolutionary and anti-revolutionary anecdotes, and how valuable for the historical information which they imparted! The actors in these convivial scenes are all now in their graves, and no surviving hand is left to depict them.*

It is gratifying to a liberal mind to see these remarkable men, some of whom had taken opposite sides in the revolution, throwing off their austerity after that event, and giving scope to the generous sentiments of pure minds. It is a lesson of toleration to the generations which follow that ought not to be lost. It is indeed a singular fact that the prominent actors in the revolution, the very leaders on the popular side, and those who made the greatest sacrifices in that conflict, had more consideration for their political opponents than the generations which have succeeded them. THEY appreciated the difficulties which embarrassed the conscientious loyalist. Hence Washington, Jay, Morris, Benson, Schuyler, Trumbull, Hamilton, Sedgwick, Troup, Wadsworth, Benjamin Rush and others of the same class, found no difficulty, on the ratification of the treaty of peace, in recognizing the virtues of those who from principle had been opposed to the revolutionary movement. "These men," said a revolutionary veteran, when speaking to the author of a number of loyalists, "became, after the peace, some of our best and most useful citizens."

That Mr. Van Schaack could bear his part in such company is evident from the fact that so many eminent men sought his society and were fond of becoming his guests. These distinguished characters were not all brought casually to his residence, for Pittsfield then was an out-of-the-way place.* There

---

* It is due to history, also, to state that all the eminent men mentioned in the text, with the sole exception, it is believed, of Eustis, were advocates for the adoption of the federal constitution. They were all FEDERALISTS. Posterity will determine as to their patriotism.

Among other men of mark in their day whom Mr. Van Schaack ranked among his friends, and with some of them he corresponded, were President Dwight, of Yale college; Dr. Aaron Dexter, professor in Harvard college; Jededian Morse, the geographer, John Brooks, Jonathan Jackson, Samuel Elliot, Thomas C. Amory, Thomas H. Perkins, Dummer, Samuel Henshaw, Uriah Tracy, George Cabot, Chauncey Goodwin, Frederic Wolcott, John Sloss Hobart, Benjamin Russell, Henry, Thomas and Elijah Dwight, and Eleazer Backus, afterward president of Hamilton college.

* The turnpike from Albany to Pittsfield was not made until 1793; up to which time the direct road from Albany to Boston passed through the south part of Berkshire county.

were in those days no railroads over land, or steamboats on our rivers, to facilitate social intercourse, and even turnpikes and stage coaches were then a novelty. Long special journeys in private conveyances, over rough and mountainous roads, were made to interchange friendly feelings as well as opinions on public matters and for mutual enjoyment, in accordance with those simple and hospitable customs which prevailed before the revolution, and which were continued among the old families until some time after the present century.

It was not uncommon for these visits to be extended through many days. Jonathan Trumbull, the second Governor of Connecticut by that name, and son of the last royal and first Republican Governor of that state, spent ten days at one time with the Pittsfield farmer who had been his father's prisoner in 1776. The ci-devant "rebel" and the ci-devant "Tory" met upon terms of perfect equality, and nothing could exceed the cordiality of their intercourse. The Governor's costume, on this occasion, was a long-tailed blue coat, light colored, small clothes with silver knee buckles, a long white vest buttoned from top to bottom, cream colored stockings, shoes with large, smooth silver buckles, a small gray, highly-powdered wig curled at the ears, surmounted by a small cocked hat with a black rose over the right eye. In short, his costume was that of a complete, well-dressed gentleman of the eighteenth century.

Mr. Van Schaack's acquaintance with the bench and bar of Massachusetts was extensive, and furnished another outlet for that hospitality and fondness for the delights of social intercourse for which he was remarkable. The judges and many of the leading members of the bar frequently repaired to his house, on the adjournment of the court at Lenox, for social enjoyment. The names of Parsons, Lowell, Dexter, Sergeant, Sewell, Dana, Minot, Tyng, Merrick, Bigelow, Strong, Sedgwick, Dewey, etc., need but to be named to convince, at least the Massachusetts reader, that the encounters of wit and raillery in which they participated could not be other than keen and rich.

Properly to interweave into these memoirs the great name

referred to in the last few pages, and suitably to commemorate
the interviews to which they were parties, in such a way as to
give the reader a full and correct idea of their social intercourse, would require such an acquaintance with characters
and such details of information as are beyond the author's
reach.*

By the customs of those days, friends could not meet without partaking of a glass of good wine or (which was very common in the country) a tumbler of bottled cider. Mr. Van
Schaack claimed to be able to regale his friends "with cider
out of his own orchard equal to champagne." It was during
the high excitement of federal and anti-federal times (and the
Federalists, it should be remembered, were in favor of a much
stronger government than their opponents) that several gentlemen from the lower part of Berkshire county met at Mr.
Van Schaack's house, as they were in the habit of doing, to
take him in their way to Williamstown College, of which they
were all trustees. The company were all animation and cordiality. Mr. Van Schaack brought forward his good cheer, according to the custom of the day. ."Gentlemen," said he, "I have
here some Federal cider and some anti-Federal cider; which
will you have?" "I will thank you, Mr. Van Schaack, for a glass
of your Federal cider," was the reply of one of the gentlemen,
and three others of the company gladly partook of that kind of
pure, strong cider. "Mr. Judson," said Mr. Van Schaack to the
only anti-Federalist present, "let me help you to a glass of my
anti-Federal cider. REMEMBER, THERE IS A LITTLE WATER
IN IT."

The old men of that day loved each other with almost
female fondness, and it is delightful to notice the evidences of
this tenderness, in their correspondence, and in other illustrations we have of their social intercourse, which was distinguished as well for its child-like simplicity as for its hearti-
ness and unaffected sincerity. We find gentlemen of three-
score-and-ten, who have filled the highest public stations in

---

* The propinquity of Mr. Van Schaack's residence to Lebanon Springs (then called
"The Pool") as they arose into notice, also brought to his door, in the summer months, many
interesting characters, and among other foreigners of distinction were the Dutch and British
ministers.

their conversations and correspondence, calling each other by
their Christian names only.

It is pleasing to see these old-school gentlemen descend to
puerilities in their intercourse with each other. The following letter furnishes an instance of the playful humor of Egbert
Benson, who at the date of the occurrence was a judge of the
Supreme Court of New York. Theodore Sedgwick was at the
time speaker of the House of Representatives of the United
States.

[TO THEODORE SEDGWICK.]

PITTSFIELD, Jan. 15th, 1799.

DEAR SIR: The stage driver this moment hailed me, and
put in my hands apparently a letter directed to "Henry Van
Schaack, Esquire, Pittsfield. Free. Theodore Sedgwick."
It was tied to a fresh fish, denominated rock fish—sometimes
bass—and, behold! when I had eagerly broken the seal, the
pages within presented to my view the following inscription
and no more:

"Merit Rewarded;
or,
A New Year's Gift
from
The President of the United States
to
that Zealous and Disinterested
Advocate and Promoter
of
Just and Efficient Government,
HENRY VAN SCHAACK.
A Continuance in His Present
Laudable
Sentiments and Efforts
will next year entitled him to a
Loaf.
January, 1799."

What do you think was my surprise and disappointment to
find, instead of political details from you, a waggish joke upon
me, sanctioned by your name? I hope you will consider it a
duty incumbent on you to call on the President, and detail to
him all the patriotic pursuits of the man to whom the forego-

ing lines are inscribed. Set forth to him with ardor those services, and solicit the chief magistrate to prepare a loaf against the commencement of the year 1800, or before, if anything can be spared. However well the President may be disposed toward me, I fear there are too many seekers to enable him to give me a slice of the loaf!

And now, my dear friend, who do you think had malignity enough in his heart to impose this novel joke on me? No Jacobin (for they can spare neither loaves nor fishes, you know,) I assure you. From the handwriting I am persuaded that the whole was the fabrication of that eccentric friend of ours, Judge Benson.

I have never attempted to dedicate or inscribe in my life. Resentment now will prompt me to it. I am torturing my brains already to see what sort of present I shall send and how to cover it. You may be sure I shall not speak of him as "disinterested," when I know he receives one thousand pounds York a year as judge, and a thousand sterling for two years as a federal commissioner.*

After I return from a visit to our friend Wadsworth, I shall probably make another visit to Albany, and laugh at my own expense and eat and drink at his. *Malgre* all I have said, I wish he was here to partake of his fish and my wine!

I have not had a line from you since you got to the seat of government. Have you cast me off, or are you so engaged in the labors of the day as not to have time to attend to your country correspondence?

I am, my dear friend,

Your affectionate and obliged humble servant,

H. VAN SCHAACK.

Mr. Van Schaack was one of the most courtly gentlemen of his day. His manners were highly fascinating, and his colloquial powers were such as to render him the delight of every company into which he was introduced. "Did you know Henry Van Schaack?" said the author to a septuagenarian,† twenty years after Mr. Van Schaack's decease. "Oh yes!" was the reply, "and how I should like to have another interview with him." The animation and delight which marked the response spoke volumes.

---

* Judge Benson was one of the commissioners for settling the boundary line between New York and Massachusetts.

† The late Judge Lyman of Northampton,

He was also very fond of the society of young persons, and remarkable for attaching them to him, making them familiar and communicative and participant of his own joyous and social emotions and excitations, but at the same time respectful, and without compromising the dignity belonging to his own advanced years and station in society.

Probably no person took greater delight in cherishing friendships than he, and he kept them up by an active and interesting epistolary intercourse. His correspondence with eminent men, members of Congress, revolutionary characters and others was extensive. He interchanged letters for a time with the eccentric William Cobbett, whose tergiversations, however, were too great to admit of its long continuance.

It is worthy of note, and indeed remarkable, how much of the private correspondence of individuals not in public stations, and even letters between brothers, for fifteen years after the adoption of the federal constitution, was taken up with public matters, evincing the deepest solicitude for the success of the new government, and for the advancement of such measures as were deemed best calculated to promote that object. The correspondence which has come under the author's eye was chiefly of the original supporters of our national constitution, and although many of these letters contain severe expressions in regard to political opponents, we shall in vain seek in them for evidences of political intrigues, or for the selfish calculations of mere politicians.

There was a native dignity in the manners and personal bearing of those composing the educated class of "old school" gentlemen, at the period of which we have been speaking, that induced the idea of aristocracy, although in truth, they were vastly more condescending, and their tender sympathies much more readily entered into the feelings and views of those in humble stations, than the loudest proclaimers of popular equality at the present day. Their was the truest courtesy. They were especially GENTLEMEN, and ever respected the feelings of those moving in the lowly walks of life. Their humanity was fully illustrated in the kind and considerate manner in which they treated their slaves and other dependents, and which was extended to the brutes that served them.

With the exception of one child, who died in early infancy, Mr. Van Schaack had no offspring; but he adopted into his family as his own child the daughter of a sister in moderate circumstances, for whom he ever manifested all the tenderness and solicitude of a parent. This was a frequent practice in the old Dutch families, and it has been pleasantly adverted to in a publication of great interest.* When this child was translated, by marriage, to a different sphere of duty, her place was immediately supplied by another who occupied the same position.

In 1807 Mr. Van Schaack removed from Pittsfield to Kinderhook Landing. Here he erected a house on the banks of the Hudson, adjoining the seat of a niece, one of his adopted children, who had been married several years and now resided at this place. It was the desire to be near her that had drawn him to this spot, so deeply seated was that *quasi* parental affection which had been fixed, as before mentioned, in the absence of children of his own.

The author is here tempted to introduce several extracts from a letter received by him from an intelligent lady† who visited Kinderhook in 1786, and Pittsfield in 1792, giving some glimpses of the manners and customs then still prevailing among the descendants of the early Dutch settlers on the Hudson, and confirmatory of the statements in a work referred to on a previous page :

"We embarked at New York in 1786, in a sloop in which Madame Dwight and myself were the only passengers. The vessel itself, the noble river, and above all the "highlands," filled me with wonder and delight. The captain had a legend for every scene, and not a mountain reared its head unconnected with some marvelous story. One of the men played on the flute and woke the gentle echoes, while the captain fired off

---

* Mrs. Grant's "Memoirs of an American Lady."
† Mrs. Eliza S. M. Quincy, wife of President Quincy of Boston.

guns to make the mountains reverberate a more tremendous
sound.   All this was enchanting to me.

"In the course of a WEEK we arrived at Kinderhook. There
we stayed at the house of Mr. David Van Schaack, in the town
of Kinderhook, several miles from the landing.   This was a
house of good, old-fashioned hospitality.   The mansion was
large* and the furniture and domestic establishment marked
the wealth of the proprietor, and were superior to those usually
met with at that period.   There were three brothers, David,
Henry and Peter Van Schaack.   The first two had no children
and had adopted those of a sister.   In this respect, and in their
general style of living, the family resembled the description
since given of the 'Schuyler Family' by Mrs. Grant.   I can
also bear witness to the truth of her accounts of the treatment
of the domestic slaves in their families.   The older men and
women among them were on the most familiar terms with their
masters and mistresses, and exercised considerable influence
over the young people of the family, especially the old women.
Still, they were respectful toward their superiors, and much
attached to their master and his family.

"We were received by this eminent and excellent family
with the greatest kindness, and I think we stayed with them
several days, until a wagon came down from Stockbridge for us.
I have always retained a lively remembrance of the hospitality
we received.   I remember Mr. Peter Van Schaack coming to
his brother's to visit Madame Dwight, and of his being blind or
nearly so—a circumstance which naturally made an impression
on a young person.

"I visited Stockbridge again in 1792, but did not pass
through Kinderhook.   During this visit I became acquainted
with Mr. Henry Van Schaack of Pittsfield, at Mr. Sedgwick's,
and I visited his family at his residence.   I still cherish the
recollection of Mr. and Mrs. Van Schaack's hospitable reception of me.   A striking feature of their mansion was the
exquisite neatness of the house and everything about it.   I
had never seen the floors of entries, stairs, kitchens, etc.,
painted, and though brought up among the natives of Holland,

* It is now the home of his great-niece, Mrs. Aaron J. Vanderpoel.

who are proverbial for their neatness, this seemed to me then 'a stroke beyond the reach of [their] art.' Parts of the house were covered with very handsome carpeting, manufactured, as I understood, by the 'Shakers;' at least so it rests in my memory.

"Mrs. Van Schaack appeared to me a very kind, matronly and dignified lady. Miss Van Vleck I soon found to be the sister of my first friend in Kinderhook, and these instances suggested the comparison I afterwards made to the same mode of adoption in the 'Schuyler Family,' as described by Mrs. Grant. I presume you have read the 'American Lady,' by Mrs. Grant, in which she gives, as far as my observation and experience have gone—in New York, Albany and Kinderhook —very correct accounts of the state of manners, etc., at that period."

The following letters were received by the author from gentlemen who are themselves objects of interest and the representatives of an interesting age:

[FROM SAMUEL S. WILDE.*]

BOSTON, April 5th, 1845.

DEAR SIR: I have received your favor of the 29th March, and willingly communicate my recollections on the subject of your inquiry; but they are few and unimportant.

I had no acquaintance with your deceased uncle, Mr. Henry Van Schaack, until after his removal from Pittsfield, after which I frequently saw him, from year to year, when I was holding the court at Lenox. He was advanced in years when I first made his acquaintance—considerably over seventy, I think. He used generally to come over from Kinderhook when the court was in session, and spend several days with us, and my acquaintance with him was limited to those occasional meetings.

I retain a pleasing recollection of his manners and his conversational and social qualities. He appeared to me an accomplished, gallant gentleman of the old school, and a favorable representative of the well-educated men of our ante-revolutionary times. He seemed to possess a general knowledge of the

---

* Judge of the Supreme Judicial Court of Massachusetts. He died in 1855, aged 84.

world and its affairs, and his historical recollections were often amusing and interesting. His understanding was good and vigorous, and his faculties continued in remarkable preservation, according to my recollection, until toward the last of my acquaintance with him. The last time I saw him he was much debilitated with disease and old age, which of course impaired his faculties in some degree, but not remarkably, and in much less degree than might have been expected, considering his bodily decay and extreme old age.

These are my general recollections of your deceased uncle, and I recollect no particulars which would be interesting.

I am, my dear sir,

Respectfully, your obedient servant,

S. S. WILDE.

H. C. VAN SCHAACK, ESQ.

[FROM EZEKIEL BACON.]

UTICA, July 21st, 1845.

MY DEAR SIR: Yours of the 8th reached me a day or two since, on my return from an eastern tour.

I regret that it will be in my power to furnish you with so few reminiscences of your honored uncle which can be of much interest in elucidating his life and character, although my impressions of both are as strong and vivid, and my acquaintance with him as familiar as could be expected from the disparity of our ages, and from the distance of our respective residences.

You do him no more than justice when you state your information respecting him to have been "that he was a gentleman of the old school and a fine specimen of that class," for he was such indeed. The general history of his life, and the particular circumstances which drove him to take what you call "a refuge" in Berkshire, I was early acquainted with. The part which, in common with your own more immediate and honored ancestor, he thought it his duty to take in the revolutionary contest, undoubtedly subjected him to many prejudices and disadvantages in the community where he resided; and even his more polished manners and habits of life were not calculated, in such a community, to add to his POPULARITY either as a public or private man, although of his high sense of honor and personal integrity I believe there never existed a doubt.

My first recollection of his person was in the winter of

1786–7, during the period of the "Shay insurrection," when I, being ten years of age, accompanied my late father, then living in Stockbridge, to see and confer with him on that matter. It was, as I recollect, on a very cold Sunday, the day on which General Lincoln entered Pittsfield with his troops to suppress that insurrection. Your uncle and my father were zealous supporters of the government, and it was, I presume, from the high and decided part which your uncle took in that contest that he was the same year chosen a member of the legislature from the town of Pittsfield, notwithstanding the prejudices under which he labored on account of his anti-revolutionary predilections and attachments.

He was, also, as I perceive you well know, a very decided Federalist of that day, on which question he and my father separated, subsequent to which their former intimacy, I think, ceased, although their personal intercourse, both in their public and private relations, was by no means unfriendly or discourteous.

He was a gentleman who exercised much liberal hospitality towards his friends who visited him, although from the circumstances before alluded to, that circle immediately about him was not probably very large. He was a man very systematic and assiduous in his business, and not fond of having that broken in upon by idle visits or gossiping conversation, as the following anecdote, which I recollect to have heard at the time, may indicate: There was a certain Mr. Jones living in the north part of the county, who, like him, was a very zealous Federalist, but, unlike him, rather an idle busy-body sort of a man, who was in the habit of calling upon Mr. Van Schaack to tell and learn the news of the day, and to talk over politics. Calling one day, he found Mr. Van Schaack engaged in his field, but immediately began to open his budget of politics and news. Mr. Van Schaack soon became very impatient and turning to Mr. Jones, said: "Mr. Jones, federalism is a very good thing in its place and at a proper time, but we must mind our business first. I wish you a good morning, sir."

Your uncle was not only an industrious, but, I believe, a very THOROUGH man in whatever he did or attempted, as the very ample and well constructed habitation which he erected on his place in Pittsfield evinced. He enjoyed life much, and was fond of anticipating its long and happy continuance, which in truth he seems to have realized, although not on the spot which he had fondly designed for his old age, at the time. As illustrative of which, I recollect to have heard this further anecdote: When finishing his barn, he had placed at the entrance of his stable door a very large and massive flat stone as a stepping-stone for his horse, remarking, as he did at the time, that he "wished to live until his old favorite horse had worn out that rock by going in and out of the door over it."

Mr. Van Schaack removed from Pittsfield, I believe, the same year in which I came there to reside, and of his after life I knew little or nothing.

To your kind inquiries of my personal health, etc., I am happy to have to say that,with the exception of one infirmity, which I can hardly expect to wholly get rid of, that of declining years, my general health is good and my enjoyment of life is quite as well as I probably deserve or can expect one who is nearly a septuagenarian, to retain.

Respectfully your obedient servant,

E. BACON.

H. C. VAN SCHAACK.

The following reminiscences were furnished to the author by a gentleman* of reputation who knew Mr. Van Schaack well, and had ample opportunities for studying his character:

"Among all the self-taught men of my acquaintance, the late venerable Henry Van Schaack excelled, being endued with strong mental powers, possessing a well balanced mind, discriminating and logical, and highly improved by early culture."

"He commenced, while a boy, reading history, geography and memoirs of distinguished characters, the latter being his darling study. Possessing a tenacious memory, he retained what he read through a long life. Even while a young man he had treasured up such a fund of knowledge of general sciences as to render himself not only agreeable but instructive even to graduates of highest standing.

"Although Mr. Van Schaack never affected the Chesterfieldian graces, he was the most finished gentleman, take him on all occasions, I ever knew. He would pass through the literary circles and among the *elite* more like a dandy rival, without committing himself in word or action. But he excelled

---

* Rev. Daniel Burhaus, D. D., who married a niece of Mr. Van Schaack.

in the drawing-room among ladies and gentlemen and could be in constant CHIT-CHAT without ever saying a foolish word, or making the least mistake in his *congé* or balance—never in want of words, always chaste and diffusive, refined and highly classical. His *forte* not only lay in knowing what to say and when to laugh, but he also knew what few great talkers do know—when to stop. But the most remarkable fact is untold. No one ever heard an invidious word in anything he said or did, by any individual of the various circles through which he passed, but always the reverse. The *literati* would frequently remark, after Mr. Van Schaack had retired: "What a remarkable man that Mr. Van Schaack is. They say he never received any other education than at a common writing school, and yet he is logical in his reasoning, classical in his language and appears to be at home on every subject." The latter would applaud him as the most polite man of the age ; the ladies with unfeigned hilarity would exclaim: "Delightful old gentleman." "*Beau monde*," the other sex would respond. "Yes," would be the reply, "and happy would it be for many if they would copy from his example."

He never flagged in his suavity of manners until rising four-score, and there was a neatness and polish about him until his dying day.

Mr. Van Schaack, although inclined to corpulency and thick set, yet was a noble figure ; round and full features, high forehead, dark blue eyes that bespoke strong conceptions and deep thought, which analyzed subjects and principles as they passed through his mind ; seldom misjudging, and from an equanimity of temper and polished politeness, he had a singular faculty of timing his remarks and guarding his expressions, as seldom wounding the most fastidious in public, unless his religious or political principles were assailed, and then he was most writhing, and often sarcastic in his rebukes, so much so that no one was ever known to provoke him a second time.

"His religious views were the result of deep thought. Although in early life taught the tenets and formalities of the Dutch Church, Reformed, by reading and reflection he became attached to, and united himself with, the Church of England,

and of course after the revolution he became a warm, although tolerant, member of the Protestant Episcopal Church.

"In his politics he considered civil government insecure without religion, and before the revolution he was a loyal subject of the British crown, and therefore through the struggle, although a warm friend to his country, for his oath's sake, he could not for conscience's sake take any active part in defense of the colonies, for which he severely suffered in person and purse. But the moment Great Britain acknowledged the independence of the United States, he considered himself absolved from being a LIEGE SUBJECT and declared himself a CITIZEN of the republic, and became, and continued until his death, a zealous and able defender of the Washington school, both with his pen and tongue; and he so far exceeded the scribblers of the age as to be well known and esteemed as one of the first noble advocates and defenders of the federal and wise administration of Washington and Adams. As such he was recognized, and corresponded with the most distinguished patriots of the age throughout the Union, and especially in New England and his native state of New York."

After his removal from Pittsfield to Kinderhook Landing, Mr. Van Schaack lived more retired than he had before done. He kept himself well informed, however, with public affairs, in which he took a lively interest, ever exercising that watchfulness of the proceedings and conduct of our public functionaries which becomes the patriotic duty of every citizen under our republican form of government.

He enjoyed excellent health until near the close of his life, and his mental faculties and cheerfulness of spirit remained unimpaired until the day of his death. His physicians (as he had become accustomed to say) were DOCTOR COB and DOCTOR HOE. The former article he used as a flesh brush, and the latter he was wont to exercise himself with in his garden.

As late as 1811, and when he was seventy-nine years old, he traveled from Kinderhook to Williamstown, over rough mountainous roads in autumn, to attend to his duties as one of the trustees of the college at that place.

Mr. Van Schaack departed this life on the 18th day of July, 1823, in the ninety-first year of his age, and his body was interred in the church-yard at Kinderhook, in the same grave in which were reposing the remains of his wife, who had been dead eight years. A vacancy, purposely left on the monument which he had caused to be erected over her grave, is now filled, pursuant to his intentions, with a simple inscription commemorating his own decease.

APPENDIX.

A.

[From "THE AUTOGRAPHIC COLLECTORS," by LYMAN C. DRAPER, LL.D., Burns & Sons, Publishers, New York, 1889.]

Hon. Henry C. Van Schaack, of Manlius, N. Y., made extensive general autograph collections in his day. He was born at Kinderhook, N. Y., April 3, 1802. For sixty-four years he practiced law; declining public employments, he devoted himself to his profession and to literary pursuits. His chief literary productions were: "Life of Peter Van Schaack, LL.D." (his worthy parent); "A Kinderhook Mansion;" "Henry Cruger," the colleague of Edmund Burke; "Captain Morris, of the Illinois Country;" "A History of Manlius;" and (in manuscript) "A Life of Major Harry Van Schaack"—a man of marked character, who figured largely in the early French and Canadian wars, and also during the Revolutionary period in the New England States—which his descendants intend publishing, in accordance with the author's wishes. He was fond of saving historical newspaper scraps and left many volumes systematically arranged, twelve of which relate exclusively to historical and biographical selections, and three to the history of Onondaga county, N. Y.

His very valuable collection of autographs was designed to illustrate the period of the war of the American Revolution—among which were at least eighteen full letters of the signers—all bound in three fine volumes, fully illustrated, with engravings, sketches, newspaper articles, etc., descending to his children—Mrs. Wm. G. Hibbard, of Chicago; Mrs. A. J. Vanderpoel, of New York; and Peter Van Schaack, of Chicago.

Mr. Van Schaack died at Manlius, N. Y., Dec. 18, 1887, in his eighty-sixth year, leaving behind him a stainless name, and a reputation for ability, goodness and integrity, second to none of his day and generation.

B

We hear from Kinderhook that on Wednesday, the 2nd instant, as four men, two boys and a negro were hoeing corn in a field near that place, they were surprised and fired upon by six Indians and a French-man, which wounded one of the men, a boy and a negro fellow, when they, with two others, took to their heels. The seventh, named John Gardenier, ran towards their arms, that were nigh at hand; and having dispatched two of the Indians, a third closed in upon him, and, in the scuffle, the Frenchman came up, and seeing Gardenier get the better of the Indians, he knocked him down with his piece and afterwards scalped him, when the Indians made off and carried their dead with them. Some short time after, Gardenier came to himself, and with some difficulty reached the fort. He was so stunned with the blow he received from the Frenchman, that he was insensible of his being scalped until he was in-formed by the people, who discovered the blood, but remembered the whole of their proceedings before, and said he could have killed three of the Indians had not the second gun he took up missed fire.

On the receipt of the above news the sum of twelve pounds was imme-diately raised, by a few gentlemen in this city, and sent to John Garde-nier for his gallant behavior, to support his wife and family during his illness, and it is to be hoped that those gentlemen who would willingly infuse a martial spirit in the armies now going against our enemies, will follow an example so truly worthy of their imitation.—The New York Mercury of 14th July, 1755.

C

ALBANY COUNTY, 20th January, 1775.

MR. GAINE: The following resolutions of the inhabitants of Kings District, in this county, will explain the occasion which produced them. The measure was deemed a prudential one, by the magistrates of the district, and it has fully answered the intended purpose:

KINGS DISTRICT, 24th day of Dec., 1774.

At a meeting publicly named by the clerk of the district, and requested by a number of the principal inhabitants present,—five of the King's Justices for the county of Albany, and a great number of the principal people belonging to said district: Whereas, it appears to this meeting that some individuals in the northeast part of this district have associated with divers people of a neighboring district, and combined together to hin-der and obstruct Courts of Justice in the said county of Albany; this meet-ing, deeply impressed with a just abhorrence of these daring insults upon government, and being fully sensible of the blessings resulting from a due obedience to the laws, as well as convinced of the calamities and evils attending a suppression or even suspension of the administration of justice; have therefore unanimously come into the following resolutions:

First—That as our gracious sovereign, King George the Third, is lawful and rightful king of Great Britain, and all other dominions thereunto belonging; and as such, by the constitution, has a right to establish courts, and is supposed to be present in all his courts.

Therefore we will, to the utmost of our power and at the risk of our lives, discountenance and suppress every meeting, association or combination which may have a tendency in the least to molest, disturb, or in any wise obstruct, the due administration of justice in this province.

Second—That we will as much as we can, in our different capacities, encourage, promote and enforce a strict obedience to the aforesaid authority.

Third—In as much as that life, liberty, and property and bands of society are secured and protected by the laws, we do for the further security of these blessings mutually covenant, agree and engage, that if any obstruction, hindrance or molestation is given to any officer or minister of justice, in the due execution of his office, we will separately and collectively (as occasions may require), aid and assist in the executive part of the law, so that all offenders may be brought to justice.

Signed by order of the meeting.

ABRAHAM HOLMES,
Clerk for King's District.

D

Mr. Printer: Please give the following piece a place in your paper:

"A community whose very vitals, civil discord, under the baleful influence of public commotions, seems to be tearing away from the political body, may be fitly considered as emblematical of that world (wherever it be) which is under the more immediate influence of the infernal potentate, who first introduced disorder and confusion into the wise and benevolent system established by the Creator. It is not meant here that this infernal spirit (if there be a superior and first in rank among devils) is not absolutely under a divine control, however mysterious and inconceivable the idea. The frequent dispossessions effected by the Savior and his Apostles and servants by the power confessedly received from Him, are at once instances and proof of His divine power, and that those spirits are under the absolute control of the Supreme Magistrate of the universe. This is the thought I would suggest upon this occasion, viz: that the wisdom of the Supreme Ruler permits these scenes of confusion to take place at once to make us thoroughly understand and properly prize and improve the blessings of government, order, and peace, and practically to fix our attention and affection on that world where these blessings are realized in all their perfection and glory.

"That the government of this commonwealth is much [I hope not inextricably] embarrassed, in consequence of the late commotions, and by the present temper of a great part of the people, cannot be denied or secreted.

"That it is the duty of every faithful subject to contribute as there may be opportunity all the assistance he possibly can to extricate government out of trouble is alike undeniable. The means most proper to effect the end may be less clear. Different persons will differ on this point. Indeed the same person, in different attitudes and under the operation of different connections and prospects, may vary from himself. To me, this appears indisputably the best method: first, to investigate, with a candid scrupulosity the causes which have originated the present confusion and embarrassment; in the next place, to carry our views into probable consequences, and thence to infer the measures proper for government to pursue. In prosecuting my plan, I shall think myself entitled to the candor of my readers, after assuring them that my character and inclination concur to preclude all and every expectation from government.

In investigating the causes of the present confusion and embarrassment our views will be necessarily carried back to past, though not very remote, facts and occurrences.

In the fourth year of the reign of George the Third the British parliament passed an act whose object was the raising a revenue from the American colonies for defraying the expense of their defense, protection and security. Some things, singular and new, in this act excited particular attention, and seemed to have occasioned the first consternation and alarm in the Colonies, respecting their rights and immunities as British subjects. Before the consternation thus occasioned was over, the memorable Stamp Act had its existence. The frenzy it produced, particularly in the town of Boston, and the steps taken to prevent its operation and effect, are too well known to require being particularly mentioned.

In the year 1766, if my memory serves me, the Stamp Act was repealed by another more alarming than those which had preceded it. It was declared "that His Majesty in parliament, of right, had power to bind the people of these colonies by statutes in ALL cases whatsoever." Not to be particular, divers subsequent acts of the British parliament came over, which we considered as evidently intended to support and carry into effect the right just claimed and asserted, to bind us in all cases whatsoever. These several acts were considered as infringing more or less on the rights of the colonists, and utterly incompatible with the privileges granted by charter to divers of the Colonies; and, of consequence, as grievances which threatened them with a total loss of their privileges. Humble remonstrances for redress of those grievances were repeatedly addressed to the King and parliament. I do not recollect my having seen more than one or two of the remonstrances and petitions sent for this purpose; therefore am not able to determine for myself as to the propriety of those applications, that is, whether they were humble and respectful. Of this I am sure, they failed of success; and it was then said, were treated with contempt.

From what I recollect, and from the consequences which followed, however, I think it probable that those supplications to the King and parliament carried in them such clear and undeniable claims of right, and such a manly sense of the wrongs done us by the British government, as fully convinced them that America never would be brought to submit to their impositions but by force. For although the destruction of the India Company's tea was the ostensible reason for the armament under General Gage, yet as this was private property, and the common course of law might have righted the sufferers, it will appear to every considerate person who will be at the pains to take an attentive retrospect of the manœuvres of that period that the armament must have been intended to give the completest effect to the claim of right to bind the British colonists in all cases whatsoever. This was the idea then generally entertained of the matter.

A determined, spirited opposition, or a tame and slavish submission, to British power, had now become the only alternative. No one then upon the stage can have forgotten the frequent publications of this period, in which the rights of America were strongly asserted, the claims of the British government refuted, and the destructive and shocking consequences of submission held up to the people in glowing colors. It will be sufficient for my purpose only to mention the votes and proceedings of the town of Boston, at their meeting begun the 28th of October, 1772 published in a pamphlet.

Every one must remember the general agitation occasioned by hope and fear, at this period. To oppose the most formidable power in Europe, or to commence as slaves was alike shocking. In this situation, however, that strong sense and love of liberty natural to Englishmen determined in favor of opposition;—not opposition to the military force, but to the civil authority of Great Britain as then administered in this province. This was judged the easiest, safest and only practical measure that could be pursued to prevent the execution of laws deemed tyrannical, oppressive and ruinous. Partly from motives of interest, partly from those of envy and revenge, and partly from principle, and this, I believe, ever has been and ever will be the case in all public commotions. The people, instigated by leaders who will probably come within the same predicaments, stopped the proceedings of the courts of law in Berkshire. They afterwards did the same in the county of Hampshire. In short, the course of law was totally obstructed, and committees of correspondence, etc., substituted in their room; and, under their administration, we did pretty well.

To encourage us to commit those outrages on government, we were told that humble and dutiful petitions for redress of grievances had been presented to the King and parliament and not only had failed of procuring it, but had been treated with contempt. Our opposition was not only encouraged by gentlemen who then took the helm, and who now hold the first places of honor and trust in the commonwealth, but they were also countenanced [and this with the people at large is sufficient justification], by Congress. Their resolve runs thus: "Resolved, that this Congress do approve of the opposition made by the inhabitants of the Massachusetts Bay to the execution of the late acts of Parliament, and if the same shall be attempted to be carried into execution by force, in such case all America ought to support them in their opposition."

That this principally respected the stopping the courts of law here in 1774 will not be made a question, if a subsequent resolve of the same Congress is attended to. "Resolved, that this Congress do recommend to the inhabitants of the colony of Massachusetts Bay to submit to a suspension of the administration of justice where it cannot be procured in a legal and peaceable manner under the rules of the charter and the laws founded thereon, until the effects of our application for a repeal of the acts by which their charter rights are infringed are known." The artful manner in which the resolve is expressed will not be objected against the present application. Honest acts are necessary in urgent cases. And cases may happen where art is not only justifiable but laudable.

From the preceding review of the past, this consequence seems to be fairly deduceable, viz.: That the first efficacious measure for obtaining a redress of our grievances in 1774 was the breaking up of the courts of law by an unlawful assembly.

This is a matter which merits attention also. During the foregoing period the political writers, who were very numerous, to stimulate the people to a prompt and spirited opposition to the oppressive system of British policy, dwelt profusely, and in some instances extravagantly, upon the evils which were apprehended as a consequence of that system being established; and, on the other hand, by a misjudged exaggeration, raised too high, much by the people's expectations from the blessings of liberty and independence, and thus laid a sure foundation for disappointment and chagrin.

If these several matters are taken into account, that a natural propensity of the mind encouraged and brought into act is thereby strengthened; that the opposition to the administration of justice was encouraged, and effectual, in 1774; that like circumstances, whether real or imaginary only, will be likely to operate on the mind in a similar manner at any other period; that the people had been led by those then at the helm of the political ship to believe that if she could be but steered into the haven of independence, or in other words, if we could only be rescued from British tyranny, perpetual ease and freedom from public burdens and troubles must be the certain consequence;· that the common herd are more influenced by passion and present feelings than by a just view of remote consequences or probabilities. If it be considered, at the same time, that the constitution of this commonwealth is liberal in the extreme, that it is founded on principles of equal liberty, and almost throughout calculated to inspire the people with a high sense of their importance as the source of all powers, it will not, it cannot, be difficult to find a cause adequate to the effects we have lately seen and still see. The difference in the circumstances of the people now and twelve years ago is allowed. But what is this difference to those who cannot or do not distinguish? In 1774 we were opposed to expected and probable evils. The people are now prompted to opposition from circumstances and feelings, not so far as my observation has reached, by any foreign influence. They did not consider that by virtue of their own solemn compact they were bound to pray for a redress of their grievances. They did not consider that this method had been unsuccessfully pursued previous to their forcible opposition to British tyranny. It is agreed their conduct is now absolutely wrong and wicked, but are there no palliatives in the case?

Great commotions in governments well established are not always productive of lasting evils; they are seldom the occasion of any good to the subject. The people generally come off with loss. In infant governments very serious consequences may be expected from them. To form a probable conjecture with respect to those which may take place among us, divers things should be considered; the love of liberty, natural to this people, now confirmed and become habitual; the power of strength of this habit in consequence of a successful struggle for ten years for the dear bought blessing; the high-raised expectations of perpetual freedom from burdens in the enjoyment of it occasioned by misjudged exaggeration, in order to incite the people to engage in that struggle, disappointed; the natural expectation of like effects, from like causes in similar circumstances; the high importance to which the people were raised by the political writers several years preceding the revolution; this importance established by the principles of equal liberty, the revolution principles and ill-judged declarations of right and power in the people with which the constitution of this commonwealth abounds; their late complete disappointment; the chagrin of infamy as well as disappointment; the hope of relief from Great Britain, and, added to this, the uneasiness known to exist in sister states; these several articles, though distinctly of small moment, uniting their force and influence upon the corrupt and vindictive tempers of the illiterate, or ill-taught, unprincipled and hardy boors and illiberal yeomanry of the commonwealth may lay a foundation for probable conjectures respecting the issue of the late commotions.

My character and disposition have concurred not only to prevent my joining or encouraging the people in their late unjustifiable and wicked attempts to overthrow the government, but everywhere to oppose them so far as dependence and prudence would permit me to do it. This notwithstanding, as I have ever been cautious of giving unnecessary offense, I have had considerable opportunities to make myself acquainted with their feelings; and from all the information I have been able to obtain on this head, it is abundantly clear to me that the people within the circle

of my information, in general, far from having lost a disposition to
have the government overset by their late disappointment, that this disposition is only increased in proportion to the chagrin occasioned by it.

Now, if the temper of the insurgents at large may be learnt from those
people with whom I have had opportunity to be acquainted, what are the
measures which wisdom and the best policy would dictate in circumstances so very critical? To attend to this question has been my principal
object; a question, in my opinion, of the first importance to the happiness
[possibly the existence], of this commonwealth. In answering it, severa
matters are to be kept in view. First, that the sovereignty and indepen
dence of the commonwealth of Massachusetts are the effects of a manly
generous and virtuous opposition to tyranny, and of those noble efforts for
liberty which the civilized world generally admires and applauds. Second-
ly, that its constitution and form of government is considered as a match-
less production and effort of human wisdom. Thirdly, that the folly and
madness of overturning and destroying it must render us infamous in proportion to the honor we have got by acquiring it. Fourthly, that the
calamities and miseries we may expect from the ruin and loss of it will
probably exceed those we have experienced in obtaining it. How vastly
important, then, that government should adopt measures most proper
to secure the enjoyment of so valuable a blessing!

Many, I find, who have taken an active part in the support of government, in the late insurrection and rebellion, are disposed to consider and
treat the rebels in general as a miserable set of beings of desperate fortunes
and hardly deserving a rank among men. This appears to me both illiberal
and imprudent. I know many among the insurgents who are men of
property and principle, as far as men may be supposed to possess, principle in a time of so general corruption. In point of property, indeed, they
are much below those on the side of government. But, in point of principle, it is by no means clear that the same may be said with truth. Look
into characters, and I think it will be generally found that those who have
appeared for government are interested persons, who either are connected
with or have expectations from government or connected with those who
have such connections and expectations. Disinterested characters, and
such whose patriotic virtue only has called them forth to quell the rebellion, would not be very numerous Can it, then, be wise in government
to pursue measures which will unavoidably hold up to view a distinction,
which, for this as well as other reasons, must be disagreeable if not odious?

This, also, is a consideration in the present inquiry which ought to have
weight. The people who have been in arms [and many others equally
disaffected whose fear or prudence have kept from overt acts] are those
who fought for their liberties, and on the strength of whose nerves and
courage the preservation or loss of the constitution may very much depend. It is to be remembered also that human nature is the same in all
countries.

Great Britain, to satisfy her lust of domination and verify her own pre-

dictions respecting America, may insidiously endeavor to promote the dis-
affections already become too general among us, and to affect that by our
own madness and folly which they have not affected by military skill and
prowess.

From these observations the following general answer to my question
seems to be clearly deducible, viz: that those measures ought to be pursued by government which will most directly tend to ease the minds of
the people and conciliate their affections. Every sensible and judicious
man in the state who was at the pains to inquire into the characters of the
leaders and chiefs amongst the insurgents, to attend to their various injudicious movements, their want of a settled plan, and of men able to form
one, their want of resources and the impracticability of finding them;
carrying with them at all times a consciousness of being wrong, must
have perceived that subjugation would not be difficult at any time if government should once rouse.

To recover the affections of these people is an object equally important—perhaps not so easily obtained. Their measures they readily confess
were wrong, but they tell you at the same time their views were ultimate-
ly right, and the same which originated similar and successful measures
heretofore, in a case they at first imagined had been similar. People
possessed of such apprehensions in ordinary cases will be pretty well punished by complete disappointment. Add, in the present case, to the chagrin
and disappointment an entire subjugation, and will it not, in general, as a
punishment, come up to the measure wisdom would prescribe for a people
realizing the liberties and blessings of a commonwealth?

The two objects of government must be these: To convince the people of
the futility and wickedness of attempts to destroy the constitution, and
satisfy them they are as happy under it as they can or ought to be in a state of
society. Of the former they have full conviction already. That government has not been sufficiently attentive to the happiness and ease of the
people before their late exertions the address lately sent us is a clear
proof. If government has owned itself faulty; if by a late attention to the
complaints of the people it has tacitly countenanced exertions against
mal-administration, will it be prudent to inflict punishments obviously
calculated and intended to cowe for a while that spirit of freedom which
originated exertions that give existence to commonwealths? And would
not such punishment discover a degree of absurdity in administration?

This, however, is not a matter of the greatest consequence. Infamy is
sure to produce one [sometimes both] of these effects, viz: sordid mean-
ness or malice. The first is an absurdity in a commonwealth; the latter
ought not to be suffered to exist, much less should it be promoted and established in the breasts of her citizens. The delicate and critical situation of government at this time seems to me, therefore, to furnish sufficient

and abundant proof of the impropriety and impolicy of indiscriminate infamy as part of the punishment of the late insurrection.

It will be said by some (and I trust by few only) that capital punishment is no more than the offence universally merits. To such sanguinary
spirits it will be sufficient to say that the government is not with them in
opinion. Besides, the people know that of the number who urge severity
and affect to consider them wretches, there is a large proportion who
were as low as themselves and indebted to their exertions for the plumes
which rank them among gentlemen, and which, in many instances, furnish
their only title to the rank they hold. Government cannot, therefore, it
seems to me, suffer their deliberations upon this matter to be influenced
by the wishes of such gentlemen, but will rather fix their attention upon
past occurrences and carry their views into probable consequences.

It may be further said this is a very singular writer. Is not the government now doing the very thing he must wish, if he has any meaning? By
no means. The government has appointed commissioners to promise in-
demnity to certain persons if, on inquiry, they shall find satisfactory evidence of their penitence, etc., to promise a remission of their punishment in whole or in part, etc.

And who that has been conversant among men for fifty years, as this
singular writer has, does not know that satisfactory evidence may be produced to the gentlemen making the inquiry respecting the temper and
disposition of the insurgents, without the least foundation in truth? Any
man who wishes to be out of trouble would apparently be very sorry for
his crimes and make very fair promises, and feel at heart much more
sorry that he had not carried his point, and less affection for government
on account of this very measure. Besides, there is a great proportion of
those rendered infamous whose malignity will not suffer them to request
a restoration to their former rights and privileges. They now have opportunity to rail they would not lose.

The wishes of the writer are these: That government would inflict an
adequate punishment on such a number of her rebel sons as might be at
once sufficient to raise her to respect and dignity among the nations of the
world and effectually secure the commonwealth against further commotions and insurrections, and at the same time tender pardon and indemni-
ty to all her other rebel children (who have not left the state) indiscriminately, and without other condition than taking an oath of allegiance to the
commonwealth. From motives which a generous and noble magnanimity
would suggest, such a conduct must render the present administration
illustrious.

It ever has been and still is my devout wish, that wisdom (not caprice
or the spat of power) might mark the steps of government at this most
critical period. If the ship should live through the present storm she
may reach a haven of long rest.

D

General Lincoln's views in regard to the Massachusetts Disqualifying Act of February, 1787:

When a state, whose constitution is like ours, has been convulsed by intestine broils; when the bands of government have in any part of it been thrown off and rebellion has for a time stalked unmolested; when the most affectionate neighbors become, in consequence thereof, divided in sentiment on the question in dispute and warmly espouse the opinions they hold, when even the father arms against the son and the son against the father, the powers of government may be excited and crush the rebel.lion, but to reclaim its citizens, to bring them back fully to a sense of their duty and to establish anew those principles which will lead them to embrace the government with affection, must require the wisdom, the patience, the abilities and address of the Legislature.

Love and fear are the bands of civil society. Love is the noblest in.centive to obedience. A government supported hereon is certainly the most desirable and insures the first degrees of happiness which can be derived from civil compact. Such a government as this is always wounded when anything shall exist which makes it necessary to apply to the fears of the governed. This never will be done by a wise administration, unless the general good renders it indispensable, and it will be removed the first moment it can be consistently with the common safety.

The spirit of rebellion is now pretty fully crushed in this state and the opposition to government is hourly decreasing. This, therefore, is the most critical moment yet seen. Punishments must be such and be so far extended as hereby others shall be deterred from repeating such acts of outrage in future, and care must be taken that they do not extend beyond a certain degree, the necessity of which must be acknowledged by all. In her right hand government must hold out such terms of mercy, in the hour of success, with such evident marks of a disposition to forgive as shall apply to the feelings of the delinquents, and beget in them such sentiments of gratitude and love by which they will be led to embrace with the highest cordiality that government which they have attempted to trample under foot. This example in government will have its influence upon individuals and be productive of the best effects among contending neighbors and divided families.

These are sentiments which I suppose have their foundation in truth; and in the belief of them I have been led to examine, with some attention, the late act of the General Court, by which certain characters are for a time disfranchised. Although I revere the doings of the General Court and think their conduct will make a rich page in history, yet I cannot but suppose that if the number of the disfranchised had been less the public peace would have been equally safe and the general happiness promoted.

The act includes so great a description of persons that in its opera.

tion, many towns will be disfranchised. This will injure the whole, for multiplied disorders must be experienced under such circumstances.

The people who have been in arms against government, and their abettors, have complained, and do now complain, that grievances do exist and that they ought to have redress. We have invariably said to them, "You are wrong in flying to arms; you should seek redress in a constitutional way and wait the decision of the Legislature." These observations are undoubtedly just, but will not they now complain and say that we have cut them off from all hope of redress from that quarter? for we have denied them a representation in that legislative body by whose laws they must be governed. While they are in this situation they never will be reconciled to government, nor will they submit to the terms of it from any other motive than fear, excited by a constant armed military force extended over them.

' While these distinctions are made, the subjects of them will remain invidious, and there will be no affection existing among inhabitants of the same neighborhood or families where they have thought and acted differently. Those who have been opposed to government will review with a jealous eye those who have been supporters of it, and consider them as the cause which produced the Disqualifying Act, and who are now keeping it alive. Many never will submit to it; they will rather leave the state than do it. If we could reconcile ourselves to this loss and on its account make no objection, yet these people will leave behind them near and dear connections who will feel themselves wounded through their friends.

The influence of these people is so fully checked that we have nothing to apprehend from them now but their individual votes. When this is the case, to express fears from that quarter is impolitic. Admit that some of these people should obtain a seat in the Assembly the next year, we have nothing to fear from the measure. So far from that, I think it would produce the most salutary effects.

For my own part, I wish that those in general who should receive a pardon were at liberty to exercise all the rights of good citizens, for I believe it to be the only way which can be adopted to make them good members of society and to reconcile them to that government under which we wish them to live. If we are afraid of their weight, and they are for a given time deprived of certain privileges, they will come forth thereafter with redoubled vigor. I think we have much more to fear from a certain supineness which has seized on a great proportion of our citizens who have been totally inattentive to the exercise of those rights conveyed to them by the constitution of the commonwealth. If the good people of the state will not exert themselves in the appointment of proper characters in the executive and legislative branches of government, no disfranchising acts will ever make us a happy and well governed people.

I cannot, therefore, on the whole, but think that if the opposers to government in general had been disqualified on a pardon from serving as jurors on the trial of those who had been in sentiment with them, that we should have been perfectly safe. For, as I observed before, these people have now no influence as a body, and their individual votes are not to be dreaded, for we certainly shall not admit that the majority is with them in their political sentiments. If they are, how, upon Republican principles, can we justly exclude them from the right of government?

Pittsfield, Feb'y, 1787.

THE END.

www.ingramcontent.com/pod-product-compliance
Lightning Source LLC
Chambersburg PA
CBHW030818020726
47499CB00006B/1972